EDGEWISE

EDGEWISE

Graham Masterton

This first world edition published in
SEVERN HOUSE PUBLISHERS I
9–15 High Street, Sutton, Surrey SN
This first world edition published in
SEVERN HOUSE PUBLISHERS I
595 Madison Avenue, New York, N.Y. 10022.

British Library Cataloguing in Publication Data

Masterton, Graham
    Edgewise
    1.   Windigos - Fiction
    2.   Kidnapping - Fiction
    3.   Horror tales
    I.   Title
    823.9'14 [F]

    ISBN-13: 978-0-7278-6449-9   (cased)
    ISBN-10: 0-7278-6449-1   (cased)
    ISBN-13: 978-0-7278-9186-0   (paper)
    ISBN-10: 0-7278-9186-3   (paper)

Typeset by Palimpsest Book Production Ltd.,
Grangemouth, Stirlingshire, Scotland.
Printed and bound in Great Britain by
MPG Books Ltd., Bodmin, Cornwall.

One

Lily was beginning to slide into a deep sleep when she heard a muffled clicking noise, somewhere downstairs, like a door opening. Then a stumbling sound, as if somebody had accidentally walked into a piece of furniture in the dark.

She raised her head from the pillow, frowning and listening hard. She knew that she had locked all the doors and set the alarm. Maybe it was Sergeant, her black Labrador, trying to get out of the utility room. Sergeant was nine years old now, and he wuffled so loudly in his sleep that he kept waking himself up.

She waited and waited, but the house remained silent, except for an occasional indigestive gurgle from the central heating. She was exhausted – so tired that her neck muscles creaked – and all she wanted to do was rest her head back down on the pillow and sleep.

But then she heard another stumbling sound, and immediately afterward she was sure she could hear somebody cough. *Shit*, she thought. *Maybe it isn't Sergeant at all. Maybe it's intruders.*

She switched on her poppy-patterned bedside lamp. Her carriage clock said seventeen minutes after two in the morning. She didn't often go to bed so late, but after she had given Tasha and Sammy their supper, she had sat for over four hours at the dining-room table, working on the sales brochure for Indian Falls Park, a 350-acre development of $2.5million homes out on Ridge Road, Edina.

She opened the drawer in her nightstand and took out her

pepper spray. Then she swung her legs out of bed and reached for her cerise satin robe.

In the multiple mirrors of her bedroom closets she could see herself standing indecisively by the door, her short blonde hair tousled, her eyes puffy from lack of sleep. *Maybe you should lock yourself in your room and call nine-one-one*, she told herself. But then she thought: *No, if it's only Sergeant, you'll look like a hysterical idiot.* And besides, she had Tasha and Sammy to worry about.

She opened the door and went out on to the galleried landing, switching on the large glass chandelier that hung over the stairwell.

'Is anybody there?' she demanded, trying to sound utterly fearless. But immediately she thought: *What a dumb question. If there* is *anybody there, what are they going to say? 'Don't worry, lady, it's only us intruders'?*

She leaned cautiously over the banister rail. 'I'm warning you, I have a gun, and I know how to use it.'

There was no answer. The house remained silent. Lily waited a little longer and then walked across the landing to Tasha's room. A ceramic plaque was screwed to the door, with a picture of a stern-looking Bratz doll and the warning *Totally Stay Out*! Lily eased the door open and looked inside. Underneath her pink gingham comforter, all she could see of Tasha was a few sprigs of dark-brown hair. From the shelves all around the room, about forty Bratz and Barbies stared back at Lily with mute hostility.

She went to Sammy's room. Sammy was sprawled sideways, his blue-and-green-checkered pajamas rucked right up to his knees, and he was whistling through one blocked-up nostril as he slept. He was only eight, but already he looked so much like Jeff. That broad, Germanic face. Those invisible blond eyebrows. It was just as if Jeff had left a smaller version of himself behind, to keep a watchful eye on her.

Lily tippy-toed her way between Tonka firetrucks and mutilated Gorillazoids to give Sammy a kiss on his cheek. Sammy stirred, and raised one hand, and muttered, 'mmh never come back, never.'

'What?' said Lily. 'What did you say?'

But Sammy turned over and twisted his sheet around himself, and she realized that he had been talking in his sleep.

Lily reached out and touched his back. God, he even *felt* like Jeff. Then she tippy-toed back out of his room and closed the door.

Out on the landing she stood and listened for another few moments. The wind was beginning to rise, and she could hear the oak tree at the side of the house tapping against the weatherboards, like some old mendicant trying to get in. Maybe she should check downstairs, too, just to make sure, especially if Sergeant was so restless.

She padded on bare feet down the wide, uncarpeted staircase. Arranged on the wall were framed photographs of herself and Jeff and the children, and Sergeant, too. Near the bottom of the stairs, the largest photograph showed them by the old stone bridge at Marine-on-St-Croix. She and Tasha and Sammy were leaning over the parapet, looking down at the gushing mill race. Jeff was standing more than twenty yards away, his head lowered, as if he didn't belong to this family at all.

Lily crossed the hallway to the front door. The large fringed red-and-purple rug was kinked in the middle, as if somebody had tripped up on it, but the front door was closed and there was no sign that anybody had tried to force it.

She went through to the kitchen and switched on the lights, which flickered for a few seconds before they popped full on. The kitchen was Shaker-style, paneled in oak, with an oak-paneled island in the middle. She could see Sergeant standing behind the hammered-glass door that led to the utility room, looking more like a liquid black puddle of uncertainty than a dog. He made a huffing noise but he didn't bark.

Lily opened the door. 'What's the matter, boy? Have you been having nightmares again? Chasing after rabbits that you can't catch?'

She massaged his ears for him. She knew that he was old and sick and she ought to be thinking about having him put down, but Jeff had bought him for her when they were first married. He was the last living reminder of that happiest and silliest of times, when she had believed that she and Jeff would stay together until they grew senile, and that only death would be able to drag them apart.

She filled Sergeant's bowl with fresh water, and then she told him to settle down in his basket. He obeyed her, but mournfully, looking up at her with his amber-colored eyes.

'Good dog. Why don't you dream of tortoises instead? You'll be able to catch *them*.'

As Lily left the kitchen, she could hear that the wind was blowing even harder. Not only was the oak tree tapping, but the swing on the back verandah had started to creak – *creakk-squikk-creakk-squikk*, as if someone were pushing themselves backward and forward; or the *memory* of someone, anyhow. Lily didn't believe in ghosts, but she had been working in real estate long enough to know that some houses had spirits who stayed there long after their owners had moved away, or died.

She walked through the wide archway that led into the living room. There were folding mahogany doors on either side, but she rarely closed them. The living room was in darkness, with the floral drapes drawn, so that all she could see was the shadowy shapes of chairs and couches.

No, nobody here. It must have been the draft rattling the doors. Or maybe she had simply imagined it, as she was drifting off to sleep. Several times, between sleeping and waking, she had imagined that Jeff was still lying next to her. Once, she had been convinced that she could feel him breathing on her shoulder.

She turned around to go back upstairs. But standing in the archway close behind her were two huge figures, bulky and dark. She let out a high-pitched '*Hah!*' and stumbled backward.

Both figures were dressed entirely in black – black leather

4

coats and black denim jeans – and they were both wearing transparent celluloid masks, which gave their faces the melted appearance of severe-burns victims. The taller of the two had a strange hat that looked like a demon's horns.

'Goddamit!' Lily shouted at them, although she was more shocked than angry. 'Who the heck are you? And what the *heck* are you doing in my house?'

The figure with the demon's horns took a step toward her, and raised his hand. 'Didn't intend to alarm you, Mrs Blake.' His voice was thick and harsh, like a heavy smoker.

'Who are you? How do you know my name?'

'We know everything about you, Mrs Blake – where you work, where you do your marketing; where you spend your lunch breaks.'

'*What?*'

'Oh, yes. We know what you been up to. You and that Dane guy. Thought you'd get away with it, did you? Thought nobody would notice all of them midday get-togethers? You're a bad, bad woman, Mrs Blake.'

Lily's was shaking. 'Get back. Get away from me. I've called nine-one-one.'

'Don't exactly believe that you have, Mrs Blake. In any case, what we came here to do we can do long before the cops get here.'

The figure stepped forward again, and then again. Lily retreated behind the couch and held up her pepper spray. 'Don't you come any closer. I'm warning you.'

'We've only come here to give you your just desserts, Mrs Blake. Nothing more.'

'If you come any nearer . . .' Lily warned him. But without any hesitation the figure vaulted over the back of the couch, knocking over a brass planter filled with hyacinths. He grabbed hold of Lily's hands, and when she tried to spray him in the face, he twisted her fingers so fiercely that she dropped the spray on to the floor.

She had taken self-defense classes, and she struggled and

5

feinted and tried to kick her assailant between the legs. But he was far too strong for her, far too heavy. He wrenched both her arms behind her back and forced her to bend forward, until her face was pressed against the knotted pile of the rug. All she could so was pant with effort, and with pain.

'You know what you are, Mrs Blake? You're a witch – that's what you are. And do you know what the punishment for witches is?'

'Let me go,' she begged him. 'Listen – there's money in the house. Cash. You can have it.'

'Are you insulting my moral purpose?' the figure demanded. 'Are you trying to suggest I'm some kind of a yegg? I came here to give you your just desserts – that's why I came here, and that's what I'm going to do!'

'I have jewelry. Please. I have my children to take care of.'

'Oh, *now* you're worried about your children! Maybe you should of thought about your children when you was bouncing around on that waterbed with Robert Dane!'

'Who the hell *are* you?' Lily panted. 'Who sent you here?'

The man leaned forward, pressing his full weight on to Lily's back. She felt as if he was going to crush her ribcage. When he spoke, his lips were very close to Lily's ear, and his voice behind his celluloid mask sounded foggy and indistinct.

'We was sent by God, Mrs Blake. We was sent by God, to carry out divine retribution.'

The other figure came around the couch, and between the two of them they lifted Lily up. She had never felt so help-less in her life, and her heart was beating like a panicking bird's.

'Tasha!' she cried out, although her voice was so choked that Tasha couldn't possibly have heard her. 'Tasha! Call the police!'

'Thought you'd called the police already,' said the figure with the demon's horns. 'You weren't trying to *mislead* us, by any chance?'

'Just let me go,' Lily pleaded. 'If you let me go, I swear on my children's lives that I will never say anything about this to anyone, ever.'

The figure took hold of the lapels of Lily's robe, and tore it wide open. 'Don't think that's much of an offer, Mrs Blake. After we've done what we came here to do, you ain't going to be saying nothing about this to nobody, regardless.'

He wrenched her robe off her back and tossed it on to the floor. Now she was wearing nothing but her long white sleep-T.

'Please don't hurt me,' she said. 'You can do whatever you like, but please don't hurt me. Think of my children.'

'You don't get it, do you?' said the figure. He leaned forward until his celluloid mask was only three inches away from her face, and she could see his eyes glittering behind it like black beetles. He smelled strongly of cigarettes and onions and something aromatic, like creosote. 'The children is the reason we're here.'

'What?'

'You won custody, didn't you? You got to take sole care of them. But taking care of children – that's a very burdensome responsibility. You need to be moral, don't you, and set a good example. You need to be a shining light. No drinking, no cursing, no bad-mouthing your former partner, and no indiscriminate fornication with guys who ain't fit to wipe your former partner's rear end.'

Lily stared back at him, horrified. 'Did *Jeff* send you? Is that it?'

'You don't need to know nothing more, Mrs Blake, except that you're getting what you justly deserve.'

Lily screamed at him and threw herself wildly from side to side, trying to break free. She was so frightened and so furious that she felt as if she were going insane.

'Let me go! Let me go, you bastards! Let me go! *Let me go!*'

But the figure with the demon's horns swung his arm back

and slapped her across the face, so hard that it made her ears sing. She stopped struggling at once and dropped her head down. She could feel the side of her mouth swelling up and her left eye closing.

'Don't struggle,' the figure admonished her. 'There ain't no future in struggling.'

'There ain't no future at all,' said the other figure, speaking for the first time, and then giggling.

Between them, the two figures half-dragged and half-carried Lily into the kitchen. Behind the frosted-glass door which led to the utility room, Sergeant appeared, and stood there blackly and silently, watching their distorted images as they made their way around the island. He whined in the back of his throat but still he didn't bark.

The figure with the demon's horns stood over Lily and said, 'I want you to know that this is a sacred duty and there ain't nothing personal in it. Like, I don't want you coming back to haunt me.'

Lily said nothing. Her mouth was too swollen and she felt too numb.

The figure hesitated a moment longer, and then said, 'Look at you. You look like a witch, in that nightgown, all ready to make her peace with God.' Lily was trembling with shock. The other figure, who was gripping her arms, let out another giggle, and then a snort.

The figure with the demon's horns dragged over one of the wheelback kitchen chairs, and pushed Lily back until she was forced to sit down in it. Out of his pocket he produced a coil of washing-line cord, and lashed up her arms and her waist and her ankles, knotting the cord so tightly that it cut into her skin.

'You won't hurt my children, will you?' Lily managed to ask him, in a bruise-muffled voice.

'Do I look like somebody who would hurt a child?' the figure asked her. 'There's a whole lot of difference between divine retribution and unnatural cruelty, believe me.'

'Just don't hurt my children – or, by God, I *will* come back and haunt you, I swear. I will haunt you day and night for the rest of your miserable, worthless life.'

The figure said nothing but walked across the kitchen to the refrigerator and lifted out a gallon-sized container of spring water. He came back, unscrewing the cap.

'Do you know why witchfinders used to duck witches in water?' he asked. 'There was three reasons. One, to make them confess to their liaisons with Satan. The second, to see if they floated, or sank. If they floated, then God's own water refused to take them to its bosom, and their guilt was manifestly proven. But the third reason was to soak their clothes, so that when they were burned, they burned more slowly, and suffered the pain of their punishment for a whole lot longer than they would have done if they had been burned dry.'

'*What?*' said Lily. She couldn't understand what she was hearing. But without any hesitation the figure held the container over her head and emptied it all over her. It splashed all over her hair and her face, and drenched her sleep-T, and she couldn't stop herself from gasping.

The figure tossed the empty container across the kitchen. Then he nodded curtly to his companion, and the two of them bent down on either side of her. They gripped the kitchen chair and heaved it up until Lily was sitting on top of the island.

'What are you going to do to me?' asked Lily. High up like this, she felt even more vulnerable.

'Well, you're a witch, and this is the prescribed way for dealing with witches. As close as I could manage, anyhow. These modern homes – they may have all the modern built-in accessories, but not too many of them can boast a stake for the burning of witches, can they?'

The other figure had temporarily disappeared, but he returned only a few moments later carrying a green plastic gasoline can. Lily could hear the gasoline sloshing inside it.

'Oh God,' she said.

'Well, it might be a good idea to ask for the Lord's forgiveness, in your final moments.'

'Oh God, you're not going to burn me. Please don't burn me. I'd rather you shot me.'

'That'd be kind of difficult since I don't carry a gun of any kind and neither does my friend here.'

'Then for God's sake strangle me. But please don't burn me. I couldn't stand to be burned.'

'I gather it's pretty damned painful, for sure. But the pain you've caused, Mrs Blake, don't you think you deserve it?'

Lily tried to appeal to him again, but she was so terrified that she began to hyperventilate and she couldn't get the words out. She watched with dread as the figure unscrewed the cap of the gasoline container and began steadily to pour it all over the floor around the kitchen island, and splash the sides of the island itself. The reek of gasoline was overwhelming, and the air was distorted by its fumes, as if everything around her were a mirage.

At last, she heard a woman say, '*Please* – don't do this.' To her surprise, it was her. She was amazed that she sounded so reasonable and detached – almost as if a separate Lily Blake were pleading on her behalf. 'If Jeff sent you – if Jeff has a problem with custody – I'm sure that we can work something out. I can talk to my lawyer first thing in the morning.'

The figure with the demon's horns said nothing, but backed away from the island, toward the kitchen door, while his companion crouched alongside him, pouring a trail of gasoline across the tiles.

'You won't get away with this,' Lily insisted. 'And if Jeff sent you, neither will Jeff.'

The two figures reached the kitchen door and stepped outside, into the hallway. The figure with the demon's horns took out a cheap flip-top cigarette lighter and flicked it into flame. It dipped and guttered and made his transparent plastic mask look as if he were grinning.

'You're making a serious mistake here,' Lily warned him.

Two

There was no explosion, only the softest of *whoomphs.* Orange flames ran across the floor and then jumped up all around her, like blazing clowns. She felt a wave of heat that seared her face and shriveled the hairs in her nostrils.

The fire burned with soundless ferocity. Within a few seconds it had consumed almost all of the oxygen within the circle of flames that surrounded her. She gasped for breath, but the gases she inhaled were so hot that she had to clamp her mouth shut, and keep it shut. She could smell her hair burning, and she could see the skin on her forearms starting to redden.

Sergeant was barking now, and throwing himself up against the utility-room door. Lily was fully aware of what was happening to her, but she felt preternaturally calm. *No matter how I do it, I have to get myself out of this fire, and I have to do it now.* The oak-paneled sides of the island were already blazing – they were thickly polished with beeswax and they were crackling and popping and pouring out thick black smoke. She realized that she would probably choke to death before she was actually cremated.

She did the only thing she could think of: she bent her head forward as far as she could, hesitated for a moment, and then threw herself violently backward. Her chair tilted, rocked, but it didn't overbalance.

Desperate for air, she bent her head forward again, and threw herself backward a second time. There was a split second in which the chair was teetering on its back legs.

Then she crashed off the island on to the floor, knocking the back of her head on the terracotta tiles and jarring her spine.

Gasoline flames were still dancing all around the island, but on the tiles they had almost burned themselves out. She managed to kick herself away from the island with one blistered foot, and rock the chair on to its left side. She rocked it again, and again, until she had rolled herself clear of the fire, almost as far as the kitchen door.

She felt bruised, and half-concussed, and she was quaking with shock. The kitchen door was shut, but Sergeant was still furiously barking and the smoke alarm was screeching. That worried her more than anything. If Tasha and Sammy were still in the house, surely the noise would have woken them up, and they would have hurried downstairs to find out what was happening. She prayed that those two figures in black hadn't hurt them.

The island was still burning in the center of the kitchen, spitting out sparks. As she watched, the oak work-surface collapsed sideways, and two drawers fell out, showering cutlery all over the floor.

'Tasha!' she croaked. 'Sammy!' Her throat was raw and she couldn't shout any louder. '*Tasha!*' The two figures in black could still be in the house, and if they heard her calling out, they might come back and finish her off; but right at this moment she didn't care. She just needed to know that her children were safe.

She cried out again, but there was no reply. The fire was dying down, although the smoke was billowing much more densely. Lily lifted up her hands as if she were praying and started to bite at the cords around her wrists. The figure with the demon's horns had tied her painfully tight, and she had to gnaw at the cord until her gums bled. But the knots weren't complicated, and gradually she managed to tug one end loose, and then another. After three or four minutes she was able to untie her waist and her ankles and climb unsteadily on to her feet.

She hobbled to the utility room and let Sergeant out. He stopped barking and circled worriedly around her legs, his tail lashing from side to side.

'Steady, boy,' she coughed. 'Quiet now.'

She opened the kitchen door and stepped out into the hallway. There was no sign of the two figures. She waited for a moment and then limped toward the foot of the stairs. A horrifying apparition approached her, until she found herself standing face-to-face with her reflection in the long mirror by the front door. Her forehead and her cheeks were scarlet and her eyebrows had been singed, which gave her a mad, expressionless look. Her sleep-T was scorched, and her feet were swollen with blisters. The right side of her hair had been burned into crispy, prickly clumps.

She coughed, and coughed again, and couldn't stop coughing, but she mounted the stairs and made her way across the landing to Tasha's bedroom.

'Tasha?' The door was ajar. 'Tasha?'

She switched on the light. Tasha's comforter was pulled right back and her bed was empty. Still coughing, Lily went to Sammy's room. His bed was empty, too.

She leaned back against the wall. *Jeff*. It must have been Jeff. Who else hated her so much, and wanted the children?

She went to her bedroom and picked up the phone. Her fingers left oily black marks on the receiver, and she was shivering uncontrollably.

'Police,' she said. 'And fire department.' And then, catching sight of herself in the mirrored doors of her closet, 'Paramedics, too, I guess.'

The next morning she opened her eyes and her sister Agnes was sitting next to her bed, smiling at her. The hospital room was the palest of pale blues, and it was filled with white October sunlight. On the windowsill stood a large glass vase of white and yellow roses.

She lifted off her oxygen mask. 'Agnes,' she croaked, trying to sit up.

Agnes said, 'Ssh,' and gently pushed her back against her pillows. Then she held her very close, and kissed her.

'I'm so glad you came,' said Lily. 'When did you come?'

'First time, about three o'clock this morning. Ned drove me up here. I looked in on you but you were totally out of it, so I went home and came back again.'

Lily reached out and took hold of Agnes's hands. She wanted to say something, but her throat was so sore and she was all filled up with tears.

'It's OK,' said Agnes. 'I talked to the doctors and they said that you're going to be fine. Minor burns, bruising, smoke inhalation. Your hair's a bit singed. But nothing worse than that.'

'What about Tasha and Sammy?'

'No news so far. The police have called in the FBI.'

'Already?' Lily tried to sit up again, but she started coughing again, and had to lie back.

'It's procedure, apparently, whenever young children go missing.'

'My God, if those men have hurt them . . .'

'I'm sure they haven't, Lily. I'm sure they won't. The police think that Jeff has probably taken them.'

'They were going to burn me alive. They said they were going to burn me like a witch.'

'I know. But you're going to be OK, sweetheart. The doctor said that you should be able to go home in a couple of days.'

Lily pressed her oxygen mask against her face and took half a dozen deep breaths. Then she said, 'Is Jeff not at home?'

Agnes shook her head. 'He hasn't been seen for over a week. He left his job without saying anything to anyone, and the police say that his mother hasn't seen him since the end of September.'

'Oh, God.'

Lily lay back and all she could do was look at Agnes and hold her hands. Agnes was five years younger than she was, just twenty-nine years old, but her serious face and her brown eyes and her wavy brunette hair always made her look more mature. Lily had always thought that there was something of the Catholic saint about her.

The nurse came in, a plump girl with unnaturally rosy cheeks. 'You're awake, then, Ms Blake! I'll check your vitals and then you can have some breakfast.'

'I'd like to see a mirror,' said Lily.

The nurse looked at Agnes warily. 'I don't know if you ought to, just yet.'

'Please,' coughed Lily.

Agnes opened her pocketbook and produced a small compact mirror. Lily peered into it and saw a swollen, reddened face, glistening with lidocaine gel. One eye was purple and almost completely closed. Her eyebrows were shriveled and the hair on the left-hand side of her head was prickly, like a burned sweeping-brush. She stared at herself for a long time, saying nothing. The truth was, she could hardly believe that it was her.

'Your burns are only superficial,' flustered the nurse. 'Doctor Perlstein says you won't have any facial scarring.'

Lily nodded. 'That's good.' She handed the mirror back. 'Not quite ready for mascara, though, am I?'

'Lily . . .' said Agnes.

'It's all right,' Lily insisted. 'I didn't die, and I'm going to get my children back.'

Agnes picked up a manila envelope and opened it for her. 'I brought you this,' she said. 'I thought it might give you some hope.'

It was a color photograph of Tasha and Sammy taken in the summer when they had spent a week with Agnes and Ned in Wayzata. They were sitting on the swing in the back yard, surrounded by roses. Sammy had his left eye squinched up against the sunshine. Tasha was throwing her head back and laughing. Lily looked at it for a moment and her eyes suddenly filled up with tears.

'I'll get them back,' she said, and she was quaking with emotion. 'I don't care what it takes, I'll get them back. And those men who took them, they're going to burn in hell.'

Early that afternoon, Special Agents Rylance and Kellogg came into her room and stood beside her bed with their hands in their pockets. Special Agent Rylance was the older of the two, with a gray comb-over and dark pouches under his eyes and suspicious-looking stains on his yellow satin necktie, while Special Agent Kellogg was young and thin-faced and edgy, with a slicked-back pompadour and sideburns that made him look curiously dated, as if he had stepped out of a high-school prom in 1965 for a cigarette and unexpectedly found himself in the twenty-first century.

Already there were more than a dozen get-well cards beside Lily's bed, and it seemed as if the nurses were bringing in fresh flowers every few minutes. Agent Rylance picked up one of the cards and read it. 'Best wishes from Bennie and Fiona and Bill and all at Concord Realty. God be with you.'

He put down the card and said, 'Doctors said you could have been barbecued, Mrs Blake. You sure lucked out there.'

'Luck had nothing to do with it,' Lily coughed. 'I was trying to survive.'

Special Agent Kellogg said, 'The police pretty much filled us in on the problems that you've been experiencing with your ex-husband – the custody battle, all of that. But did he ever give you any indication at all that he might be thinking of kidnapping your kids, or trying to harm you?'

Lily cleared her throat. 'Never. I mean, Jeff always had a temper. But he was childish, you know, rather than vicious. He slammed doors and shouted and broke things. He never hit me. Most of the time, whenever he got really angry, he just stormed out of the house.'

'These two men who took your kids . . . Do you have any

idea at all as to who they might have been? Like – did your ex-husband ever mention that he was joining one of those fathers' action groups?'

'No. Jeff isn't really a joiner. He wouldn't even join a car pool.'

'The thing is, Mrs Blake, the way your children were taken and the harm that was done to you, we've come across several similar instances of this before, most of them in Minnesota and Wisconsin and Illinois. Children being kidnapped and their mothers being ritually burned to death.'

Special Agent Rylance said, 'We've been trying to track down these sickos for three and a half years now. We believe they belong to an organization calling itself Fathers' League Against Mothers' Evil – FLAME for short.'

'I still can't believe that Jeff would want to see me dead. I mean, he's very emotional, very unstable, but I don't think he's capable of killing the mother of his own children.'

'The police said that one of the guys who attacked you accused you of having an affair.' He opened his notebook and squinted at it, as if he was having trouble reading his own writing. 'A Robert Dane – is that right?'

'Sure. Robert and I dated a few times. He works for the Neighborhood Revitalization Program and that's how we met. But it's never been anything serious. I've never brought him home and Tasha and Sammy don't even know about him.'

'Would your ex-husband be jealous if he found out that you were seeing another man?'

'I don't know. Maybe. He always used to say that I'd never find anybody else to replace him.'

'OK,' said Special Agent Rylance. 'I'm just trying to get a hook on the guy.'

Lily took a few more inhalations of oxygen. Then she said, 'I'd never bring Jeff down. When he and I were first married, everything was wonderful. We were so happy that I could hardly believe it was true.'

'So what went wrong?'

17

'Money, mostly. When I met him, Jeff had a really great job at 3M, in the IT division. We saved up and bought a three-bedroom starter house in Bloomington and when Jeff was promoted we moved to West Calhoun – to the house I'm living in now. It was pretty dilapidated when we first moved in, but we started to fix it up and we were hoping to sell it in a few years and upgrade nearer to Lake Harriet.'

'But then Jeff lost his job?'

'Not exactly – 3M merged two of their divisions and Jeff was sidelined. All of a sudden he had a smaller staff and much less money and no real prospects of promotion. He had a blazing argument with the CEO and he quit. He thought he could walk straight into another high-flying job, some-place else. But of course he was that much older and the marketplace was crowded with young whizzkids. He ended up doing computer maintenance for a small company in Richfield.'

'So things got financially tight?'

'For a while. But then my friend Margaret Allison found me a job at Concord Realty. I loved the job. I *still* love it. I was only there for six months before I was promoted to area sales manager. By the end of the first year I was earning three times what Jeff was bringing home.' She shrugged, and then she said, 'I guess that made him feel less of a man.'

'So that's when the marital disagreements started?'

'First of all we had endless petty arguments about stupid things like what we were going to eat for dinner, and what color we were going to paint the den. Jeff used to say, 'Why bother asking me? You're the one who pays for it all.' Then our personal life started to suffer. You know. After a while we couldn't stay in the same room together for five minutes without having some kind of a row.'

'When was the last time you heard from him?' asked Special Agent Kellogg.

'Two months ago. It was Sammy's birthday and he

asked if he could come round and give him a present. I said absolutely no.'

'How so? That seems like a pretty reasonable request.'

'Well, you'd think so, wouldn't you? But I let him come round to Tasha's birthday party last April, and he went crazy. He ended up pulling the tablecloth and all the birthday food ended up on the floor.'

'I see.'

The nurse came in and told Lily that it was time for her meds.

'OK,' said Special Agent Rylance. 'We'll leave you in peace. But let me just ask you this: was there any place that your ex-husband ever talked about as being like a sanctuary? Someplace that he had good memories of, where he might possibly take the children to bring back some of his happier times?'

'If he had a place like that, he never told me about it. He was born and raised here in Minneapolis. Went to school here, got his first job here. Maybe his mother might know.'

'We'll ask her. She's next on our list.'

Lily said, 'You are going to find my children, aren't you?'

'Mrs Blake, the FBI's child abduction investigation center is the best in the world. We'll find them for you, and that's a promise.'

Agnes came back in. She sat on the edge of Lily's bed and stroked her arm.

'Maybe we should say a prayer,' she said.

But Lily said, 'No. I'm only going to say a prayer when I find them.'

'Is there anything else I can do?'

Lily thought for a moment and then said, 'Yes, there is. Go find some scissors for me, and a razor.'

'What?'

'Scissors, and a razor. They're bound to have some in the hospital store. I want you to shave off what's left of my hair.'

*   *   *

Lily sat up in bed with a towel wrapped around her neck while Agnes carefully shaved her head. She kept her eyes closed while the warm soapy water ran down her face and the back of her neck, and said nothing at all, so that there was no sound but the chiming of the hospital paging system in the corridor outside and the soft persistent scratching of the razor.

When Agnes was finished, she took out her mirror again, and showed Lily what she had done.

'I feel terrible, doing this to you,' said Agnes.

But Lily ran her hand over her scalp and said, 'You shouldn't. This is a fresh beginning.'

She felt strangely empowered by her baldness, as if she were a samurai warrior, or Saint Joan of Arc. Convicted witches used to have their heads shaved, too, and if she was going to be accused of being a witch, then that was what she would be. It was like a symbol of her determination to get her children back, no matter what she had to go through. She was no longer that smart, tousle-haired real-estate salesperson. She had another identity altogether, pure and strong. She was a mother who was seeking her revenge.

'You should sleep now,' said Agnes. 'You need to get your strength back.'

'You bet,' said Lily. 'And the sooner the better.'

Her boss from Concord Realty came to see her, too – Bennie Burgenheim. He shuffled shyly into her room carrying a ludicrously large bouquet of red roses and alyssum. Bennie was a big man, over six feet four inches, and he was always self-conscious about his size and his weight, which led him to tiptoe around as if he were creeping up on people.

He had a big face with a double chin and protuberant eyes, and he wore his hair brushed forward in a boyish fringe. He had taken an obvious interest in Lily ever since she had started working at Concord, and he had been even more attentive after her divorce from Jeff. Bennie was a widower himself:

five years ago he had lost his wife Marjorie when she had tried to warm up her car by running the engine with the garage doors closed, one of the most common causes of accidental death in Minneapolis in the winter months.

Bennie grinned at her, and blinked, and lifted up the bouquet.

'You bought the whole florist,' said Lily.

'Just wanted to show you how much we all appreciate you.'

'Thanks, Bennie. They're wonderful. Here – look, put them down on the end of the bed and pull up a chair. Would you like a cup of coffee or anything? The nurse can bring you some coffee.'

'I'm fine, Lil. I'm much more concerned about you. That was such a terrible thing to happen.'

'I'm OK now. I just want to get Tasha and Sammy back.'

'You will,' said Bennie. 'I'm sure you will. And listen – we don't expect you back at work anytime soon. Take as long as you like. And if there's anything else we can do for you – or *I* can do for you . . .' He took hold of her hand and squeezed it hard. For a moment she almost thought that he was going to burst into tears. But then he nodded at the green silk scarf she was wearing on her shaven head, and said, 'You know what? You look like an elf.'

'An elf? Oh, thanks!'

'You know what I mean . . . kind of little and delicate. I guess you bring out my protective side.'

'I'm OK, Bennie. I'm quite capable of protecting myself.'

'Sure, course you are,' Bennie told her. 'There is one thing, though: I guess the police and the FBI are right on top of things – you know, finding your kids and all. But a couple of years ago my brother Myron found this great private detective when he was going through all of his custody problems with his first wife. He was a little off the wall, this guy, but he was some terrific detective. He saved Myron a bundle, and made sure that he got to see his daughters, too.'

'OK,' said Lily. 'Thanks. I'll bear that in mind.' She paused, and then she asked him, 'How's the Ridge Road development coming along?'

'It's fine. Fiona's handling it for you. I don't want you worry about work at all.'

Lily smiled at him. She knew how much he liked her, and she liked him, too, as a boss and a friend. But every time she looked into his eyes she could see what he really yearned for. He wanted to see her sitting on the opposite side of the breakfast table, while he watched her admiringly and blessed the Lord for bringing him such a pretty young wife.

The last person who came to see her, late in the evening, when all of her other visitors had left, was Robert. He knocked very gently on her open door.

'OK if I come in?'

'Of course it is! I didn't think you were going to show.'

He approached the bed in his long camel-hair overcoat, staring at her. 'My God, Lil. What did they do to you?'

She touched her scarf self-consciously and said, 'Hey – it's not as bad as it looks. Half of my hair was burned so I asked Agnes to shave it off.'

'But your *face*, too, honey. Your poor face.'

He sat down on the edge of the bed and put his arms around her.

'I'm OK,' she said. 'I'm really and truly OK.'

She had promised herself that if Robert came to see her she wouldn't cry, but she couldn't help it. Tears rolled down her cheeks and then she sobbed so deeply that her chest hurt. Robert shushed her and kissed the top of her head and waited until she had recovered enough to speak.

'Oh, Robert, it's Tasha and Sammy. They must be so scared. How could anybody have taken them away like that?'

'They'll find them, believe me. You're going to have to be brave.'

Lily sat up, her reddened face wet with tears. 'I don't feel brave. I don't feel at all brave. But I feel really, really angry. I feel angry with the men who took them and I feel even angrier with myself because I couldn't protect them. I've never felt so . . . *powerless.*'

'Do the police have any leads yet?'

She told him about FLAME, and all the questions that Special Agents Rylance and Kellogg had asked her.

'Do you think Jeff had anything to do with it?' Robert asked her.

'I don't know. I never would have believed that Jeff was capable of being so vengeful. But who else could it be?'

'People can surprise you,' said Robert. 'People you thought you knew real well.' He lifted her hands to his lips and kissed them. 'I'm sorry I didn't bring you any flowers. I came straight over from a council meeting. I'll bring you some tomorrow.'

'You don't have to bring flowers. Look at all these. And they're going to be letting me out in a couple of days.'

'OK, chocolates then. Or grapes. Or a bottle of champagne.'

'I'm on antibiotics. Can't drink.'

He looked her in the eyes. He was handsome, in a rather ordinary way, with wiry blond hair and a short, straight nose and a cleft in his chin. Although he didn't say anything, there was something in his expression that told her that their relationship was over. He was a plain man, with straightforward tastes – considerate, and fun to be with, but without much depth – and she could sense that this kidnapping and this assault were too complicated for him. If he carried on seeing her, he would have to help her recuperate, both physically and mentally, and cope with the possibility that something dreadful might have happened to Tasha and Sammy.

He checked his wristwatch. 'I have to get home now. But I'll look in tomorrow, round about the same time.'

He kissed her again, and she very lightly kissed him back.

Three

S he was allowed to leave Fairview Hospital four days after she been admitted. Agnes and Ned came to collect her in their Ford Explorer and take her back to their home in Wayzata to complete her convalescence. It was a bright, knife-sharp day, and already there were signs that the winter weather was dipping south from Canada. Ned said, 'It's going to be a hard one this year.' Ned wore a Golden Gophers cap and a little ginger moustache and was given to making educated predictions about everything from January's snowfall to this season's walleye population in Lake Minnetonka.

Lily said, 'Do you think we could make a detour?'

'A detour?' said Ned. 'Sure. You want to go home and pick up some things?'

'No, I want to call on Jeff's mother.'

Ned looked at Agnes and pulled a face. 'Do you really think that's such a good idea? The police have already interviewed her, haven't they – and the FBI?'

'I know. But I need to look her in the eye and hear her tell me that she really doesn't know where Jeff is.'

'Even if she *does* know, do you think she'll tell you?'

'She loved Tasha and Sammy. She knows how unhappy they must be without me. And what do I have to lose? The FBI haven't come up with any leads yet. Nothing at all.'

'Well . . . I'm not too sure it's such a good idea.'

All the same, Ned drove them to the suburb of Nokomis, to the tree-lined street of small 1950s houses where Mrs

24

Blake lived. Next door, an elderly man was raking up heaps of red and yellow leaves, while his grandchildren kicked them and rolled in them and chased each other around the front yard. Lily couldn't help thinking of Tasha and Sammy, running through the leaves around the bandshell at Lake Harriet Park.

She rang the doorbell while Agnes and Ned waited in the car. At first she didn't think that there was anybody home, but after a few minutes she saw a shadowy shape through the hammered-glass door, like a fish rising to the surface of a lake. Mrs Blake opened up for her, keeping the door on the safety-chain.

Sylvia Blake had once been a very attractive young woman – red-haired, creamy-skinned, with green eyes and a full, generous figure – a young woman who loved to dance and laugh and go to parties. But Jeff's father had slowly died of progressive supranuclear palsy, taking seventeen years to do it, and gradually Sylvia had been reduced to a weary illusion of her previous self, with white roots in her hair and a small tight mouth that was permanently puckered in resentment.

'Lily,' she said, without any intonation whatsoever.

'Hallo, Sylvia. I just got out of the hospital and I thought I'd come to see you.'

'Oh – now you don't have the children with you? You never came to see me when you had the children with you.'

'Come on, Sylvia. You know how difficult it was. All I want to do is ask you if you've heard from Jeff.'

'I've had the police asking me that. And some agents from the FBI. Don't you think I would have told *them*, if I had?'

'Sylvia . . . can I come in?'

Mrs Blake hesitated for a moment and then unfastened the security chain. 'I don't have anything to tell you, Lily, whether you're in or out.'

Lily followed her into the living room. Although it was

so sunny outside, the windows were draped in dusty net curtains and the room was shadowy and stuffy and smelled of stale food and cigarettes. The furniture was all dark brown, with brown cushions, and over the fireplace was a dark reproduction of an ineffably gloomy fur trapper, roasting a squirrel on a stick.

'Who's that outside?' asked Mrs Blake, peering through the nets.

'My sister Agnes and her husband Ned.'

'I see. Well, I haven't heard from Jeff. I told the police and those FBI agents. I haven't heard a squeak from him since September.'

'Did he ever tell you that he wanted to take Tasha and Sammy away from me?'

Mrs Blake raised her gingery, overplucked eyebrows. 'Once or twice, when he was really mad at you. But I wouldn't say that he meant it.'

'You know that the men who kidnapped Tasha and Sammy tried to kill me, don't you? They tried to set fire to me.'

Mrs Blake shrugged but said nothing.

'They tried to burn me alive, Sylvia. Look.' With that, Lily tugged off her black woolly hat. Mrs Blake's eyes widened and her left arm jerked up as if she was suffering from a nervous spasm, but still she didn't say anything.

'Sylvia,' said Lily, 'even if you haven't heard from Jeff – even if you don't know where he is now – is there anything you can think of that might help me to find him? Was there any special place that he used to like to go to, when he was younger? Someplace he felt happy and safe?'

'This is my only son we're talking about here, Lily,' said Mrs Blake. 'You ground him down, and you destroyed his pride, and then you took his children away from him. You can't expect me to give you any help.'

'Sylvia, please. I'm not thinking about myself. I'm thinking about Tasha and Sammy. And I'm thinking about Jeff, too. If he's kidnapped those children, he's in very serious trouble. He's looking at a very long jail sentence. If I can find him . . . if I can persuade him to bring them back . . . maybe things'll go much easier on him.'

She watched Sylvia's face go through a whole kaleidoscope of expressions: doubt, anxiety, perplexity, and an odd raccoon-like furtiveness.

'Come on, Sylvia; he's not going to be able to hide for ever, especially with two young children.'

Mrs Blake said, 'You can't ask me that, Lily. Even if I knew, how could I tell you?'

Lily took hold of her shoulders and looked her straight in the eyes. 'Sylvia, you're a mother too. You know what I'm going through. Tell me.'

But Mrs Blake lifted her hands away and said, 'There's nothing to tell, Lily. Life never turns out the way we want it to, does it?'

Lily spent the weekend in Wayzata with Agnes and Ned. They had three children – Petra, Jamie and little William, who was only twenty-two months old. Every day was bright and sunny and every day was colder than the day before. The kids spun around the yard in scarves and gloves, and laughed, and chased their cocker spaniel Red, and all Lily could do was stand by the window watching them, and thinking of Tasha and Sammy.

Sammy was his father's boy; he would probably be getting along OK, doing outdoorsy stuff like fishing and watching sport and playing basketball. But Tasha was much quieter and much more sensitive, and she had been deeply hurt by their marriage breaking up. Lily was worried that all the care she had taken to restore Tasha's self-assurance might have been scattered and lost for ever.

On Sunday afternoon a gray Pontiac Grand Prix drew up outside and Special Agents Rylance and Kellogg climbed out. Agnes brought them through to the living room, where they stood in front of Lily with the solemnity of Mormons.

'I'm sorry, Mrs Blake. So far we don't have any progress to report. We've had thirty-eight different sightings of children who might have been Tasha and Sammy, seventeen of them here in the Twin City area, but one of them as far afield as Philadelphia.'

Special Agent Kellogg put in, 'We've posted pictures on the FBI website, and we've sent out bulletins to every police headquarters in the country. This is what happens automatically with missing children of tender years, but we're doing a whole lot more than that. We have informants giving us inside information on fathers' pressure groups and any other organizations that might be involved in related acivitities.'

Lily was wearing blue jeans and a white rollneck sweater but she wasn't wearing a hat. Neither Special Agent Rylance nor Special Agent Kellogg asked her why she had shaved her head, but she had an idea that they understood what she was going through, without having to be told.

'So . . . no leads so far?' she asked. She paused, and then she heard herself saying, 'Do you think they might be dead?'

Special Agent Rylance looked at her and his eyes were half-closed like a lizard's. 'I won't try to deceive you, Mrs Blake. The longer that a child of tender years goes missing for, the higher the likelihood is that they've been killed. But this is usually when we're dealing with your straightforward sex abductions. When we're dealing with your parental kidnaps, the survival rate is dramatically improved.'

'But you still don't know for sure if it was my ex-husband who arranged to have the children taken?'

'Not one hundred percent, no – I'll admit it.'

'So it could have been some pedophile group? Or a couple of psychos?'

'It could have been, I admit. But we're not inclined to think so. The longer that Mr Blake stays missing for, the higher the chances are that your children are with him.'

'So what am I supposed to do?' asked Lily. 'It's been nearly a week.'

Special Agent Rylance sat down next to her and took hold of her hand. 'I want you to try and trust our expertise, Mrs Blake. The NCAVC has truly amazing resources for finding missing children and abductees.'

'Like what? Like putting their faces on milk cartons?'

'That's one way we do it, yes. But we also have huge resources of DNA samples and fingerprint files and telephone records and minute-by-minute credit-card transactions. It's becoming increasingly difficult for anybody to vanish off the face of the earth.

He looked at Lily for a long moment, 'We'll find your children for you, Mrs Blake, don't you worry about that.'

But a week became two weeks, and in the middle of November the cold weather system came sweeping down from Alberta and suddenly the streets of Minneapolis were whirling furiously with snow.

Lily returned to her house, but after a few days she went back to work for Concord Realty, because she couldn't stand sitting by the phone all day waiting for a call from the FBI, or sitting on the children's beds trying to remember what it felt like to have them there. She was even beginning to forget what their voices had sounded like.

Her parents telephoned her every evening from Escondido, in southern California. Douglas Frazier was seventy-four now, with a bad heart, and Iris Frazier had recently dislocated her hip, so they couldn't make the trip to Minneapolis, especially now that winter was closing in. But they tried to reassure her that it was only a matter of time before somebody would recognize Tasha and Sammy on a street corner someplace, and bring them home. Every time she put down the phone, however, she believed them a little less.

Agent Kellogg called her too, sometimes three times a

day, no matter where she was or what she was doing. But each day the calls were the same. 'We had a sighting in Presque Isle, but it turned out to be a false alarm. Sorry.'

The snow grew thicker and thicker and the lakes turned to stone. WCCAM Radio 830 forecast that this was going to be the worst winter in the Twin Cities area since 1864, when temperatures had dropped to minus forty-five. A strange hush descended on Minneapolis, as SUVs crept around like tumbrels, and people stalked around like drunken scarecrows on Stabilicer boots, and even diesel fuel started to freeze.

'We had a sighting in St Louis Park. We had another sighting in Mankato. Both false alarms. Sorry.'

But on the second day of December, just as she was leaving the house, the mailman came across the snowy front yard and handed Lily a second-hand manila envelope, stuck down with Scotch tape. The previous addressee's name had been heavily crossed out in blue ballpen and her own name and address written to one side. Lily turned it this way and that; then she carried it back inside the house, took off her gloves and opened it up.

Inside, she found a yellowed old photograph, about ten by eight, stuck to a piece of cardboard. It showed a small boy in a striped T-shirt and dark shorts standing outside a barn, holding a piece of wood shaped like a rifle.

She felt the stubble on her head prickle, and her hand started to tremble. *Jeff. This was Jeff, when he was a boy.*

She went across to the phone and punched out Sylvia's number. The phone rang and rang for over two minutes before Sylvia eventually answered.

'Blake residence?' said Sylvia, as if she wasn't too sure about it herself.

'Where is this?' Lily demanded. 'This place in the photograph?'

'It's Christmas in two weeks. I thought if we could find them . . . maybe I could see them at Christmas.'

'*Where is this?*' Lily screamed at her. '*You knew about this place and you didn't tell me?*'

'You don't have to yell at me. I forgot all about it till this weekend, when I was tidying up Jeff's old room. Then I remembered you asking me if he had a favorite hideout.'

'Sylvia, I need to know where this is, and I need to know right now.'

'There used to be an abandoned farm about a mile away – Sibley's place. It's all built up now, mostly, but the old barn is still there. When he was a boy, Jeff used to play in that barn all day sometimes, pretending he was a cowboy. He used to walk around with a spent match in his mouth and his eyes all slitty and telling me that he was Clint Eastwood.'

Lily was still trembling. 'Sylvia, if I find out that Jeff took my children there . . .'

'I'm trying to help you, Lily. You don't have to get so mad at me. You think that *I* don't want to see those children, too?'

Lily held up the receiver in front of her face, staring at it in anger and disbelief, as if she could throttle it. But then, with an effort, she quietly hung it up. Angry as she was, she knew that Sylvia was more confused and worn-out than malicious, and she didn't want to antagonize her, in case she needed to ask her for any more help.

She dialed the number that Special Agent Rylance had given her.

'Mrs Blake?' said Special Agent Rylance. He sounded very weary.

'I think I might have found Jeff's sanctuary – the place where he used to go when he wanted to get away from the world.'

'Give us twenty minutes, Mrs Blake. We'll call round and pick you up.'

It started snowing again, quite suddenly, and they had to drive to Nokomis at a crawl. Even though it was only ten thirty a.m. the sky was dark, and all of the vehicles on Forty-Second Street had their headlights on.

Special Agent Rylance looked at the back of the photograph. '*Jeff, Sibley's Barn, 1981.* You don't want to get your hopes up about this, Mrs Blake. All the same, I wish your mom-in-law had shown it to us before.'

'Ex-mom-in-law,' Lily corrected him.

They rolled slowly past Sylvia's house, kept on going until they reached a new development of three- and four-bedroomed houses, built around a curving hill and landscaped in descending terraces. This morning the hill was deeply buried in snow, and a crowd of twenty or thirty young children were tobogganing. Lily couldn't stop herself from looking carefully at each of their faces, just in case they happened to be Tasha or Sammy. Totally illogical, she knew. Totally impossible. But she still couldn't help herself.

Special Agent Rylance frowned at the large-scale local map that was unfolded on his lap. 'Here we are . . . Sibley's End. This is where the old farm used to be. The barn is actually marked here – look. Sibley's Barn, *circa* 1882. Take a left here, Greg, then we should see it up on the right-hand side.'

Sibley's End turned out to be a small collection of two-story brick homes with snow-covered SUVs parked in their driveways, and a motley collection of snowmen standing in their front yards. Special Agent Kellogg parked at the very far end of the development, where there was a black overgrown tangle of briars, and they all climbed out of the car. Between the briars they found a narrow zig-zag pathway that led to what was left of Sibley's Farm – a half-acre triangle of snowy field. In the far corner of the field stood a dilapidated barn, its roof sagging and most of its green paint weathered away.

Lily pushed her way through the briars and started to trudge across the field, with Special Agents Rylance and Kellogg following close behind her. In the near distance, they could hear the whistling and screaming of airplanes

at Minnesota International, as they lined up for their slot
to take off. A fat gray rabbit jumped and scurried across
the field and vanished into the briars. Lily couldn't help
thinking about Sammy. He used to love the story about Brer
Rabbit and the Briar Patch.

*'Hang me just as high as you please, Brer Fox,' says Brer
Rabbit, says he, 'but for the Lord's sake don't throw me in
the briar patch.'*

'Nobody's been here since the snow started,' said Special
Agent Rylance.

Special Agent Kellogg approached the barn's main door.
It had collapsed on its runners years ago, but there was still
a small access door in the middle, which was fastened with
nothing more than a long twist of rusty wire.

'Looks like this wire could've been disturbed not too
long ago,' said Special Agent Kellogg.

'Kids, probably,' said Special Agent Rylance.

'I very much doubt it, Henry. Kids don't play in smelly
old barns any more. They stay in their well-appointed
centrally heated bedrooms, playing with their X-Boxes.'

'Well, let's take a look inside anyhow.'

Special Agent Rylance unwound the wire and wrenched
open the door. He took a flashlight out of his coat pocket
and cautiously climbed into the barn. After a moment he
reappeared and said, 'Empty. No sign that anybody's been
here, either.'

Lily and Special Agent Kellogg stepped into the barn
too. It was high and gloomy, although scores of shingles
had slipped, so that dull gray daylight filtered through to
the floor. The agents' flashlights flickered from one side to
the other, and up to the hayloft, criss-crossing each other
like lightsabers, but there was nothing here except heaps
of dusty, dried-out straw, and two rusty plow-blades, and
part of a half-dismantled generator.

'Sorry, Mrs Blake,' said Special Agent Rylance, laying
his hand on her shoulder.

Lily looked around one last time. She was just about to step back out of the door when she glimpsed a small button shining on the floor, almost completely hidden amongst the straw. She turned to Special Agent Kellogg and said, 'Here . . . can you point your flashlight down here?'

She bent down and picked the button up. It was new, plastic and pearly, and there was a tiny shred of torn cotton attached to it, blue and green.

She felt breathless. 'This is Sammy's,' she said, holding it up in front of the flashlight. 'This is a button from Sammy's pajamas.'

Special Agent Rylance came forward and peered at it. 'You're sure about that?'

'He was wearing blue-and-green-checkered pajamas when he was kidnapped, wasn't he? This is from the same pajama top – I'm sure of it. He *was* here. He *was* here. So it must have been Jeff who took him.'

'Too bad you picked it up,' said Special Agent Rylance. 'Might have had a partial on it. All the same . . .' He reached into his inside pocket and took out a crumpled brown envelope. 'I'll send it to the lab, see what they can make of it. And we'll get some forensics people round here a.s.a.p. Greg – do you want to call Murray Halperin for me?'

Lily bent over again and quickly started to flick away the straw, trying to find any more evidence that Sammy had been here. But Special Agent Rylance quickly took hold of her arm and said, 'No, Mrs Blake. If Sammy was here, then this is a crime scene, and you mustn't disturb the evidence. It could make all the difference between finding your children or not finding them.'

Lily stood up straight and stared at him. 'What do you mean – "not finding them"? You promised me that you were going to find them. You *promised*.'

'*Quickly*, was what I meant, Mrs Blake. Finding them *quickly*.'

But Lily could see by the way he glanced across at Special Agent Kellogg that he hadn't meant 'quickly'. Tasha and Sammy had been missing now for forty-six days, and the FBI's own statistics were increasingly pessimistic with every hour that passed.

Special Agent Rylance escorted her back across the Brer Rabbit field. Their breath smoked in the mid-morning gloom.

As they climbed into the car, Special Agent Rylance said, 'There's one consolation, Mrs Blake. If you're right about that button, and it *is* Sammy's—'

'It is. I'm sure of it.'

'Well, if it is, we have much less reason to be concerned for Tasha and Sammy's safety. If they were brought here, then it's almost certain that your ex-husband took them, and I very much doubt that he would injure them in any way.'

Lily looked back toward the old barn. 'What will they do – the forensics people? Will they be able to tell if Jeff was there?'

'They'll look for footprints, fibers, cigarette butts – you name it. If anybody drove a vehicle across that field on the night that Tasha and Sammy were taken, they would have left very deep tire tracks, and since it started to freeze only a few days later, the chances are that those tire tracks are very well preserved. We'll also start a house-by-house inquiry, to see if any of the residents in this development saw anything unusual.'

Lily looked around. 'If only snowmen could talk,' she said.

Four

B ut the snowmen remained mute, and the people who lived in Sibley's End had seen nothing, and the FBI forensic team found no tire tracks or distinctive footprints or any other material evidence. The single pajama button with the shred of blue-and-green cotton attached to it was the only indication that Jeff had taken Tasha and Sammy. Even then, Lily had bought Sammy's pajamas on sale at Dayton's, so there was no conclusive proof that the button was his.

Christmas came, and the Twin Cities sparkled with lights and decorations, and it snowed for three days solid. Lily took Petra, Jamie and William to the Holidazzle Parade at the Nicollet Mall, and then for pizza and frozen custard at Marco's. She found it painful, taking them out, but to watch them clapping and laughing at the marching Santas was a more endurable pain than sitting at home, in her dark and empty house, waiting for phone calls that came less and less frequently.

She spent Christmas Day with Agnes and Ned and the children. Before lunch they bowed their heads around the table and said a special prayer for Tasha and Sammy and their safe return. Lily had bought Tasha the new Bratz disco doll, and a talking robot for Sammy. She wrapped their presents in gold and silver and left them under the tree, as a way of showing that they were not forgotten, and that she expected them to be home soon.

She was standing in the kitchen with Agnes, talking and

drinking a glass of red wine, when Ned came in and said, 'Lily? Couple of gentlemen visitors for you.'

For a split second she thought: *Not Special Agents Rylance and Kellogg, please. Not with bad news, not on Christmas Day.* But then Bennie Burgenheim appeared, with snow melting on the shoulders of his big red padded windbreaker.

'Lil! Happy Christmas!' He came tip-toeing into the kitchen and gave her a kiss. 'I brought you a present,' he said. He turned around and held his hand out. In the doorway behind him stood a thin-faced man wearing a long black overcoat and carrying a gray wide-brimmed hat. The man gave Lily a small, tight smile and lifted up his hat by way of acknowledgement. He had dense black eyebrows and black glittery eyes and a narrow, bony nose. His chin was blue, as if he hadn't shaved since the day before yesterday.

'Lily, want you to meet John Shooks. John – this is Lily Blake, who I was telling you about.'

'Bennie,' said Lily, trying not to sound too irritated. 'Do you want to tell me what's going on here?'

'For sure. John is the private detective who helped out my brother Myron. I thought since Christmas had come and the FBI still hadn't found where Tasha and Sammy were taken to, maybe John could have a try.'

'Bennie, I know you mean well. But I really believe that the FBI are doing everything that anybody possibly *can* do.'

'I'm sure they are, Lil. But what do you have to lose? You know what it's like when we're having a tough time shifting an unattractive property. Sometimes it helps to bring in somebody new, so that they can look at the problem from a fresh point of view.'

'Agreed,' said Lily. 'But selling a clunker is a whole lot different from hunting for somebody who's taken your children. Those FBI agents told me that they have very carefully planned procedures, so that they don't spook the people they're looking for.'

'Of course they do, Mrs Blake,' said John Shooks, 'and quite right, too.' He had a dry Minnesota accent like a creaky door, and a slight lisp, so that 'course' came out 'coursh'. He stepped forward and put down his hat on the kitchen counter. 'One of the great difficulties when you're looking for parental kidnappers is that their victims are often willing accomplices to their own abduction.'

'What do you mean? My children wouldn't have gone with their father willingly.'

'Maybe not to begin with, granted. But you can guarantee that he's giving them the time of their life. And you can also guarantee that he's been working on them since day one, undermining their feelings for you. It doesn't take much.'

Agnes snapped, 'Tasha and Sammy could never stop loving their mother, *ever*, no matter what Jeff might say to them.'

Shooks raised one eyebrow. 'With all due respect, ma'am, young children can be very easily manipulated. They're young children, after all: they're *supposed* to be suggestible. That's how they learn things. And it doesn't take much in the way of amusement parks and rocky-road ice cream to convince a pre-teen kid that life with Daddy is a whole lot funner than staying at home with Mommy, tidying her bedroom and washing dishes and doing her geography homework.'

'I don't think my children are like that,' said Lily, defensively.

'What? They don't like roller-coaster rides? They don't like ice cream? They don't prefer swimming to schoolwork? Unusual kids, if you don't mind my saying so, Mrs Blake.'

'I really don't need your help, Mr Shooks. Bennie – thank you for bringing Mr Shooks around. I appreciate what you're trying to do. But I think it's best if we leave this investigation to the proper authorities.'

Shooks smiled at her. Although he was so dark and thin

and saturnine, there was something strangely kind about his smile, as if he really understood what she was suffering. 'OK,' he said, 'the decision is entirely yours. Bennie's quite right, though. Sometimes – if you look at a problem from a different angle – it can unravel itself right in front of your eyes. As if by magic.'

'Would either of you gentlemen like a drink?' asked Ned. 'I still have about two gallons of my famous Christmas punch left over. Bennie? How about you, Mr Shooks? Care for a drink?'

'Thanks, but no,' said Shooks, still smiling at Lily.

'I'd better take a raincheck, too,' said Bennie. 'It's solid ice out there, and I think I'm going to need my wits about me.'

'I'm sorry you've had a wasted journey,' said Lily.

Bennie put his arm around her and gave her a hug. 'Not at all. You know that I'd do anything for you, Lil. I just thought it might be worth giving John a crack at finding Tasha and Sammy for you. Like I said, he really helped out my brother Myron with his two daughters. Every time his ex-wife Velma tried to take them away, John found her in a couple of hours flat. In the end I guess she got tired of trying. He never heard from her again.'

Shooks picked up his hat and turned to go. As he reached the door, however, Agnes said, 'Do you *really* think you could find Lily's children, Mr Shooks?'

Shooks smiled at the floor. 'Believe me, ma'am, I wouldn't have come here otherwise. Not on Christmas Day.'

Agnes looked at Lily. 'Lily – maybe you should let him try. As Bennie says, what do you have to lose?'

Lily said, 'I don't want to mess up anything the FBI might be doing, that's all. You see these stories on TV when ordinary cops arrest undercover cops by mistake, thinking they're criminals, and blow the cover on a drug bust or something.'

'I understand your concern, Mrs Blake,' said Shooks, 'but

we're not dealing with a sting operation here, and I don't have any more power of arrest than anybody else in this kitchen. All I intend to do is find your children and bring them back to you, unharmed, and as quickly as possible.'

'But how can you do that, if the FBI can't do it?'

'Because I'm not the FBI, Mrs Blake, and I can call on resources which the FBI are unable or unwilling to employ.'

'Like what, for instance?' asked Ned. 'You mean, like' – and he silently mouthed the next two words – '*the Mafia?*'

'No, nothing like that. There are forces in this world which are a great deal more powerful than the Mafia. More trustworthy, too.'

Lily could feel her heart beating, quick and hard – adrenaline, released by the possibility that Shooks could actually do what he claimed he could do.

'How long do you think it would take you to find my children? I mean – supposing I *did* ask you to look for them?'

Shooks turned his head slightly and fixed her with his glittery eyes. 'Hard to tell exactly. Depends how far away they've been taken. But no more than three or four days, I shouldn't imagine.'

'If you're such a genius at finding people, how come you're not more famous? How come the FBI don't use you?'

'Because what I do, Mrs Blake – it comes at a very high price. Not always financially. Sometimes, in terms of money, it comes extremely cheap. But all the same, some people can't afford it; some people can afford it but don't want to pay it.'

'I don't understand.'

'You would, if you were to retain me.'

'Give us a ballpark figure,' said Ned.

Shooks said, 'I'm sorry. I'd have to consult my resources first, find out what they were looking for.'

'A thousand? Two thousand? Ten thousand? What?'

'You can name your price,' put in Bennie. 'Concord Realty will pay. We just want to see Lily get her kids back.'

'How much did your brother pay?' asked Shooks.

Bennie thought about it, and then frowned. 'I don't know, to tell you the truth. He never told me.'

'Exactly,' said Shooks. He turned again to leave, but Lily knew that she couldn't let him go. If he could really find Tasha and Sammy for her in three or four days, she didn't mind what it cost. She didn't even mind if she had to sell the house and live in some low-rent apartment in Cedar-Riverside.

'Mr Shooks . . .' she said, and he stopped where he was, patiently waiting for what she was going to say next.

He met her the next morning at eleven a.m. at Sibley's Barn. It had stopped snowing and an orange sun was suspended in a pale-gray sky. She wore a shaggy fox-fur coat and a shaggy fox-fur hat and thick shaggy boots. When she crossed the Brer Rabbit field Shooks was already waiting for her, in his long black coat and his wide-brimmed hat, and a very long black scarf, his breath smoking.

'How did you sleep?' he asked her as she approached. She was taken aback. It seemed an incongruous question from a man who barely knew her. Yet somehow it made sense. He wanted to know how excited she was.

'Not very much, as a matter of fact,' she told him. 'But then you must have known that.'

'I've looked inside the barn already,' he said. 'No physical evidence, just as the FBI told you. No footprints, no fingerprints, no fibers.'

'So now what?'

'We find out what happened here first.'

'How can we do that, if there's no evidence?'

Shooks smiled. 'I said no *physical* evidence. But people leave more than physical evidence. They leave a resonance, an echo. A smell of themselves.'

41

'The FBI tried manhunting dogs. They couldn't pick up any scent at all.'

'I'm not talking about that kind of a smell. Here – come into the barn and I'll show you what I mean.'

Lily hesitated for a moment, but then she stepped through the access door into the barn and Shooks followed her. She stood amongst the straw while he circled around and around her, trailing his fingers against the walls.

'What are you looking for?' she asked him.

He stopped circling. 'They were here all right. I can hear them.'

'You can *hear* them? What do you mean?'

He approached her with his hands held up to the sides of his face He stopped only two or three feet away from her, and it was then that she saw that his eyes had rolled up into his head, so that only the whites were exposed. She took a step away from him, and then another. He looked grotesque, like a death mask.

'*Where are we going?*' he suddenly said. But he didn't speak in his own voice at all. He sounded high and childish. In fact, he sounded exactly like Sammy.

Lily felt her scalp crawl with fright. This wasn't ventriloquism, or mimicry. Somehow, this was Sammy talking through Shooks' lips.

'How are you doing that?' she demanded. 'That's Sammy! How are you doing that?'

'*Mommy's going to be worried,*' said Shooks, and this time he spoke in Tasha's voice. '*I think you should take us back home.*'

'*Don't you want to come on vacation?*' he replied, and now he was talking like Jeff. In fact he sounded so much like Jeff that Lily couldn't stop herself from turning around, to see if Jeff was standing behind her. '*Mommy won't mind if we take a few days' vacation. We can swim on the beach, we can go horseback riding. We can do anything you want.*'

'*But does Mommy know?*' asked Tasha.

'*I'll call her. I promise. The trouble was, she didn't want me to see you so the only way was to have those friends of mine sneak you out of the house.*'

'*I'm cold,*' said Sammy. '*I don't want to go on vacation. I want to go back to bed.*'

'*Don't you worry. My friends are bringing a car for us. There are blankets in the back, and it'll be warm. You can sleep on the way.*'

Lily slowly approached Shooks and said, 'Jeff? Jeff, listen to me, Jeff. Where are you taking them?'

But it was Sammy who answered. '*I don't want to go on vacation. I want to go home.*'

'Jeff!' shouted Lily, taking hold of Shooks' upraised wrists, and shaking him. 'Jeff! Where are you taking them, Jeff?'

There was a long pause. Somewhere up in the eaves of the barn an owl flapped, and gave a hollow moan that was unnervingly human. Shooks slowly closed his eyes, and when he opened them again, his black glittery pupils had reappeared. He looked at Lily's hands, gripping his wrists, and he gently but firmly pried himself free.

'You heard them, then?' he asked her.

'Of *course* I heard them. You spoke like Sammy and Tasha and you spoke like Jeff, too. How did you do that?'

'It's a well-known phenomenon, Mrs Blake. Scientists call it "auditory persistence".'

'What?'

'It's very simple. After we say anything, our words continue to resonate for a very long time – days, or even weeks, depending on where they were spoken, and with how much vehemence.' He tapped his forehead with his fingertip. 'Anybody who has the sensitivity can pick them up. It's a talent. I inherited it from my great-great-grandfather, on my mother's side, who was a Mdewakanton Sioux. The Sioux call it "ghost talking".'

'So that was actually *them* – their actual voices – Tasha and Sammy and Jeff?'

Shooks nodded. 'Absolutely. You heard them for your-self. And so far as I'm concerned, those voices prove beyond any shadow of a doubt that your ex-husband kidnapped your children and tried to have you killed.'

'So where is he now?'

'It sounds like he was planning on going someplace warm. Who knows – Mexico maybe?'

'I thought you could find out.'

'Oh, yes. But not me personally. I don't have the man-trailing skills for that. But I have an acquaintance who does.'

'Then what are we waiting for?'

'You remember what I was saying at your sister's house – about the price that has to be paid?'

'Yes. So what? I'll pay anything.'

'I know. But I have to warn you that my acquaintance may not be tempted.'

'I don't understand.'

'I think you'd better meet him. Then we can see if he's willing to help.'

'All right, then. When?'

Lily went back home, feeling jumpy and impatient and unnerved. The house was chilly and silent. The long-case clock in the hallway had stopped, and the log fire in the living room had burned out. She went into the utility room and Sergeant was dozing in his basket. He looked up at her sadly. She could have believed that Sergeant was pining for Tasha and Sammy more than she was.

She hunkered down beside him and ruffled his ears. 'Don't you worry, boy. Mommy's found a man who can bring them back to us. I hope so, anyhow.'

Sergeant made a whining noise in the back of his throat and licked her hand.

The phone rang. It was Special Agent Kellogg. 'We had a sighting at Estherville, Mrs Blake, a few miles over the border in Iowa. Two kids, very similar to Tasha and Sammy in appearance, but the Iowa State Police have just emailed us pictures and I'm afraid it isn't them. Sorry – I was hoping to give you a belated Christmas present.'

Lily was tempted to tell him what Shooks had managed to find out in Sibley's Barn – that Jeff had taken the children and had probably headed south. But she decided against it. She guessed that Special Agents Rylance and Kellogg would be pretty irked if they found out that an amateur was interfering in their investigation, especially a part-Native-American amateur who could talk in other people's voices.

She took Sergeant for a walk. The streets were snowy and the world was utterly hushed. The oaks were bare of leaves but they were clustered with hundreds of black crows, as if the souls of all the children who had ever died in Minneapolis had gathered together, to hold a vigil. She still believed that Tasha and Sammy were alive, but she wondered how mothers could bear it when their children were killed. The emptiness and the sense of loss must be almost maddening.

She was walking across the empty park when her cell phone rang. 'Mrs Blake? This is John Shooks. My acquaintance says that he can see us tomorrow, at noon.'

'Did you tell him that I can pay him anything he asks?'

'That didn't really arise.'

'What do you mean? I have to get my children back. Whatever he wants, he can have it.'

'I'll call for you tomorrow, Mrs Blake.'

He hung up. Lily checked her screen but he hadn't left a number. She stood in the middle of the park, surrounded by snow and silence, and for the first time in her life she felt as if she were the only person left alive on the entire planet.

Five

The next morning, while she was sitting in the dining room drinking a cup of coffee and working on a brochure for the Shingle Creek development, the doorbell chimed. She opened the door and it was Bennie, with a boiled bell hat that was two sizes too small for his head.

'Bennie, come on in!'

'I was on my way to Tangletown – thought I'd call by.'

'Like some coffee?'

He stamped his snowy galoshes on the mat. 'No, no. I can't stay long. I've got a viewing at the Starling property.'

'Well, if you can sell *that* old ruin for the asking price, you're a better realtor than I am.'

He took off his padded coat and his hat, and perched his hat on top of the banister post. 'Did you meet John Shooks yesterday?' he asked her.

'Yes, I did. And I really think we're making some progress. He's coming round later this morning and bringing a friend of his.'

'That's good,' said Nat. 'That's good.' But then he said, 'I *hope* it's good, anyhow.'

'You *hope* it's good? The way you talked about him before, he's the best detective since Sherlock Holmes.'

'I don't know, Lil. Maybe it's nothing. But I met my brother Myron yesterday and told him that Shooks was going to be working on your case. He said fine, good, he'll definitely get your kids back for you. But for some reason he didn't seem too easy about it. I asked him if there was

46

anything wrong, and he said no. Then I asked him what Shooks had charged him, because I wanted you to have some idea of what you were letting yourself in for, cost-wise. And he said, it wasn't the money.'

'It wasn't the money?'

'That's what he said. I didn't know what he was talking about, either. So I asked him: if it wasn't the money, what was it? And he said, it was his conscience.'

Lily sat down at the dining-room table. 'His *conscience*? He didn't explain himself any more than that?'

Bennie dragged out a large green handkerchief and blew his nose. 'I told him that I still didn't understand what he meant. And I told him that if he knew of any risk in doing business with Shooks, he needed to warn me about it, because I certainly don't want *you* to come to any harm. But all he said was, when you do business with John Shooks, the price he asks you for is the price you're going to have to pay, come hell or high water, so think long and hard before you agree to it.'

Lily didn't know what to say. She couldn't imagine what Shooks could ask her for that she wouldn't be prepared to give him. She wanted Tasha and Sammy back, at any price, and even if Shooks asked her for a million dollars, she was sure that she could find some way of raising it.

Not only that, she was a seasoned negotiator and she knew exactly how to cut a deal and draw up a contract. Before she entered into any kind of arrangement with Shooks, she would make sure that all of the angles were covered, legal and financial, and that he wasn't able to spring any unpleasant surprises – like finding Tasha and Sammy but refusing to hand them over unless she trebled his fee. Not that she believed he would.

Bennie said, 'Maybe I'm making something out of nothing at all. Myron can have his funny moods, you know – laughing his socks off one minute, all doom and gloom the next. I thought he was real happy with what Shooks did for him, which is why I introduced him to you. I just thought I'd better give you the heads up, in case.'

'Well, I appreciate it,' said Lily. 'But it sounds to me as if Myron could be feeling guilty about taking the children away from Velma and getting the court to cut down her alimony. I mean, once the dust has settled, some husbands and wives do regret how crappy they've been to each other, while they were going through their divorce. I know *I* did. Well – *now* I don't, after what Jeff's done. But I did before.'

'Maybe you're right. I hope so. And I hope you get those kids back, real quick.' Bennie peered at his wristwatch. 'I'd better be heading off. I arranged to meet those people at eleven thirty.'

But he didn't immediately reach for his hat or his coat and Lily sensed that he had something more to say.

'What is it?' she asked him.

He pulled a tight, embarrassed smile. 'I'll tell you something, Lil: you must be psychic. I don't really know how to tell you this, especially since I feel so fond of you. But I've been going through your sales figures for the past two months, and I guess you know that you're way, *way* below target. And not showing a whole lot of improvement.'

'It's been a tough couple of months, Bennie – you know that. The market's been really sluggish.'

'Well, yes, sure, but I've had some negative feedback about you from some of our clients. Most of the local people we deal with – they're aware of what happened to you – the kidnap, the way you were nearly burned alive. Quite understandably they're not one hundred percent comfortable buying and selling their homes with you.'

'What?'

'They're not unfeeling people, Lil. Far from it. But they know how traumatized you must be feeling. All they want to discuss with their realtor is customized kitchens and walk-in dressing rooms and escrow. They don't want to be treading on eggshells in case they accidentally mention fire hazards or child security.'

'I see.'

'There's one thing more . . . your hair. The way you keep your head shaved, with that scarf and all. Quite a few clients have gotten the impression that you're undergoing chemotherapy, and to be honest with you, Lil, it doesn't put them in a very upbeat state of mind.'

'Oh. They think I have cancer? How depressing for them.'

'I know. I know it doesn't sound very caring. But if people think that their realtor has cancer, it doesn't put them in a very buy-receptive state of mind.'

'Bennie, shaving my head is a symbol. It's a female-warrior thing. It's a witch thing. It means that I'm determined to get my children back.'

'I know that, Lil, and so does everybody else at Concord Realty. But we can't afford to make our clients feel uneasy.'

'So what are you suggesting? You want me to grow my hair back?'

'It's not just that, Lil. I think you need to take some time off. If you want to carry on with the Mystery Lake promotion, that'd be fine. But I think you need to stay home – concentrate on finding your kids and sorting your life out. Then we can talk about the way ahead.'

'The way ahead,' Lily repeated, nodding her head. 'OK, Bennie, if that's how you see it.'

'Lily – you know how I feel about you, don't you? I mean me personally – *me* – regardless of all of this trauma.'

She didn't answer, but lifted his hat from the banister post and handed it to him. 'I'll see you, Bennie. Thanks for dropping by. Good luck with the Starling property, huh?'

John Shooks arrived at her door on the last reverberating stroke of eleven. Outside, a big black 1987 Buick Electra with green-tinted windows was parked at an angle in her driveway. Its engine was running and its exhaust was smoking in the cold.

'Are you ready?' asked Shooks. 'It's only about an hour away – not even that.'

'Where are we going?' asked Lily, closing the front door behind her and double-locking it.

'Black Crow Valley, about six miles south of the Minnesota River. We're going to be meeting my acquaintance George Iron Walker.'

'And he's the one who can find Tasha and Sammy for me?'

'He's the one who knows how to do it, yes.'

Shooks opened the car door for her. It creaked on its hinges. Inside, the seats were covered in worn black leather and there was a strange pungent smell like Russian cigarettes. As they drew away from the curb, it started to snow, only lightly at first, but by the time they reached Bloomington it was coming down thick and fast.

'So your friend's agreed to help me?' asked Lily.

'Let's just say that he's agreed to discuss what you want.'

'I never visited a reservation before.'

Shooks wiped the windshield in front of him with the sleeve of his coat. 'You're not going to visit one now. George Iron Walker – he's not a hermit or anything like that, but he prefers to live way out on his own. He says that he needs the silence, so that he can hear the spirits all around him.'

'Oh.'

They drove for a while without talking. The highway ahead of them was so blinding white that Lily imagined she could see shapes dancing across it, like ghosts.

After a while, she said, 'How did you get to be a private detective, Mr Shooks?'

He sniffed. 'By default, I guess. I used to be a newspaper reporter, for the *Minneapolis Star Tribune*, but I always relished the investigation part of it more than the writing part of it.'

He was silent for a while, smiling to himself. Then he said, 'The trouble was, I relished it a little too much. I dug up a couple of juicy scandals involving city dignitaries and under-age girls and I was politely but firmly told that my services to the media were no longer required. You have to play the game if you live in a city like Minneapolis, Mrs Blake. All your readers want to know is how lucky they are to live in such a prosperous, happy, morally uplifting place.'

'You have Native American blood in you. That's really interesting.'

'You think so? I'm only about an eighth Native. Like, my left leg is Sioux and the rest of me is German and Canadian. And I find it irksome, more than interesting.'

'You can do that incredible thing with the voices.'

'Oh, sure. And I can always tell when the wind's going to swivel around, hours before it actually does. But my Sioux relatives all expect me to feel as resentful of the white man as they do, and my white relatives all think that I'm one-eighth inferior.'

They were driving due westward now, along the south side of the Minnesota River, though the blizzard was so intense that Lily could see nothing but the pines that bordered the highway, shaggy with snow. After twenty minutes, without any warning, Shooks turned off 101 and headed along a narrow, bumpy road that ran alongside an ever-thickening forest. The road looked as if it had been cleared that morning by a snow-plow, but fresh snow was already beginning to drift across it and clog up the tire tracks.

'Not too far now,' said Shooks, as the Buick bounced and creaked over the furrows.

'It's not getting there I'm concerned about,' said Lily. 'It's getting back.'

'We'll be OK. Besides, we could do worse things than spend the night in the company of George Iron Walker. He's a fascinating man, George, especially when it comes to Native American culture. He knows it all: how the beavers all got together and made the world ready for men to live in – all that stuff.'

'The beavers did that? I thought it was God.'

'It's just one of those Mdewakanton legends. But George takes it all very seriously. He's very political, too, when it comes to Native American affairs. You know the casino at Thunder Falls? It was George who was mainly responsible for getting that built, and, believe me, the reservation was transformed overnight. All of those millions of dollars of gambling money . . . the Mdewakanton got themselves power, sewage, health centers . . . an indoor swimming pool. There's even a George Iron Walker Orthodontic Clinic.'

Lily looked out of the window. Ahead of them, on their left, the forest began to rise higher. It may have been an optical illusion, but she was sure that she could see ten or eleven pale-gray animals running between the trees.

'Are those *wolves*?' she said.

John Shooks peered in the direction that she was pointing. 'I don't see anything.'

'I could have sworn they were wolves.'

'Hmm, well. Maybe they were stray dogs. You get a lot of stray dogs around the this area, scavenging for scraps.'

'They looked way too big for dogs.'

'Maybe they were witches.'

'*Witches?*'

'Many Native Americans used to believe that wolves were witches in animal form. In the Lakota language, the word for *wolf* and *witch* is the same.'

The Buick began to slide sideways and he had to spin the wheel left and then right to correct it. Then he said, 'Actually, we'd be much less at risk if they *were* wolves. There isn't a single recorded instance in North America of a wolf killing a human being, ever. But there are plenty of stories in Native American mythology about witches who could burn down people's lodges from fifty miles away, just by thinking angry thoughts about them, or skin human babies like rabbits.'

Lily didn't say anything. She didn't like to talk about fire, or mutilated children. She still woke up in the middle of the night gasping for air, thinking that her skin was burning and her hair was frizzing. And she didn't want to imagine what harm could be done to lost and defenseless children – especially children who had been snatched out of their beds in the middle of the night, and didn't know how to get home.

'You OK?' asked Shooks.

At last they came to the top of a rise, and saw below them a low single-story house with a verandah running all the way around it. It had a single brick chimney, which was sullenly smoking into the falling snow. To one side of the house stood a rust-colored stable, with three pick-up trucks parked around it, as well as a newish blue Subaru Forester.

Shooks circled the car around in front of the house and blew a loud, dirge-like blast on his horn. Almost at once the front door opened and a tall man in a red checkered shirt and jeans appeared. He came bounding down the steps and opened Lily's door for her.

'Welcome to Black Crow Valley,' he said, holding out his hand. 'My name's George.'

'Glad to know you, George,' said Lily, looking up at him and blinking against the snow. 'I'm Lily.'

As she climbed out of the car, she realized how tall George actually was – at least six feet four. He was also strikingly handsome, with short-cropped hair, a broad forehead, and a firmly defined jaw. His eyes had that knowing, confident twinkle that she had always liked in good-looking men, even though she would never have admitted it.

Around his tree-trunk of a neck he wore several tight silver necklaces and a dangling arrangement of feathers and bones and beads that looked like a dreamcatcher.

'Come inside,' he said. He took hold of her elbow so that she wouldn't slip on the steps. 'You couldn't have picked a worse day to visit me, weatherwise. Forecast says it's going to snow all night, and most of tomorrow, too.'

'Those Canucks have a lot to answer for,' said John Shooks.

'Don't be too hard on them.' George Iron Walker smiled at him. 'They don't only give us their crappy weather. They come down here to gamble in their thousands, and they give us all of their crappy money, too.'

He led Lily into his living room. It was wide and low and very warm, with a huge log fire blazing. The walls were hung with multi-colored Native blankets, and with old framed photographs of notable Mdewakanton chiefs, and famous Sioux encampments. The furniture was antique, in the overweight Sears Roebuck style of the early 1900s, and every armchair and couch was heaped up with huge tapestry cushions.

Next to the fire a girl was kneeling. She had high cheekbones and glossy black hair, which was beaded and braided all the way down her back. She was wearing a dark-red polo-neck sweater and tight jeans, and even though she was kneeling, Lily could see that she was very tall and longlegged.

'Hazawin,' said George, and the girl turned toward them. She was almost beautiful, although Lily thought that her features were a little too asymmetric and a little too sharp. What was most striking about her, though, was her eyes, which were misty purple, and completely blind.

'Hazawin, this is Lily. John Shooks you've met before.'

The girl smiled sympathetically in Lily's direction. 'Glad to meet you, Lily. Sorry about the circumstances.'

'I told her why you were coming,' George explained. 'Hazawin can help us. She has a very close affinity to the spirit world.'

'The *spirit* world?' asked Lily.

Shooks said, hurriedly, 'I haven't really filled her in yet, George – not on the spirit stuff. I was hoping that you could do that.' He turned to Lily and said, 'I'm not too good at this one-with-nature malarkey. Like I said, I'm only one-eighth

Mdewakanton. Voices, yes. Weather forecasts, yes. Spirits, only so-so.'

'Please,' said Hazawin, 'why don't you sit down and let me bring you some tea? Do you like herbal?'

'Hey – wouldn't say no to a Wild Turkey if you have one,' said Shooks. 'Straight up, no ice. No umbrella.'

With complete assurance, circumnavigating the furniture without once touching it, Hazawin stood up and walked out of the living room. Lily wondered if she ought to follow her into the kitchen and offer to help, but George came over and took off her coat and said, 'Please . . . sit down.'

She sat on the end of one of the couches, furthest from the fire. She was feeling awkward now, and she was beginning to wish that she hadn't come, but she couldn't really ask Shooks to drive her straight back to Minneapolis.

George sat down opposite her. Not only was he wearing necklaces and feathers, but several silver bracelets, one of which was fashioned in the shape of twenty or thirty beavers, all swallowing each others' tails. He jabbed at the fire with a long poker, so that it roared up even higher, and its light danced in his eyes.

'John told me what happened to you, Lily,' he said. 'There are very few feelings in life that are worse than being betrayed by somebody you thought you could trust – somebody who loved you.'

'Well, you're right about that,' Lily agreed. And he *was* right. Up until now, she had never been a vengeful person. She knew that she could be irritable, and lose her temper quickly, but her tempers never lasted for long, and in the end she had always been forgiving, and willing to compromise. Now, however, she wanted to see Jeff suffer. She wanted him to suffer just as painfully as she was suffering, or even more. Her hatred for him was so strong that it made her mouth dry, as if she had been trying to eat ashes.

'I understand that the FBI still haven't been able to locate your children,' said George.

Lily nodded. 'Today is the sixty-ninth day, and they don't even know if they're still in the continental USA.'

'John – you believe their father has probably taken them south? Mexico, maybe?'

'That's my surmise, George, yes.'

George sat back, and stared at Lily for so long that she had to look away. Eventually, he said, 'There *is* a way of finding your children, and bringing them back. When I first tell you what it is, you probably won't believe me. But even if you *don't* believe me, you can trust me.'

Lily looked back at him for a long moment, and then she said, 'All right, then. I trust you.'

'Good. But first of all, we have to reach an understanding.'

'You mean you want me to pay you some money?'

'Not in this particular case. But it does involve something of very significant value.'

'Go on.'

He stood up and walked across to a dark oak bureau in the far corner of the living room. He opened it up, took out a folded map, and brought it back to the fireside.

'Here,' he said, spreading the map across the couch. 'Do you know where this is?'

Lily frowned at it. It showed a lake, with surrounding forests. She thought she recognized the shape of it, but she couldn't quite be sure. After a while, George rotated the map anti-clockwise and said, 'How about this? Does this make any sense?'

'Oh, yes. Now I know where it is: Mystery Lake.'

'Your company is marketing some land there, I understand.'

'That's right, yes we are. It's going to be a very profitable development, eventually. I think the official description is "a superior lakeside community for active professionals". In other words, an upscale enclave for lawyers and doctors and entrepreneurs, with a yacht marina and a Tom Fazio golf course.'

'Mystery Lake is a sacred place for the Mdewakanton,' said George.

'I didn't know that.'

'Of course not. I wouldn't have expected you to. The spirits leave no traces that white men can see. But it was here that Haokah appeared to Little Crow and warned him that his land was going to be dragged away from under his feet, like a blanket. And so it was, of course – in the Treaty of 1851, when Little Crow surrendered the north side of the Minnesota River to the white men and the Mdewakanton were forced to leave the hills and the lakes which had been theirs since the time before time.'

'I see.' Lily paused, and blinked at him. 'Well, actually, to tell you the truth, I *don't* see.'

'Do you know who Haokah is?' asked George. 'Haokah is the god of thunder, and the god of the hunt. He cries when he is happy and he laughs when he is sad.

George pointed to a hook-shaped spit of land that extended into the lake on the north-west side. 'This is the place where Haokah appeared to Little Crow. They were both reflected in the water so that they appeared to occupy two worlds at once – the world of men and the world of spirits, simultaneously.'

He waited for a moment, obviously expecting Lily to ask him something, but she didn't know what he expected her to ask.

In the end, he said, 'I want this place.'

'Excuse me? You want this place? This little piece of land here? You mean – if you can find my children, you want me to buy it for you?'

'That is the price.'

Lily blew out her cheeks. 'I don't know, George. I don't have the development plan here with me, but if my memory serves me, that's exactly where they're thinking of building the jetty for the yacht marina.'

'I know that. I've seen the plans for myself.'

'That piece of real estate, George . . . I couldn't tell you what it's worth, not off the top of my head, but—'

George lifted his hand. 'To the Mdewakanton, Lily, it is worth far more than money. To the Mdewakanton, it is priceless.'

Lily studied the map with a concentrated frown. Maybe – if the yacht marina were to be built a hundred yards further to the east, and some concrete pilings put into the lake to construct a new jetty – well, it would obviously cost a whole lot more, but maybe not too much more. Quarter of a million dollars? Her house was worth at least $450,000 and she could always remortgage. And if Bennie helped her, like he had promised . . .

'OK,' she said. She knew how rash it was to offer him a piece of real estate that wasn't even hers, and she could feel her cheeks flushing. 'If you can bring my children back to me, unharmed—'

'You swear? You realize what the consequences could be, if you don't?'

'I swear, George. When Tasha and Sammy are safely sleeping in their beds at home, this piece of land will be yours.'

'Very well,' said George. He folded up the map and put it aside. 'This will be an historic moment for the Mdewakanton people.'

'Well, I'm glad about that,' said Lily. 'But how exactly are you going to get my children back?'

Six

Hazawin brought in a tray of herbal tea, in hand-decorated mugs. The tea smelled like nothing that Lily could put a name to, yet for some reason it reminded her of something. A room. A garden. A face turning to smile at her.

'What is this, Hazawin?'

'Verbena, and some other herbs. It will help to protect you against anybody who wishes you harm.'

'Heap powerful medicine,' said John Shooks. 'Not as powerful as Wild Turkey, but pretty powerful.'

George was standing at the window. Outside, the snow was still falling, and Shooks' car was almost buried.

George turned around and said, 'Lily, have you ever heard about the Wendigo?'

'The Wendigo? Sure. I saw a movie about it once. It's some kind of forest spirit, isn't it?'

'It's a demon that inhabits the north woods,' put in Hazawin. 'It is called by many different names – We-tee-go, Wi-ti-ko. But most white people know it as Wendigo, because of the famous story by Algernon Blackwood. And, of course, that movie you saw.'

'Some people think that Algernon Blackwood invented the Wendigo,' said George. 'But it has been spoken of by the Sioux for centuries. The name actually means "flesh-eater", and in particular, "cannibal".'

'Cannibal?'

'Yes. The elders of the Sioux tribes used to tell their

people that if ever they were tempted to eat human flesh, they would gradually turn into a Wendigo – a lonely, hungry, predatory creature, doomed forever to hide in the forests, with nothing to eat but any unwary hunters who might happen to wander their way.'

Uninvited, Shooks poured himself another whiskey and knocked it straight back. 'The popular theory is that the Sioux elders invented the Wendigo to discourage their tribespeople from feeding on each other when food got short in the middle of winter.'

'Of course, the story's been embellished, over the years,' said George. 'Some Dakota story-tellers say that the Wendigo swoops down from the sky, seizes your shoulders in its claws and makes you run along so fast that your feet catch fire. That's what happens in the Algernon Blackwood story. A French Canadian guide gets snatched up, and—'

' *"Oh! Oh, my feet of fire! My burning feet of fire!"* ' John Shooks quoted, and widened his eyes at Lily in a way that she didn't really understand. Was he warning her? Or mocking her? Or was he mocking George and Hazawin?

Hazawin said, 'Some naturalists believe that the Wendigo may even be a real, crypto-zoological creature, like Bigfoot, or the Yeti.'

There was a moment's silence. A log in the front of the fire suddenly lurched and gave off a thick shower of sparks.

'And you're telling me all this – why?' asked Lily.

George said, 'This may be difficult for you to believe. But the Wendigo is a real force of nature. Not a Yeti. Not a hairy beast with a long tongue and claws. It smells, though – not like lions, like Algernon Blackwood said it did. More like overheated metal, after a lightning-strike. The nearest way I can describe it is to say that it's the spirit of the hunt. It's the very essence of the Native American connection between man and the world he lives in. Lost now, mostly, but not entirely.'

'So you're trying to tell me that the Wendigo is real?'

'Yes.'

'Have you ever seen one? Has *anybody* ever seen one?'

'Nobody has ever seen the wind, Lily, but the wind is real enough to blow down the grandest of trees.'

'So what you're telling me is: you're planning on using the Wendigo to find my children?'

Hazawin said, 'George has done it before, Lily, six or seven times.'

'I can't believe this.' Lily put down her mug and stood up. 'I'm sorry, George. I'm sorry, Hazawin. I think we've been wasting each other's time. John – do you think you can drive me home?'

Hazawin repeated, 'Lily – George has done it before, and every time the children have been brought home safe.'

'Look at Myron Burgenheim,' said John Shooks. '*He* has his kids back, doesn't he?'

Lily hesitated. 'I guess.'

'Well, then. What do you have to lose? If the Wendigo *can't* find Tasha and Sammy, what harm's been done? But if it *can* . . .'

'But you're talking about a *demon*. The whole idea of it – it's absurd.'

George said, 'The Wendigo is not a demon in the Christian sense, or the Islamic sense. It's not like Beelzebub, or Iblis. The Wendigo comes from the Native American need to survive, in the harshest of conditions. The Wendigo *is* our need to survive.

'Once the Wendigo goes in pursuit of somebody, it always finds them and it never loses them – *ever*. It doesn't matter how fast you go; it doesn't matter how far you go. The Wendigo will come after you and it will follow you one step behind you until the time comes when it can take you without being seen.

'If you feel it close behind you, if you feel it breathing down your neck, you can turn around as quick as you like, but it'll still be behind you. You might sense that it's in the room with you, but you won't be able to see it. It's so thin that when it turns edgewise on, it's invisible.'

'And it can really find Tasha and Sammy?'

'If it doesn't trace them by the end of this week, then you will have every right to say that this is absurd. But if it doesn't – I shall be very surprised.'

Lily looked from George to Hazawin to John Shooks. With the snow falling steadily outside, and the fire spitting, this all seemed like a dream. It reminded her of the time when she was seven years old and she had visited her grandparents' house on a snowy day just like this. She had been standing in their pear orchard, listening to the utter silence, when she had heard a trudging noise. A naked man had suddenly appeared, as if from nowhere, carrying a bunch of branches. He'd had a beard like a bush of traveler's joy, and bright red cheeks, and a big round belly.

'Hallo!' he had exclaimed. 'A little snow-fairy!' Then without another word he had trudged off again, between the pear trees, and disappeared. She hadn't told her grandparents about this encounter, because she'd thought they would be angry with her, or think that she was making it up. But years later, when he died, she had learned that a Swedish fruit-grower called Bertil Arnesson had lived close by, and that in winter he had been in the habit of taking a sauna and then going for a walk in the snow, lashing himself with birch-twigs as he went.

George said, 'Maybe the best thing we can do is take you to meet the Wendigo for yourself.'

'I thought you said that it was invisible.'

'Most of the time, it is. But you will see its brightness, and you will feel its presence, unmistakably, when it arrives.'

Lily hesitated. But she couldn't stop herself from thinking about the last time that she had seen Tasha, almost completely buried under her quilt, and Sammy, sprawled across his bed with his hair tousled and his mouth wide open, and the loss she felt was physically painful. What if this *was* insanity? What if this *was* a dream? So long as she could get Tasha and Sammy back, she didn't care.

'All right,' she said. 'Where do we have to go to meet it? Is it very far away?'

'The Wendigo is nowhere and everywhere,' said Hazawin. 'All we have to do is go outside, into the forest, and call it. It will come.'

John Shooks tipped one more drink back. 'Dutch courage,' he explained. 'I'm only one-eighth brave, remember?'

They stepped out on to the verandah. The day was enormously quiet – so quiet that Lily could hear the snowflakes falling all around her, like people whispering. George pointed to the birch woods off to the right. 'We'll go up this way. The Wendigo prefers plenty of cover.'

He took Hazawin by the hand and the two of them started to climb toward the woods, their boots squeaking in the snow. George was wearing a thick black bearskin coat and a bearskin hat to match. Hazawin was dressed in an ankle-length sheepskin coat decorated with embroidery and beads, and sheepskin ear-muffs. Slung across her back was a long leather bag, with feathers and fringes on it.

Shooks held out his hand to help Lily down the steps, but she said, 'I can manage, thanks.'

She followed George and Hazawin up the hill. Shooks stayed a little way behind her, as if he were worried that he might have upset her.

'You're probably thinking this is totally crazy,' he said.

'Yes, I am.'

'I didn't want to tell you too much about it before we came here – you know, the Wendigo and everything – in case I put you off.'

'It's all right, Mr Shooks. I understand perfectly.'

'Like George said, the Wendigo isn't a demon like the demon in *The Exorcist*, or anything like that. It's more of a *force*.'

'I realize that. I'm trying to keep a very open mind here.'
The snow was falling so thickly that George and Hazawin
had almost disappeared. Shooks said, 'I've used other Native
spirits, too, in my investigations. Crow in particular. Crow
is great for finding lost property. Coyote – Coyote has a
nose for adultery like you wouldn't believe. He can sniff
out marital unfaithfulness like rotten chicken.'

Lily didn't answer. She was struggling too hard to catch
up with George and Hazawin.

It took them nearly ten minutes to reach the edge of the
birch woods. By the time they were making their way between
the trees they were all breathing heavily and their cheeks
were inflamed with cold. Birds rustled in the branches above
them and Lily could hear rabbits scampering through the
snowy undergrowth.

They reached a small clearing. In the center of it rested
a huge sandstone boulder, the size of a dining-room table.
George guided Hazawin right up to it, and brushed the snow
off the top of it with his sleeve. Hazawin lifted her leather
bag off her shoulder and opened it, taking out two human
thigh bones, painted in red and yellow and tied with hanks
of hair, as well as a polished copper mirror and a necklace
made of three separate strands of wood and bone beads.

She laid the mirror flat on top of the boulder. Then,
without any hesitation, she took a small bright knife out of
her pocket and cut the ball of her thumb, so that five or six
drops of blood fell on to the mirror's surface. Unfazed,
George wrapped up her thumb with a strip of cotton, and
knotted it.

'The Wendigo always demands a blood sacrifice,' he
explained. 'Even if you give it no more than a token.'

Now Hazawin picked up the bones and knocked them
loudly against each other. 'Wendigo, I call you to this place!'
she said, very softly. Then, a little louder, 'Wendigo, spirit
of the forest, I call you to this place!'

She began to knock the bones quicker and quicker, in a

complicated rhythm that sounded like a skeletal horse
cantering across a hard-frozen prairie. 'Wendigo! Wendigo!
Spirit of the forest! Hunter of men! I call you to this place!'
   Lily glanced at Shooks uneasily. She wasn't sure which
disturbed her more: the possibility that the Wendigo might
really appear, or that George and Hazawin might both be
seriously unhinged. But Shooks gave her a 'don't worry'
type of look that was plainly meant to reassure her.
   Hazawin knocked the bones more slowly now, but still
in a complex, scattered rhythm. 'Wendigo! I feel you close
by! Wendigo! I hear your breathing!'
   Breathing? Lily listened hard. She couldn't hear
breathing, but she could hear something else – the softest
of hissing noises, like a TV set that has been left on long
after the night's programs have finished. Except that *this*
hissing noise seemed to be coming closer, and circling
around them, somewhere off to Lily's right.
   'Wendigo, listen to me!' Hazawin called out. 'There is a
man to be hunted, and hostages to be returned to the lodge
where they belong! Your reward will be great! In return for
the hostages, the place where Haowake appeared to Little
Crow will be given back to the Mdewakanton!'
   The hissing sound seemed to be coming from behind
them now. Lily couldn't stop herself from turning around,
but there was nobody there. All she could see was the thin,
scaly trunks of the silver birch trees, and the snow-crusted
tangle of the briars.
   Hazawin lifted both thigh bones and rattled them together
faster and faster. 'Wendigo, listen to me! Wendigo!'
   For a very long moment, there was silence, and darkness, and nothing but the snow falling. Lily thought: *This
is bullshit; why am I doing this?*
   Then – behind the trees – she saw a dim flicker of silvery
light – tall and attenuated, like the figure of a very thin man.
   '*Wendigo!*' Hazawin screamed. '*Wendigo!*'
   The light flickered again, and this time Lily was sure that

she could make out a face in it, but it was too blurry to see if it was a man or an animal. One second it looked like somebody with dark smudgy eyes and his mouth wide open; the next it resembled a deer, or a wolf.

'Wendigo!' sang Hazawin, and her voice was high-pitched and triumphant. 'Wendigo!'

Hazawin was rapping her bones together at hysterical speed. For some reason that she couldn't understand, Lily began to feel a deep sense of dread, as if she had set some appalling sequence of events in motion – a sequence of events that it was already too late to stop. She turned anxiously to Hazawin, but as she did so, the light reappeared close behind Hazawin's shoulder, and now she could see that its mouth was stretched open in what looked like a furious but silent scream.

She turned to Shooks, and the light appeared close behind *him*, too. It seemed to be everywhere at the same time. She spun around again, and again, and it was still there, only a few yards away from her now, yet still indistinct, as if she were seeing it through a fogged-up window.

Lily lost her balance and her sense of direction, and she fell sideways in the snow. She struggled to stand up but she fell over yet again, on to her knees.

'– Wendigo – hear me – *Wendigo* – listen to me –'

Lily cowered down and pressed her hands over her eyes. Whatever it was that Hazawin and George Iron Walker had summoned up from the woods, it would eventually have to go away, wouldn't it? But as she knelt there, she could hear that hissing noise approaching her, nearer and nearer. She didn't dare to uncover her eyes, but she could sense that the Wendigo was only a few feet away. It was darkness and bitter cold and the smell of impenetrable forest. It was hunger, and desperation, and a need to stay alive that was close to the very edge of madness. It was humanity reduced to its grimmest levels of self-preservation, or perhaps it wasn't human at all but some kind of animal that could walk on two legs and think like a human. *I will bite into your neck, I will tear with my teeth at your soft intestines, I will wrench the flesh from your thighs.*

'Wendigo!' screamed Hazawin, so shrilly that she barely sounded sane. *'Wendigo!'*

Lily had felt mortal fear only twice before in her life. Once, of course, when the two men from FLAME had broken into her house and taken Tasha and Sammy. And once when a boyfriend had taken her home in his '74 Mustang and insisted on sex. When she had laughingly refused, he had produced a craft-knife, and held it against her neck, and sworn that he would cut her throat wide open.

'Wendigo!'

Instantly, in response, the birch wood was filled with the harshest scream that Lily had ever heard, either from a human or an animal. It rose higher and higher until it set Lily's teeth on edge. Then, abruptly, it stopped. Lily felt a huge wave of pressure pass over her, as if she were being swept away by an icy-cold sea. Then she heard a slamming noise, like a massive door.

After that, the woods fell silent. Lily slowly took her hands away from her eyes and lifted her head. George and Hazawin were kneeling about ten feet away from her, close to each other. John Shooks was sitting with his back to a birch tree, brushing snow from his hair with his hand.

'Shit,' he said. 'Shit.'

Lily stood up, and looked around. 'So was that it? That was the Wendigo?'

'That was the Wendigo,' said Hazawin. She sniffed, and said, 'You can still smell it. Like hot iron.'

Lily sniffed too, but all she could smell was trees. 'So now what?' she asked.

'The Wendigo has seen you, felt you. Now it knows who you are. It knows what you want, and what you can offer in return.'

There was a very long silence between them. Snow kept on falling.

'Will it do it?' asked Lily, at last, trying to sound composed, even though she was still trembling. 'Will the Wendigo go looking for Tasha and Sammy?'

'Oh, yes. I believe so, yes.'

'You're not completely sure?'

'You can never be completely sure – not with the Wendigo; not until it arrives at the place where your children first went missing and picks up their scent. When it does that, you will know for certain that it has chosen to hunt for them.'

'You mean it's going to come to my *home*?'

George came over and took hold of both of her hands. 'Don't lose your nerve, Lily. The Wendigo is pretty damned frightening, I admit. But it's a Native American spirit, one of us. When it agrees to track down somebody for you, it will track them down, and it is always true to its promise. The white man betrayed us with their so-called treaties, time after time. That's how we lost our lands and our livelihood. But so long as you honor your bargain, the Wendigo will never let you down. Neither will I, or Hazawin.'

'George, for God's sake. It really scared me.'

'Of course it scared you. Don't you think it scares me, too? It is one of the most terrifying of all Native American spirits. But that's why we send it out to look for people. It's relentless. It's unstoppable.'

They stood in the woods for a while, looking around, as if they half-expected the Wendigo to make a repeat appearance. But then John Shooks said, 'Screw this, I need a drink,' heaved himself on to his feet and started to trudge his way back toward the house. Hazawin followed him, her head bowed, listening to his footsteps to guide her, and then Lily and George.

'I know this is a very different world,' said George, as they descended the slope. 'I know that you find it hard to understand.'

'Just answer me one question,' said Lily. 'Is this a scam?

68

If it *is* a scam, you should tell me now, and I'll go away and leave you alone and say nothing to anybody.'

'You really think I would trick you?'

'You want that land at Mystery Lake, don't you?'

'Of course. But you don't have to give me that land until your children are safely home. That's our bargain, isn't it?'

'All right. But if you put me through all of this, and I find out that you've been taking advantage of my feelings for my children, I swear to God that you'll *really* find out what frightening means.'

George laid a hand on her shoulder and smiled at her. 'You are a very determined person, Lily. I like determined.'

Seven

That evening, she was whipping up eggs for a cheese-and-tomato omelet when the doorbell chimed. She crossed the hallway wiping her hands on a kitchen towel. Through the spyhole in the front door she could see Special Agents Rylance and Kellogg, with snow on their shoulders, their noses red with cold. She opened up at once.

'What is it?' she asked.

Special Agent Rylance raised one leather-gloved hand to reassure her. 'It's OK, Mrs Blake. We don't have any news about Tasha and Sammy. But we may have some kind of a lead to the people who took them.'

She led them into the living room. 'You look frozen. Can I get you something hot to drink?'

'No, we're fine,' said Special Agent Rylance. 'We don't want to take up too much of your time.'

'Here, sit by the fire,' she said.

Special Agent Rylance unbuttoned his overcoat and sat down. 'We had a report less than an hour ago that these FLAME lunatics have attacked another estranged wife – in Winona this time – and kidnapped her son.'

'That's terrible. Was the woman badly hurt?'

'That's the reason we came around to see you personally,' said Special Agent Kellogg. 'The woman suffered third-degree burns and she died on the way to hospital. We didn't want you to hear it for the first time on the TV news.'

Lily said, 'Oh my God. How can anyone be so sadistic?'

'Hard to understand, isn't it? But people do all kinds of terrible things to each other, every day of the week.'

'The woman was only twenty-nine,' said Special Agent Rylance. 'Her son was four.'

'Do you think it was the same men who tried to kill me?'

Special Agent Rylance nodded. 'A neighbor saw them leaving the apartment. One of them was wearing a head-dress like the one you described, with horns.'

'The neighbor also saw their vehicle, a black Toyota SUV.'

'We'll find them, Mrs Blake,' said Special Agent Kellogg. 'And when we do, there's every chance that we'll be able to locate your ex-husband, too.'

For a moment, Lily was tempted to tell Special Agents Rylance and Kellogg what had happened in Black Crow Valley that afternoon – the chanting, and the bone-rattling, and the dim, flickering light behind the trees. But it all seemed so unreal, and she didn't want them to know how gullible she had been. How could a Native American spirit find Tasha and Sammy when the FBI couldn't? A Wendigo? Much more likely that it was a hoax – a set-up constructed from strobe lights and loudspeakers.

Special Agent Rylance said, 'We'll keep you informed of any developments, Mrs Blake. Meanwhile – as usual – if *you* hear anything . . .'

'Of course,' Lily told him.

Lily was spooning Purina Dog Chow into Sergeant's bowl when the FLAME story came on to Channel 41 news that night.

Jerry Duncan, the newscaster, said, '. . . Ms Whitney's robe was drenched in water. Then she was tied to a kitchen chair, doused in gasoline and set alight. She died of her burns before the ambulance could reach the Community Memorial Hospital.

'Her four-year-old son Dean was kidnapped from his bedroom and so far his whereabouts remain unknown. Police are looking for his father, Morris Whitney, whose last address was in Goodview. Mr Whitney was apparently involved in a series of legal wrangles with his former wife over access and alimony.'

Lily immediately stood up and walked through to the kitchen, just as a wedding picture of the Whitneys was flashed on to the TV screen. They were both laughing. Lily couldn't help thinking how ordinary they looked: Mr and Mrs Happy Average.

Jerry Duncan continued, 'Less than an hour ago, Channel 41 News received a webcam message from a man claiming to represent the men's action group FLAME – Fathers' League Against Mothers' Evil. In recent months, FLAME has been committing increasingly violent acts against mothers who have been granted custody of their children after a divorce. In three cases they have kidnapped the children and presumably handed them over to their fathers, although all efforts by law enforcement agencies to find these children or their fathers have so far met with no success.

'The FLAME representative – who said that his name was "Victor Quinn" – claimed that FLAME was responsible for burning Ms Whitney alive, and that more mothers would face a similar fate unless they were prepared to be far more reasonable about custody, access and maintenance payments.'

The silhouette of a man appeared – a man wearing a headdress that looked like a pair of devil's horns. Behind him was a solid orange background, with the word 'FLAME' painted on it in letters that were supposed to look like fire.

The man said, in a flat, dry, Minnesota accent, 'Today, we executed another witch.'

Lily started to tremble. She had had so many nightmares about this man, but she had never believed that she would ever see him again or hear his voice. But here he was, right in front of her. She was so shaken that she had to pull out a chair and sit down.

'Witchcraft is no longer a crime punishable by death,' the man continued. 'It used to be, in the thirteen original colonies, and some people think that it still should be. Women may not work spells any longer, or consort with Satan, but they are still regularly using trickery and deceit to destroy the happiness of decent and hard-working men, and to deprive them of their right to fatherhood. If that isn't witchery, we don't know what is.'

My God, thought Lily. She knew that her own behavior had been far from saintly while she and Jeff were breaking up. At times she had been unforgivably spiteful and awkward, and she had never made it easy for Jeff to keep up his relationship with Tasha and Sammy. But no matter how mean-minded she might have been, no woman deserved to be burned alive for it.

The phone rang. She was trembling so much that when she picked it up, she nearly dropped it.

'Mrs Blake? This is Special Agent Kellogg. Are you watching the TV news?'

'Yes. Yes, I am.'

'You can see this man "Victor Quinn"? Is he the man who broke into your home and kidnapped Tasha and Sammy?'

'Yes. I'm sure of it. I'd know his voice anywhere.'

'Are you OK? This hasn't disturbed you too much, has it?'

'I'm shaking like a leaf, to tell you the truth.'

'Would you feel better if I came around?'

'No, that's OK. I'll be fine. It was a shock, that's all.'

'OK, Mrs Blake. I'll probably call you again tomorrow. Thanks for the ID. I believe it could help us a lot.'

'Just find him,' said Lily. 'Just find him, and find my children.'

She went to bed early that night. It had stopped snowing for a while, but the roof was thickly covered and the whole house creaked like a ship at sea. She picked up *Minnesota Monthly* and tried to finish off the cryptic crossword she had started yesterday, but none of the clues seemed to make any sense at all. '*Brushes with insects help crones to become airborne.*' What the hell did that mean?

She closed her eyes. Her head fell back against the pillows. She began to breathe deeper and deeper, and her fingers opened so that her ballpen rolled out of her hand and dropped on to the floor.

She dreamed that she was walking through the birch woods. She wasn't alone. She could hear footsteps all around her, and people whispering, but she couldn't see anybody. She realized that she was lost, and that she had no idea where she was going, or how she was going to get out of the birch woods before it grew dark.

On either side of her, behind the trees, she saw pale-gray shapes running through the undergrowth. *Wolves*, she thought. But maybe they weren't wolves. Maybe they were witches. *Oh God I'm frightened. Oh God I'm frightened.* The branches scratched her face and caught in her hair, as if the birch trees themselves were trying to stop her from escaping.

Her heart beat faster and harder, and she started to run. Up ahead of her, she thought she could see a light flickering – a dim, silvery light, like a figure from a black-and-white movie.

The light flickered again, and again. As she came nearer to it, she saw that it was making its way between the trees on two legs, yet it was strangely hunched, and it had an odd, jerky gait, as if it were a four-legged animal that had been trained to walk like a man. It was then that she realized what it was, and she stopped, her chest constricted so tightly that she could hardly breathe. *It was the Wendigo.* It was turning around and around, in some kind of slow, spasmodic dance. When it turned to face her, she could dimly see it. But when it turned edgewise, it vanished altogether – *dissolved*, as if it simply wasn't there.

She took two or three steps backward and tried to run away, but now the branches and the briars snatched at her clothes even more viciously, and she became inextricably entangled. She struggled and fought and twisted from side to side, but the more she struggled, the more entangled she became.

'*Gaaaahhhh!*' she cried out. '*Gaaahhhhhh!*'

She opened her eyes. Her bedside light was still on. Her magazine was still lying open on the quilt in front of her. But there was something different. Her bedroom door was wide open, and she was sure that she had closed it. She always did.

Frowning, she climbed out of bed and shucked on her slippers. She looked out on to the landing. There was nobody there. She didn't expect anybody to be there. Since the kidnap, she had fixed deadlocks on every door and window and upgraded her security alarm so that nobody could possibly enter the house without setting off sirens and flood-lights and alerting the local police.

Yet she had the strongest feeling that somebody had been here. She felt that somebody had somehow managed to enter the house and climb the stairs and look at her while she was asleep.

She sniffed. She could smell something, too. It was curi-ously *metallic*, like a red-hot poker. She sniffed again. *No*, she thought. *I'm imagining it.*

It was then that she heard voices, downstairs in the living room. She froze, and listened. A man's voice, and then a woman's.

She stepped back into her bedroom and picked up the phone. She was about to punch in 911 when she heard the woman speak again. '*I have jewelry,*' she said. '*Please. I have my children to take care of.*'

She felt a prickly, tightening sensation all the way up her back, as if scores of centipedes were crawling up it. That woman's voice: there was no mistaking it. That woman's voice was *hers*.

The man's voice said, '*We was sent by God. We was sent by God, Mrs Blake, to carry out divine retribution.*'

And that was him. That was the man who had appeared on TV tonight, calling himself 'Victor Quinn'. She was listening to *herself*, and to the men who had kidnapped Tasha and Sammy.

Treading as lightly as she could, she went back out on to the landing, and looked downstairs toward the living-room archway. A fitful light was shining out of the living room. It flickered and jerked like the light from a black-and-white movie projector, so that even the chairs in the hallway appeared to be jumping.

My God, she thought, *the Wendigo. It's here. The Wendigo is inside the house.*

She lifted up the phone again, but then she hesitated. If she dialed 911, what was she going to say to the police? '*I have intruders . . . a Native American spirit and two men who aren't really here, and me?*'

She crept along the landing to the top of the stairs. She was too frightened to go down, but she wanted to listen. The voices rose and fell in volume, and she could hear the same hissing sound that she had heard in the birch woods when the Wendigo had first appeared.

'*The children is the reason we're here.*'

'*What?*'

'*You won custody, didn't you? You got to take sole care of them.*'

'*Did Jeff send you? Is that it?*'

There was silence for a few seconds, and then the two men from FLAME suddenly appeared, dragging Lily between them. Their images were unfocused and quivering, as if they were TV pictures from a scrambled satellite signal, but Lily was still shocked. She backed into the doorway of Tasha's bedroom, irrationally terrified that the men might look up and see her there, watching them, a witness to her own assault.

As the men wrestled her toward the kitchen, Lily saw the faintest twist of silvery light come out of the living room, and follow them. As it did so, the long-case clock struck a single chime for two thirty, and she realized now what the Wendigo was doing. It had been two thirty in the morning when the two men from FLAME had broken into the house and tried to set her on fire. The Wendigo was reconstructing everything that had happened that night, in real time.

She kept well back in the bedroom doorway, but even so the silvery light appeared to hesitate by the foot of the stairs, and for an instant she saw a long, distorted face, like a portrait seen from a very acute angle. Then the light disappeared altogether, and she could only hear voices, coming from the kitchen.

The man with the horns: '*Do I look like somebody who would hurt a child? There's a whole lot of difference between divine retribution and unnatural cruelty, believe me.*'

Lily: '*Just don't hurt my children – or, by God, I will come back and haunt you, I swear.*'

Lily ventured back to the top of the stairs, but she wasn't sure that she wanted to see herself set on fire. She listened to herself threatening and pleading, and Victor Quinn lecturing her about witches and witchcraft, and she saw Quinn's accomplice carry a can of gasoline across the hallway.

It was then that her phone rang, making her jump. She hurried back to her bedroom, closed the door, and answered it. 'Yes?'

'Mrs Blake? It's John Shooks. Didn't wake you, did I?'

'It's here! The Wendigo's here, in my house!'

'You're sure about that?'

'I've seen it! It was in the living room and now it's in the kitchen!'

'Listen – you don't have to be scared. It won't hurt you. How long has it been there?'

'I don't know, but it's replaying everything that happened on the night that Tasha and Sammy were kidnapped. It's like a three-D movie; it's unbelievable.'

'Well, the Wendigo is a pretty unbelievable kind of a spirit, Mrs Blake. You heard for yourself what *I* can do – that ghost talking. But the Wendigo can do much more than hear things; it can *see* them, too, and bring them back to life.'

'I've just seen myself! It's *me*, with those two men!'

'I know, Mrs Blake. The Wendigo is like one of those trackers who can look at a single broken branch and tell you exactly who stepped on it, and how heavy they were, and which direction they were headed. Probably what they ate for breakfast, as well.'

'But how did it get into the house? Every door's locked and it didn't set the alarm off.'

'It *slid* in.'

'What?'

'It *slid* in, like a sheet of paper. The Wendigo has height, and breadth, but no thickness. Only two of its dimensions ever appear in our world. The rest of its substance never leaves the world of the spirits. You can see it from the front. You can see it from the back. But edgewise it's invisible.'

'You're sure I'm not in any danger?'

'Of course not. The Wendigo's working for you. It just needs to find out what happened that night and pick up the scent.'

'So what's it going to do now?'

'It's going to follow that scent, Mrs Blake. It's going to follow that scent – and it's going to keep on following that scent until it finds your kids.'

Lily heard footsteps outside her bedroom, and the muffled sound of children crying. *Oh, no!* she thought. *Tasha and Sammy!*

She dropped the phone and whipped open her bedroom door. She was just in time to see the dark, semi-transparent figures of the two men from FLAME, one of them carrying Tasha over his shoulder, the other carrying Sammy. Both children were gagged. They were kicking and struggling but the men were much too strong for them.

'*Stop!*' she shouted. '*You can't have them! Stop!*'

But the instant she cried out, the figures all vanished, and there was nobody on the stairs at all. She leaned against the banisters, and for the first time in over a month she let out a heart-wrenching sob.

'You can't have them,' she whispered, hopelessly. 'Stop.'

At the foot of the stairs she saw a brief twist of silvery light, and an indistinct collection of shadows that could have been a face looking up at her. Then that disappeared, too.

'Hallo?' said the tiny voice of John Shooks, from her telephone receiver. 'Hallo, Mrs Blake – are you still there?'

Although the figures had vanished, Lily thought: *I know where they're going to go next. If the Wendigo is recreating all of this kidnapping, exactly as it happened, those two men are going to take Tasha and Sammy to the barn, to meet up with Jeff.*

God, I might see Jeff, too. This is so totally unreal.

She went back to her bedroom and picked up the phone. John Shooks was still trying to get her attention.

'Mrs Blake?' he was saying. 'Are you still *there*, Mrs Blake?'

'I can't talk to you now, Mr Shooks. I'm going to follow them.'

'What?'

'I'm going to Sibley's Barn. I want to see what happened for myself.'

'Mrs Blake – I have to advise you against it. The Wendigo won't *deliberately* do you any mischief, but you're dealing with some heap powerful forces here.'

'I'm not a Native American, Mr Shooks.'

'Don't have to be, to feel lonely and scared in the forest.

You ever *been* in the forest, Mrs Blake, hundreds of miles from no place at all? The forest has a great dark heart of its own, believe me. You don't want to start interfering with an influence like that.'

'Thanks for the warning, but I'm still going.'

Lily dropped the phone back on the bed. Then she opened up her closet and pulled out a thick black sweater, a pair of jeans and some thick cream socks. She quickly dressed, and then she hurried downstairs and put on her fur coat and boots.

Outside, the street was icy and silent. At two thirty in the morning most good residents of West Calhoun were fast asleep under their comforters, dreaming of golf, or making love to the redhead next door, or stock options. Lily opened her garage and climbed into her bright-red Buick Rainier. As she started it up, two shaggy gray dogs trotted across her driveway and paused to stare at her. Their eyes gleamed yellow in her headlights.

She drove due east and then south to Nokomis. The roads had been salted, but there were still slippery ridges on some of the tighter corners, and she had to drive frustratingly slowly.

She drove through Sibley's End, as dark and silent as every other development, and parked as close to the Brer Rabbit field as she could, by the briars. The night was stunningly cold, with a north-west wind that made a fluffing noise in her ears. Beyond the treeline she could see red and white lights from the airport, and she could hear the whining of airplanes as mechanics tried to keep them from icing up.

Sweeping the beam of her flashlight in front of her, she trudged across the field toward the awkward, angular silhouette of Sibley's Barn. Its roof was covered in snow, and it seemed to be leaning at even more of an angle than it had before. Even the icicles on its eaves were leaning at an angle.

She was only twenty yards away when she thought she saw a nervous white light in one of the windows. She switched off her flashlight, and stopped, and listened. Nothing at first, but the buffeting of the wind in her ears. *This is mad*, she thought. *There's nobody here. No Wendigo. No Sammy and Tasha. You've lost your marbles and you don't even know it.*

She walked right up to the barn and peered in through a narrow triangular crevice at the side of the access door. A chilly draft was blowing through the crevice and made her right eye water. But, as far as she could see, the barn was deserted: straw, packing-cases, broken generator – nothing else.

Come on, Lily, this is crazy. Go home. Talk to John Shooks in the morning. She turned to leave, but she had only walked two or three paces before she heard that hissing noise. It was like static. It was like loneliness. It was like trying to reach somebody on a radio set – anybody – but there was never any reply.

Lily turned back, and pressed her eye to the crevice again. This time she was convinced that she could see a shape standing in the far corner of the barn, under the shadow of the hayloft. The shape was dim and unsteady and out of focus, but she could tell that it was very tall, as tall as a deer standing on its hind legs – yet it seemed to have a man-like face. Or maybe that wasn't a face at all – maybe it was nothing more than a horse-collar hanging on the barn wall behind it, and maybe the entire figure was nothing but a tarpaulin draped over one of the feed-stalls. Yet the hissing continued, and the shape appeared to move, lifting its arms in a mechanical, disjointed way that reminded Lily not so much of a man, or a deer, but a praying mantis.

With no warning at all, a man in a brown leather coat walked across her line of sight. It was Jeff.

She knew that it wasn't the real Jeff – nothing more than a visual echo of Jeff – but she couldn't stop herself from saying 'You . . . *bastard!*' out loud. Out of shock, out of fury, out of sheer disbelief.

Jeff said, 'Thanks, guys. You've been amazing.'

Now a big, broad-shouldered man in black came into view. He wasn't wearing his horns now. He had a squarish head, with hair shaved very short. But when Lily heard his voice she knew who he was.

'It's a brotherhood thing. It's man standing up for man. You don't have to be grateful for that. If we don't look after our own, ain't nobody else is going to do it for us.'

Jeff looked in another direction and said, 'We're going on vacation, kids. The greatest vacation ever.'

'But I have *school*,' said Tasha, although Lily couldn't see her.

'You've been let off school. I've talked to your principal and she thinks that it's more important for you to take a vacation with your dear old dad.'

'Where are we going?' asked Sammy.

Now Tasha appeared. Her chestnut-brown hair was tangled and she looked pale and tired. She was wrapped up in a thick blue blanket but she still looked cold. Lily felt as if her chest were being crushed.

'Mommy's going to be worried,' she said. 'I think you should take us back home.'

A second man in black circled around Tasha and grinned at her with his two front teeth missing. He had an almond-shaped head and long greasy black hair that was swept straight back from his forehead. 'Don't you concern yourself about your mommy,' he said. 'Your mommy's real hot on this idea.'

Victor Quinn said, 'Shut up, Tony.'

Jeff walked out of sight and Lily could hear him talking to Sammy. 'We can swim on the beach; we can go horse-back riding. We can do anything you want.'

'I'm cold,' said Sammy. 'I don't want to go on vacation. I want to go back to bed.'

'Sorry, kid,' said Victor Quinn. 'This ain't really up for negotiation. You're going on vacation whether you like it or not.'

Jeff, for some reason, shouted, '*Hey!* Come back here!'

It was then that Sammy appeared, running straight toward the door. Lily took a step back in alarm. She could see Sammy's face – his eyes wide, his mouth tight, grimly determined that he was going to get away. Jeff made a grab for him and caught the front of his pajamas. He swung him around and lifted him right off his feet.

That was too much for Lily. She seized the edge of the access door and wrenched it open.

'Put him down, you bastard!' she screamed. '*Put him down!*'

There was a wave of icy-cold pressure, just like the pressure that Lily had felt in the birch wood. She almost felt as if she were being lifted off her feet. Then there was a deafening slam, and she found herself standing in an empty barn – no Jeff, no Sammy, no Tasha. No Victor Quinn and no sign of his toothless friend Tony.

Lily thought she saw an elongated shadow in the far corner, but it turned away from her and vanished. And at the very instant it vanished there was a loud cracking noise, and a huge section of the barn roof collapsed in an avalanche of snow and wooden shingles. Then another section fell in, almost on top of her.

The whole barn gave a groan that was almost human, and lurched to one side. Two central beams fell sideways and bounced against each other on the floor. The hayloft dropped and a rusty block-and-tackle missed Lily's shoulder by inches. She turned around and threw herself back through the access door, jarring her shoulder. She leaped into the snow and rolled over and over.

The noise was extraordinary. It was more like a massacre than a building falling down. Nails were shrieking as they were dragged out of timbers; rafters were shouting as they tumbled on top of each other. And there was the ceaseless clattering of roof-shingles, like hundreds of people running for their lives.

When Lily climbed back on to her feet, she saw that the entire ramshackle barn had been leveled, and not a single upright had been left standing.

What had John Shooks warned her? *'You don't want to start interfering with an influence like that.'*

She walked slowly back to her SUV, nursing her shoulder. She looked back two or three times, but she didn't see any more lights flickering, or any shape that could have been something from the forest, with its great dark heart.

She met Bennie at the Bakery on Grand, which was only two blocks away from his apartment. It was five after twelve, and the place wasn't yet crowded. They sat at a corner table and the waiter brought them warm, crusty baguettes and two glasses of red Lirac. Bennie immediately cracked open a baguette, buttered it thickly and started to push pieces into his mouth.

'The bread is so darn good here. I don't know why I order anything else.'

'Bennie . . . there's something I have to ask you.'

'Sure, whatever.'

She didn't quite know how to explain what she wanted. It was obvious that Bennie's brother Myron hadn't told him about the Wendigo, and she could understand why. What was she going to say? *'I've employed a Native American forest spirit to find Tasha and Sammy, and I need a really valuable piece of real estate to pay for it.'*?

On the wall behind Bennie hung a mirror with a stripped-pine frame and she could see herself in it, pale-faced, with shadows under her eyes because she hadn't been sleeping. She had tied a lavender-colored silk scarf around her head and she was wearing a purple roll-neck sweater, and somehow they made her look even more anemic.

'Seeing that guy on the news last night – that really shook me,' she said.

'Hey – I'll bet it did. They had his picture on the front page of the *Tribune* this morning, too.'

'The FBI seem to be pretty confident that they're going to catch him.'

'Well, I darn well hope that they do. And I hope he gets the needle. I don't usually believe in the death penalty, but for what this guy's done . . .'

Lily sipped her wine. 'I met with John Shooks yesterday morning.'

'How did that go?'

'Well, it was interesting, to say the least. He introduced me to a Native American tracker.'

'Really? A real live Native American tracker?'

'That's right. He's a Sioux, and he's supposed to be the best in the business. Apparently, he can find anybody, no matter how carefully they've covered their tracks. He thinks he can find Tasha and Sammy in two or three days. In fact he's already started looking for them.'

'That's great news, Lil. You know that we're all praying for you, don't you?'

Lily gave him the thinnest of smiles. 'Thanks, Bennie. You've been very understanding, all of you.'

Bennie was about to stuff another piece of baguette into his mouth, but he stopped himself. 'What is it?' he asked her. 'There's nothing wrong, is there?'

'It's the price,' said Lily. 'This tracker – well, he's asking for a lot, and I've already agreed to give it to him.'

'OK . . . How much is "a lot", exactly?'

'I'm not too sure. I need *you* to tell me that.'

'Me? I don't understand.'

'You know the residential development at Mystery Lake? You know that spit of land where they're planning to build the marina?'

'Of course. What about it?'

The waiter came across the creaky, boarded floor and asked them if they were ready to order. 'Sure,' said Bennie.

'I'll have the bean and butternut soup, and then the roast duck. How about you, Lil?'

'I'll just have the eggs *en cocotte*, thanks.'

'You're missing something if you don't have the duck,' Bennie told her. 'They stuff it with oranges and rosemary, and they roast it until it's almost black.'

'I can taste some of yours, can't I?'

'Of course you can,' said Bennie, taking hold of her hand. 'What's mine is yours, Lil. You know that. So . . . what about this spit of land at Mystery Lake?'

'That's what the tracker wants, in return for finding Tasha and Sammy.'

'He wants the *land*?' Bennie stared at her as if she had said something in a foreign language. 'What the hell does he want the land for?'

'I'm not too sure. It's supposed to be sacred to the Mdewakanton Sioux. It's the place where some god appeared to one of their chiefs.'

'Jesus,' said Bennie. 'I hope you haven't forgotten that it's also the place where we're going to be constructing a picturesque New England-style jetty for the tying up of very high-end leisure craft.'

'I know, Bennie. But that was what the tracker asked for.'

'What about money, for Christ's sake? Won't he take money?'

'He's not interested in money. Only the land.'

'I don't know, Lil. I don't know what to say to you. I'm as anxious as you are to get Tasha and Sammy back safely, but *this* – this is out of the question. Apart from anything else, that land doesn't even belong to Concord Realty; it belongs to Kraussman Resort Developments, Inc., and there is no way that Philip Kraussman is going to give half of his harbor to some – Sioux.'

Lily squeezed his hand tight. 'Bennie, I've thought about it, and it wouldn't take too much of a change. They could build another jetty about fifty yards further east. It would only take concrete pilings and maybe some extra dredging.'

'Lil, sweetheart – even if you could afford to buy that piece of land and defray the extra cost of building another jetty, Philip Kraussman simply wouldn't agree to it. I'm not being bigoted here, but Mystery Lake is going to be one of the most exclusive residential resorts in Minnesota, if not the whole north-west, and the kind of people who are going to be buying homes there – well, they won't want to have Native Americans for neighbors. You know the problems: the alcoholism, the trash, the rusty old trailers.'

Lily said, 'I don't think the Mdewakanton want to live on this land, Bennie. They just want it back, because it's holy. Because it's *theirs*.'

Bennie shook his head. 'Those treaties we did with the Indians – they may seem to be unfair. OK, they *were* unfair. They were daylight robbery. But those were different times, Lil. Pioneering days. It was every man for himself, and every woman, too. Besides – if it hadn't been for those treaties, there wouldn't be any Twin Cities. All you'd have here would be wall-to-wall wigwams.'

'Bennie, I promised. I made a deal.'

'Well, I'm real sorry, Lil. But you can't make deals with something that isn't yours. You'll have to go back and tell this tracker that he's going to have to settle for something else. My friend Lewis runs a Cadillac dealership in Roseville. I can get him a terrific deal on an Escalade.'

'I can't go back to him. He's started to look for Tasha and Sammy already, and I don't have any idea where he is. Besides, he made it absolutely clear that he wouldn't consider anything else.'

Bennie sat back. 'You've really committed yourself, haven't you?'

'I was desperate, Bennie. I didn't have any other choice. I'm *still* desperate.'

Bennie thought for a while. Then he said, 'OK . . . I'll

tell you what I'll do. I'll take Philip Kraussman to lunch and see if I can sweet-talk him into some kind of a compromise. Maybe I can persuade him that a gesture to the Sioux could be good public relations. He may want a guarantee that no Native Americans are actually going to *live* on that piece of land. But maybe he wouldn't object to a memorial stone, or a plaque, or a totem pole, or whatever.'

'Bennie, you're an angel,' said Lily. She stood up, leaned over the table and kissed him on the forehead.

'Hey – don't start counting chickens. We still don't know how much Philip Kraussman is going to ask for it. And I don't think that moving that jetty is going to be anything like as easy as you think it is.'

'I trust you,' said Lily. 'I really trust you. I'm sure you can do it. You can't even imagine know how grateful I'd be.'

The waiter brought Bennie's soup. Outside, the sky had grown very dark, almost charcoal gray, and a strong wind had got up, so that snow whirled across the sidewalk like Catherine-wheels.

Eight

She heard nothing for two days. She phoned John Shooks every few hours, but his cell was switched off. *'This is John Shooks. Leave me a message or leave me alone.'*

Robert called unexpectedly and asked if he could take her out to dinner. She said yes, because she was feeling so edgy, but an hour later she changed her mind. What on earth could she talk to Robert about? How a Mdewakanton spirit was hunting for her missing children? Robert's idea of a supernatural manifestation was a 'miracle' gust of wind that had blown his golf ball away from the rough. She called him back and said sorry, but no.

'I'm disappointed,' said Robert. 'I'd really love to see you again. You know – catch up.'

'I'm sorry, Robert. But I'm not the woman I used to be.'

'I booked a table at Goodfellow's, if that makes any difference.'

'That's great. I love Goodfellow's. But take somebody who's not going to put you off your Thai-spiced pork loin. Take somebody who can make you laugh.'

'OK, if I really can't twist your arm. I understand. I'll call you sometime. Take care of yourself. I miss you.'

'Yes,' she said. 'You too.'

I'm lying, she thought. *I don't miss him at all.*

Next she called Agnes, but Agnes was helping at a neighbor's birthday party. She could hear the children screaming in the background. Then she called Fiona at

Concord Realty, but Fiona was out of the office, showing off a newly restored property in Loring Park.

She decided to go out shopping, and maybe stop for a pastry and a cappuccino at Café Latte, and she had just buttoned up her coat and pulled on her woolly home-knitted hat when the phone rang.

'Lily,' said a faraway voice. 'Lily, this is Jeff.'

For a moment she couldn't believe what she had just heard. 'Jeff? *Jeff*? Where the hell are you?' She couldn't help visualizing the 'Jeff' she had seen in Sibley's Barn, picking up Sammy and swinging him around. 'What the hell have you done with Tasha and Sammy?'

'Tasha and Sammy are OK, they're fine. They're both well and they're having a really great time.'

Lily could hardly breathe. 'You bastard! You *bastard*! You utter, unutterable bastard! Bring those children back to me today! Bring those children back to me today or by God I'll kill you with my bare hands!'

'Lily – I've only just found out about those guys from FLAME. I didn't realize what they were doing. I just didn't realize.'

'What do you mean, you didn't realize, you bastard? You total absolute sadistic bastard! They set me on fire! They tried to burn me alive, you bastard! I nearly died!'

'Lily – listen to me, please. You don't know how sorry I am. I never realized they were going to do anything like that. If I'd have known . . .'

'How could you not know? How could you be so stupid and so cruel? How could you take Tasha and Sammy away from me like that? I hate you! I hate you!'

Lily was so angry that she stalked across the hallway and smashed a framed photograph of Jeff with her fist. Then she smashed it again, and again, until all the glass was shattered and her fingers were smothered in blood.

'You have to let me explain,' said Jeff. 'You have to let me apologize.'

'*Apologize?*' she screamed at him. 'There's no possible way to say you're sorry for what you've done. No way at all. Bring Tasha and Sammy back here now!'

'Those guys . . . they said they were a fathers' support group. They came up to me, after that last custody hearing, and they said they could help me. They didn't say anything about burning people.'

'I don't want to hear this, Jeff. All I want to hear is that you're bringing them back. Either that, or tell me where you are, and I'll have the FBI come get them.'

'Lily, sweetheart, listen to me! I wanted my own children, that's all! I wanted to see them grow up! They're my children as much as yours!'

'So you thought you'd kidnap them and cremate their mother?'

'I swear on our children's lives that I didn't know they were going to burn you. I've only just found out now. I saw that woman on the TV news, the one they killed in Winona. I called Larry at 3M and he told me that they had tried to kill you, too. That was the first I knew about it, sweetheart, I swear!'

Lily sat down on the stairs. 'I don't believe you, Jeff. I never believed anything you said before and I sure as hell don't believe this. Don't tell me you haven't checked the FBI website for parental kidnappings? Tasha and Sammy are on it, along with you, and *you* are named as being wanted for conspiracy to murder. As if you didn't know.'

'I have no computer here, Lily. Besides, it just didn't occur to me. I wanted to get as far away as I possibly could. Put the past behind me. Start a new life.'

Lily suddenly felt very tired. Her knuckle was bleeding and she sucked it, so that it wouldn't drip into her sleeve.

'Jeff, I want you to bring them back home. You and I can argue about this later.'

'I'm not going to do that, Lily. They're here with me; they're very settled, and that's the way it's going to stay. I just needed you to know that I never intended you any harm. I'm very sorry for what those guys did to you, and I'm so happy that you're OK.'

'*OK?* You think that I'm OK? I'm going out of my mind here, Jeff! The burns healed up, oh sure! Only a few disfiguring scars on the side of my face! But ever since you took Tasha and Sammy away from me I haven't been able to eat, or sleep, and now I can't even go to work, in case – guess why? – in case I depress my clients! You stupid, selfish, gutless piece of shit!'

'Lily, sweetheart – *I didn't know!*'

Lily took a deep breath, to steady herself. Then she said, 'Where are you, Jeff?'

'I'm sorry, I can't tell you that. And don't try to trace this phone call. I'm using a disposable cell.'

'I'm going to give you one last chance, Jeff. Bring Tasha and Sammy back. I have somebody out looking for you – somebody who's going to find you, no matter where you hide.'

She could almost hear Jeff smiling and shaking his head. 'Nobody's going to find us, Lily. Not the FBI, not you. Nobody, never.'

With that, he cut the connection. Lily stared at the receiver for a while, but then she went across the hall and slotted it back into its socket. She felt completely drained, as if she didn't even have the strength to go to the kitchen and wash her cuts under the faucet. Jeff's face smiled at her from the opposite wall, through a crazed arrangement of bloodied glass.

You bastard, she thought. She picked up the phone again and punched out the number that Special Agent Rylance had given her.

Shortly after six, Bennie came around.

'You want a drink?' she asked him. She held up the large balloon glass she was carrying. 'I've just opened another bottle of shiraz.'

'*Another* bottle?' he said, hanging his hat on the banister post.

'I had a phone call this afternoon – from Jeff.'

Bennie glanced across at the broken photograph. 'Don't tell me. He hasn't any intention of bringing them back.'

'You're a very astute man, Bennie – very astute. You sure you don't want a drink?'

'No, thanks – it's pretty treacherous out there. Besides, I had more than a few glasses at lunchtime, with Philip Kraussman.'

'You saw Philip Kraussman? Come on in, for God's sake. Take a load off. I didn't know you were going to see him so soon.'

Bennie followed her into the living room and sat by the fire, holding out his hands and then chafing them noisily together. 'We were scheduled to meet in any event, to discuss property densities and building permissions. But I took the opportunity of asking him about that spit of land.'

'So what did you say?' said Lily, sitting in the armchair opposite him, and tucking up her legs.

'I told him that we'd been doing some background research on Mystery Lake – you know, to give our promotional brochure some "cultural depth". I said that we'd discovered that the Sioux consider this particular site to be deeply sacred, and what a terrific chance that offered us to do some first-rate public relations.'

'Public relations? This was the place where the god of thunder appeared and told the Mdewakanton that the white man was going to steal their land. Which of course they did.'

'That's the whole point, Lil. And that's exactly what I told Philip Kraussman. If Kraussman Developments were to *return* that particular piece of land to the Indians – with something of a media fanfare, of course – Philip Kraussman would look like a man of great historical awareness and generosity of spirit, instead of the grasping chiseler which he really is. OK – he's building a high-security lakeside enclave for stinking-rich young professionals; but nevertheless he feels empathy with those who originally lived and hunted on this land and for whom it still holds enormous mythical significance, even today.'

Lily stared at him over the rim of her wine glass. 'My God, Bennie. You do have a way with bullshit. What did he say to that?'

'We-e-ll, to tell you the truth, he was still a little cagey about it. Philip Kraussman is a very cagey man, as you know. Never does anything spontaneous. Always looks for the wrinkles. So I suggested that he could attach a covenant to his donation, insisting that the land is to be used for memorial purposes only – no right of domicile. In other words: totem poles, fine – but tepees or trailers, absolutely not.'

'So . . . don't keep me in suspense. What was the outcome?'

'You'll be relieved to know that he agreed. So when your Native American tracker finds Tasha and Sammy for you, and brings them home, you can give him what you promised.'

'Bennie! That's terrific! Did Philip Kraussman give you any idea how much he wants for it?'

'Nothing. Like I told you, it's a donation. Kraussman Developments will probably get more tax relief for it than it's actually worth. Maybe Philip Kraussman might ask you to meet the legal costs of drawing up the deeds and the covenant, but that's all.'

Lily put down her glass on the side-table, got up from her chair and took hold of Bennie's hands.

'Hey,' he said, frowning at the Band-Aid on her finger. 'You've cut yourself.'

'It's nothing. Nothing at all. Especially not now.'

'Glad to be of service; that's all I can say.'

'Bennie, you're wonderful. After that call from Jeff I thought that today was going to be the second worst day of my life, but you've changed all that completely. Now it's the second best.'

'Hey – only the second best?'

'The *best* will be the day that Tasha and Sammy come home.'

'Of course. Stupid me. But when they do, I want to be here to help you celebrate.'

She kissed him, on the lips. He tasted of brandy. 'Are you sure you won't have a drink?' she asked him. 'Come on, have a glass of wine to celebrate. I don't know how you did it. I mean, Philip Kraussman must be the meanest man in Minneapolis. But you did it. Your honeyed words persuaded him.'

'After twenty-six years in realty, I should be able to persuade anybody to do anything.'

Lily sat on the arm of his chair and stroked his hair. 'Seriously, Bennie. You're wonderful. I've been so worried about this. That call from Jeff really upset me, but at least I know now that Tasha and Sammy are safe, and I know that my tracker is on his way to finding them, and that I can pay him when he brings them home. Thank you.'

She kissed him again, and this time he kissed her back. 'You're a fantastic woman, Lil. I've always thought that.'

She sat up straight and stared into his glasses for a long time, blinking, as if she were hypnotized. Then she said, 'You're right, Bennie. You're right. I *am* a fantastic woman. I'm also very drunk.'

She was still wrapped in her thick white bathrobe at ten a.m. the next morning, feeling as if she had tumbled head-first down three flights of stairs. She had just poured herself a strong cup of mocha, with a large spoonful of clear honey in it, when the doorbell chimed.

Special Agent Rylance and Special Agent Kellogg were standing on the doorstep, both wearing Ray-Bans. The sun was shining so brightly off the snow that Lily had to shield her eyes with her hand.

'We're sorry to disturb you, Mrs Blake. We have some news.'

'That's all right.' She tapped her forehead. 'This is self-inflicted. After Jeff's phone call – well, I had a little red wine to calm myself down. A *lot* of red wine, as a matter of fact.'

She led them through to the kitchen. A large pine table had replaced the original counter. 'How about some coffee?' she asked them.

'That would be very welcome. We've been up since four thirty.'

'I could cook you some breakfast, too, if you're hungry. Except that the smell of bacon would probably make me puke.'

'That's all right,' said Special Agent Kellogg. His 1960s pompadour was looking unusually spider-like. 'I'm sure we can find ourselves a diner.'

'Did you find out where Jeff was calling from?' Lily asked him.

'No trace, I'm afraid. Like he told you, he was calling from a pre-paid cell.'

'But there has been something of a development,' said Special Agent Rylance. 'We're not one hundred percent sure what happened yet, but it could have given us a useful new lead.'

He looked reluctant to continue, and turned to Special Agent Kellogg, but Lily said, 'What?'

'OK. The Fourth Police Precinct received a call at about ten after three this morning from a resident in the Willard-Hay district. She was complaining of hissing noises from the apartment building next door, and she was worried that there might be a gas leak. Then she heard a whole lot of banging and crashing and she thought she heard somebody screaming, too.

'The police went to investigate and they found that the top-floor apartment had been totally wrecked. They also found parts of a man's body.'

Lily said nothing, but sat with her coffee mug held in both hands, feeling that Special Agent Rylance was going to tell her something dreadful.

'We haven't been able to identify the man yet. There wasn't enough of him left. But we found papers and note-books and DVDs and other materials which leave us in no doubt at all – this apartment is the headquarters of the Fathers' League Against Mothers' Evil.'

Special Agent Kellogg said, 'We even found the orange-painted wall that they used for their webcam broadcast on Channel 41. You know, with FLAME written on it.'

Special Agent Rylance laid one hand on Lily's arm. 'We're going through the papers and the notebooks right now, to see if they contain any information that might lead us to Tasha and Sammy.'

'So somebody actually hit back at those bastards,' said Lily. 'Do you have any idea who it was?'

'At the moment, no. Theoretically, it could have been anybody who thought that FLAME were going too far. A feminist group. A religious fanatic. Maybe the boyfriend of one of the ex-wives who were burned to death.

'But a couple of factors have really got us stumped. Whoever it was, they were physically very powerful – almost *inhumanly* powerful. The man who was found in that apart-ment – well, there was only one leg, and half of a pelvis, and a long slew of intestines. God only knows what happened to the rest of him. We're still looking.

'The other thing is, the apartment door was locked, so whoever trashed the place must have stolen a key or owned a key in the first place. We're thinking that it could have been an inside job – maybe a member of FLAME who became disillusioned and sickened with what they were doing, and wanted to stop them from carrying on.'

'I don't know what to say,' Lily told him. 'Maybe, "Thank God."'

'Well, that's kind of our feeling, too,' said Special Agent

Kellogg. 'And we hope to have some more news for you before the end of the day. There's a whole mountain of stuff for us to go through, but the police at the Fourth Precinct are helping us out.'

Special Agent Rylance sipped his coffee. 'Meanwhile . . . if anybody contacts you . . .'

'What do you mean?'

'It's possible that somebody may call you and claim responsibility for stopping FLAME. It happens sometimes, when some unpleasant characters get whacked, like corrupt politicians, or oppressive landlords. Whoever kills them calls up their victims to ask for their approval, and maybe their congratulations too. Not much point in being a hero if nobody knows about it.'

'OK. Sure. You want some more coffee? I have some cookies, too, if you'd like some.'

'We'll be fine, thank you, Mrs Blake. You just take care of yourself, you hear?'

'Catsup sandwiches – they're good for hangovers,' said Special Agent Kellogg. 'Catsup sandwiches, generously sprinkled with dried chili seeds.'

Immediately after Special Agents Rylance and Kellogg had left, Lily picked up the phone and dialed John Shooks. This time, Shooks answered.

'Mr Shooks! Did you hear what happened?'

'Did I hear what happened about what? I've been sitting in my car all night, surveilling a property in Powderhorn Park. For no purpose whatsoever, as it turned out. No adulterers went in; no adulterers came out.'

'It's FLAME. They had a headquarters in Willard-Hay. Somebody trashed it and killed a man who was in there.'

'Well . . . that's good news,' said John Shooks, cautiously. 'Isn't it?'

'Whoever did it, they tore this man to pieces. There was nothing left of him except one leg and some of his insides.

The FBI agent said that the killer must have been in-humanly strong. *Inhumanly.'*

'Yes?' said Shooks.

'The door was locked, too. The FBI thought that the killer might have had a key.'

'That sounds like a reasonable theory to me.'

'He *might* have had a key. On the other hand, supposing he *didn't* have a key? Supposing he *slid* in, like a sheet of paper?'

'Yes,' said Shooks.

'Yes? What do you mean, "Yes"?'

'I mean, yes – you're right. There's only one thing that could have found out where those guys were holed up, and there's only one thing that could have entered their apart-ment without unlocking the door, and there's only one thing that could have torn that guy to shreds and taken two-thirds of his mortal remains for a trip across the city.'

'The Wendigo,' said Lily.

'The Wendigo,' said Shooks.

Lily could hardly breathe. 'For God's sake! I didn't know that anybody was going to get *killed*!'

'Mrs Blake, the Wendigo is a tracker and a hunter. Like all trackers and hunters, when he eventually locates what he's been tracking and hunting – he kills it. And eats it. Didn't George Iron Walker make that clear to you? The word "Wendigo" means "cannibal". He told you that.'

'Oh, God,' said Lily. 'I didn't understand.'

'Well, what do you think that the Wendigo itself was going to get out of this particular assignment?'

'The land – the spit of land at Mystery Lake. I thought *that* was the price.'

'It's George Iron Walker who wants the land. Kind of an agent's fee, if you like, for putting you in touch with the Wendigo. The Wendigo isn't interested in land, sacred or otherwise. The Wendigo wants human flesh.'

'But why did it kill that man from FLAME?'

'It's following the scent, Mrs Blake, like I told you. It followed the scent from your house to Sibley's Barn, and from Sibley's Barn it obviously followed the scent to this apartment in Willard-Hay. And when it came across one of the men who was responsible for abducting your children, it took him. The Wendigo is working for *you*, Mrs Blake. Don't tell me you didn't want to see those dirtbags dead. They wanted to see *you* dead, after all.'

'It can't just go around tearing people to pieces! Not on *my* behalf!'

'It can, and it does. Sorry if you were laboring under any kind of misapprehension.'

'But what happens when it finds Tasha and Sammy? It won't hurt them, will it?'

'Of course not. It's made a solemn and binding promise to bring them back safe.'

'And Jeff?'

Lily could almost hear John Shooks shrug. 'Jeff? Well, Jeff is a horse of another color.'

'What do you mean? The Wendigo will kill him? It can't! It mustn't!'

'You surprise me. I thought you hated Jeff with a rare vengeance, Mrs Blake.'

'I do! I detest him! But he's still the father of my children! And no matter what he's done wrong, no matter how callous and cruel he's been, he's still a human being!'

'Hmm. It seems we have something of a dye-lemmer here.'

'There's no dilemma, Mr Shooks. You have to get in touch with George Iron Walker and call the Wendigo off, right now, before it's too late.'

'I don't think it's possible to do such a thing, Mrs Blake. Once the Wendigo sets off on its hunt, there's no stopping it. Remember that a deal works both ways. You asked the Wendigo to find your kids for you, no matter what it took. And what the Wendigo takes is human beings.'

'You're playing with words, Mr Shooks! I didn't mean that at all! If I'd known that the Wendigo was going to kill people, I wouldn't even have considered asking it for anything! Call George Iron Walker and tell him to stop it!'

'I can try, Mrs Blake. Don't hold out much hope of success, though.'

'You want me to call the FBI and tell them what you and George have been doing?'

'Oh – summoning up a Mdewakanton forest spirit and sending it off to eat people? I wonder which particular federal statute that's in contravention of?'

Nine

She drove round to see Bennie. Concord Realty occupied a large open-plan office on Hennepin Avenue South, carpeted in plum, with potted palms and soothing music and scenic photographs of Lake Harriet and Lowry Hill. Fiona saw her as soon as she came in and waved. Fiona was fortyish, with blonde upswept hair and huge dangly earrings. She had taught Lily almost everything she knew about closing a property sale. Never take 'I'll call you tomorrow' for an answer. Don't even take 'Let me think about it'.

Bennie came out of his office carrying a stack of brochures. As soon as he saw Lily, he put them down and came over and kissed her. 'Good to see you, Lil! How are things shaping up? Got any news?'

'Kind of. Look – I need your help with something. I was wondering if you could tell me how to get in touch with your brother Myron.'

'Myron? What for?'

'Well, you know what you said about him and John Shooks. I'd like to talk to him about it.'

'John Shooks is not giving you any trouble, is he? If so, he'll have me to deal with.'

'Not exactly. I just need to talk to Myron, that's all.'

'Lil – if there's anything wrong . . .'

She took hold of his hand. 'I know, Bennie. And thanks. And thanks again for what you did with Philip Kraussman.'

'Hey, it's nothing. Really.'

*   *   *

Myron was manager of a winter-wear store on Cedar Avenue called Cold Comfort. When Lily called around, he was in the stockroom at the back, checking through boxes of Bugabootoo children's boots. He was thinner than Bennie, and going bald, but there was no mistaking that he was Bennie's brother.

'Lily, this is some surprise!'

Lily smiled. 'Bennie told me where to find you. Boy, this is like Aladdin's Cave in here.'

'Just having a stock clearance. We've got some great ladies' windbreakers if you're interested. Artificial fur-lined hoods. Give you a real big discount.'

'Actually I wanted to talk to you about John Shooks.'

Myron took off his heavy-rimmed eyeglasses and stared at her with a serious expression. He had a slight cast in his right eye, so that she wasn't quite sure if he was looking at her directly.

'John Shooks? Well, he got my kids back for me, when nobody else could. He'll find yours, too, believe me.'

'Did he find your kids himself, or did he have some help?'

'Any particular reason for that question?'

'There is, as a matter of fact. I'm beginning to wonder what I've gotten myself into.'

'Well . . . first couple of times Velma took them away, Shooks found them himself. Didn't take him more than two or three hours. First time, they were round at her friend Gussie's house. Second time, they were staying at the Best Western University Inn. Don't ask me how he knew where they were.'

Lily didn't say anything, but she could imagine how Shooks had found them. He would have listened to the conversations that Velma had left behind her, still suspended in the air, telling her children where they were going.

'What about the third time?' she asked.

'Well, I don't really want to talk about that, if you don't mind.'

'Myron – I need to know. I'm worried that something really bad is going to happen. To tell you the truth, I'm worried that somebody's going to get hurt, or even killed.'

Myron actually flinched. 'I don't know. I don't know what to say to you. I don't know what happened myself.'

'Did John Shooks take you to meet George Iron Walker, and a blind Native American girl called Hazawin?'

Myron said, 'That last time, Shooks tried to find Velma, but he couldn't. He said that she hadn't left any clues behind that he could follow.'

'But he knew somebody who *could* find them?'

'That's right.'

'Somebody or *something*.'

Myron nodded, looking miserable. 'I didn't really believe in it. But I didn't know what else to do. I didn't want to involve the police – Velma had a restraining order against her and I didn't want to see her get into any more trouble.'

'So George Iron Walker said that he'd send the Wendigo to look for her?'

'That's right.'

'And what did he ask for, in return?'

'Hardly anything at all. Just some old Native American blanket that we used to have in the window, as part of our display. I don't think it was worth very much.'

'So you went to Black Crow Valley and met George Iron Walker and Hazawin? And they took you into the woods, and you saw the Wendigo?'

'I don't exactly know what I saw. There was some kind of a flickery light, that's all.'

'Then what happened?'

'Three days later I had a phone call from my daughter Ellie. She said that she and her sister were in Seattle. Velma had taken them there, to a house that she had rented near Richmond Beach. Velma's folks originally came from Seattle, so I guess that was a natural place for her to go.'

Lily said nothing, but waited for Myron to continue.

Myron seemed to be very jumpy. He kept glancing around the stockroom, as if he were half-expecting somebody else to appear, out of thin air.

'Ellie said that Velma had taken them on to the seashore, for a walk. Sometime during that walk Velma disappeared. Ellie didn't know how, and neither she nor Ruthie saw anything unusual. As far as they knew, they were the only people around.

'Ellie and Ruthie searched that seashore for hours. They called Velma over and over, but there was no reply. When it started to grow dark they went back to the house. They didn't want to call the police because they knew that Velma would get into trouble for taking them.'

Myron paused again, and then he said, 'I caught the first flight to Seattle and brought them home.'

'You didn't tell the police either?'

'Velma was unstable. She was always unstable. That was why she lost custody of Ellie and Ruthie in the first place. How the hell was I supposed to know what had happened to her? Maybe she walked into the ocean. More likely she just wandered off. Why make things more complicated than they already were?'

Lily said, 'You've never heard from her since?'

'Nothing. Not a word. It was like she'd vanished off the face of the earth. After two months I stopped paying her alimony into her bank account.'

'No reaction?'

Myron shook his head.

'What do you really think happened to her?' asked Lily.

'I don't know, Lily. I don't *want* to know.'

'Did George Iron Walker tell you what the word "Wendigo" means?'

'Look,' said Myron, 'I have no way of finding out what happened to Velma and neither does anyone else. If the Wendigo took her, there's nothing I can do about it. And even if I was sure that the Wendigo took her, who would believe me?'

'I would.'

Myron said, 'Yes – but nobody would believe *you*, either.' He paused, and put his eyeglasses back on. 'As far as I'm concerned, Lily, things have turned out for the best. I've got the kids back, I don't have to pay alimony. I'm sorry for what happened to Velma. I won't be able to get her off my conscience, ever, but that's the price I have to pay.'

She tried calling Shooks again, but all she got was that infuriating voicemail response: '*Leave me a message, or leave me alone.*'

'Mr Shooks,' she said, 'I'm going out to Black Crow Valley myself, to talk to George Iron Walker. Give me a call back as soon as you can.'

It was only a quarter after noon when she climbed into her Rainier and turned out of her driveway, but the sky was so dark that it could have been a quarter after midnight. Huge snowflakes began to tumble across the highway, and she could see people hurrying for shelter. Normally she never would have ventured out in weather like this, but she didn't know how much time she had left before the Wendigo found out where Jeff had taken Tasha and Sammy. It might be too late already.

She drove as fast as she dared, sliding sideways around corners and running red lights if she could see that there was no other traffic around. It took her less than twenty-five minutes to reach the turn-off that led to Black Crow Valley. The snow was falling so furiously now that she almost missed it. She jammed on her brakes and the Rainier skidded for thirty yards before it stopped. She backed up, with two fountains of slush spraying from her front wheels.

The track that led to George Iron Walker's house had been thickly blanketed with freshly fallen snow, so that it was almost impossible to follow. Six or seven times Lily drove into the ditch that ran alongside it, or up on the verge, and the Rainier's suspension jarred and banged.

Off to her left the forest looked even more forbidding than the first time she had come here, with Shooks. She was beginning to regret that she had come here. Supposing she turned around, and said nothing, like Myron? Nobody would ever know how Jeff had been killed, or by whom. And didn't Jeff *deserve* to be punished, after he had sent those men from FLAME to burn her alive?

But she kept on driving. She couldn't behave like Jeff and Myron. It wasn't in her nature. Her father and mother had always brought her up to respect other people's lives, no matter who they were. She remembered her father paying for an old woman's groceries, when she discovered that she had lost her purse. Not only that: he had driven her all the way back to her home. 'What did it cost me?' he had said to Lily afterward. 'Eight dollars and fifteen minutes.'

Lily peered ahead of her with narrowed eyes. Her windshield wipers were whacking wildly from side to side but they could barely keep up with the rapidly falling snow. She couldn't yet see George Iron Walker's house, and she wondered if she might have taken a wrong fork. She seemed to remember that the forest had gradually risen up on a gradient on her left-hand side, yet it was still level, and the trees seemed to crowd together much more closely than they had before.

The Rainier jolted over a series of spine-jarring ridges, and Lily had to wrestle to keep it on the track. As she straightened it out, she thought she glimpsed something running through the forest, about fifty yards away – something large, and gray, and very fluid, like a wolf. She wiped the side window with her glove. She saw it again – only for an instant, but as it disappeared behind the trees it appeared to be rising up on to its hind legs.

For some reason she felt a deep sense of uncertainty. This wasn't natural, this place. It wasn't normal. She wasn't afraid of wolves, especially since Shooks had told her that wolves never attacked people. But what kind of wolf could stand up and run like a man?

She carried on driving, but every few seconds she glanced anxiously into the trees. Now the forest began to rise, and she realized that she was on the right track after all. The snow began to ease off, too, and she adjusted the windshield wipers to a less hysterical speed. She crested the hill, and there below her was George Iron Walker's house, with smoke pouring listlessly out of the chimney, and George Iron Walker's SUV parked outside.

As she drove slowly down the hill, though, she saw an explosion of snow burst out of the forest, off to her left. In the middle of the snow, barely visible, was some kind of animal, with hunched-up shoulders. It was black, although she thought she saw some brown brindling as well. She thought it might have been a bear, but it was running so fast that it had disappeared behind the back of the house before she had time to be sure.

She parked, and climbed down from her Rainier. This time, nobody came out to greet her. *Well*, she thought, *they didn't know that I was coming.* She mounted the front steps, keeping her eyes open for the 'bear', or whatever that animal had been. Wolves might hesitate to attack humans, but bears had no compunction at all.

In the middle of the door hung a tarnished brass knocker, with a face like a snarling wolf. She lifted it up, and was just about to knock when Hazawin opened the door. She was wrapped in a dark maroon blanket, and her hair, which had been tightly braided when Lily had last seen her, was flowing glossy and loose over her shoulders.

'Hallo?' she said, her misted purple eyes staring at nothing at all. 'Who is it?'

'It's Lily – Lily Blake. I'm sorry – I really should have called ahead, shouldn't I?'

'Don't worry about it, Lily. We're always pleased to have visitors. Why don't you come along in?'

Hazawin closed the door behind them and said, 'How about something hot to drink?'

Lily looked around the living room. It was gloomy and cold. None of the table-lamps was switched on, although Hazawin wouldn't have needed them. But the log fire had burned right down and a bitter draft was blowing down the chimney, stirring the ashes into little dancing ash-devils. Lily had the feeling that nobody had been in here for several hours.

'Is George here?' she asked.

'He won't be too long. He's been on the phone all day today. Casino business. Are you sure you won't have anything to drink?'

'OK . . . maybe a cup of that verbena tea?'

'Of course.'

Hazawin went into the kitchen while Lily sat down beside the fire and held out her hands toward the fading warmth of the last few embers. She had felt uncomfortable on her first visit, but this time she felt distinctly uneasy, although she couldn't have clearly explained why. This house had a feeling of unreality, out here in the middle of the forest, surrounded by wolves. It was like Grandma's house in Red Riding Hood, or a dream from which she couldn't wake up.

'Did John Shooks get in touch with you?' Lily called out.

'John Shooks? No.'

'I asked him to get in touch with you.'

At that moment, George Iron Walker appeared from the direction of the bedroom. His hair was wet as if he had been taking a shower, and he was buttoning up a red-and-black flannel shirt.

'Lily! Good of you to call by.' He leaned over and kissed her cheek. His lips felt cold. He even had an aura of cold around him, as if he had just come into the house from outside.

'Sorry to drop in without notice,' said Lily. 'I thought that John Shooks would have called you.'

'He probably tried, but I've been tying up the phone all

day. Hey, look at this fire! Let's stack some logs on here!' He knelt down on the diamond-weave hearth-rug and started to riddle the ashes.

Lily noticed that there were small scratches on the backs of his hands, like briar scratches. 'Did you hear what happened?' she asked him. 'Somebody broke into the offices of the Fathers' League Against Mothers' Evil, and killed one of them. Tore him apart.'

'Yes, I heard about that.'

'The police can't work out who did it. Apparently the door was locked.'

'Maybe it was one of their own. They're all psychos.'

Lily hesitated, and then she said, 'I'm not stupid, George.'

'Did I say you were?'

'*You're* not stupid, either. You know why I'm here.'

George bowed his head for a moment, and then turned to look at her. 'You want me to call off the Wendigo.'

'I didn't realize it was going to *kill* people. For God's sake, George. Those men from FLAME, they tried to kill me, but that doesn't give *me* the right to kill them – not without a trial, not without proper justice. And Jeff. My ex-husband. I don't want him hurt. Whatever he's done, he's still Tasha and Sammy's father.'

George carefully placed a log on the fire, and then balanced another one on top of it. 'There is no way that I can call off the Wendigo, Lily. It's not like a bloodhound. Once it agrees to hunt for somebody, it will go on hunting them right to the ends of the earth, until it finds them.'

'Isn't there something that Hazawin can do . . . some kind of incantation? Some kind of spell?'

'Hazawin can call the Wendigo out of the woods, but once it's been summoned she can't control it. You made a deal, Lily – you made a deal with me and a deal with the Wendigo, and you can't go back on it now.'

Lily said, 'Tell me something: what's really in this for you?'

110

'I don't understand what you mean. I was trying to help you to find your children – nothing more than that.'

'You wanted that spit of land from Mystery Lake. That's worth a quarter of a million dollars, at least. Yet when you helped Myron Burgenheim to find his children, all you asked for was a blanket from out of his store.'

George looked serious. 'That was no ordinary blanket, Lily. That blanket was once wrapped around the shoulders of Oye-Kar-Mani-Vim, the trackmaker, and the greatest ever taker of Chippewa scalps. It means as much to the Mdewakanton as that spit of land.' He crumpled up a sheet of newspaper and tucked it under the logs. 'I've spent my whole life trying to give my people the dignity and the independence which was taken away from them by the white man. That was why I fought so hard for that casino, so that they could have economic freedom. But it's not just about the present, and the future. It's about the past, too. I'm trying to bring together as many sacred artifacts as I can, and recover as many sacred places as possible, to give us our identity back.'

'You have to stop the Wendigo,' said Lily. 'I don't care how you do it. I'll make sure that you still get the land at Mystery Lake, whatever.'

Hazawin came in with Lily's tea, and set it down beside her on the hearth. She turned toward her and said, 'I'm sorry, Lily. If only there *was* some way of stopping it. But not even the most powerful of wonder-workers could do that.'

George lit the newspaper and the fire flared up. Hazawin knelt beside it, in the same way that she had been kneeling when Lily had first seen her. Lily sipped her tea, but it seemed to have an odd haylike taste to it, and she could only drink half a mug. She was tempted to ask George about the wolves she had seen in the forest, but for some reason she decided that it would be more prudent if she didn't. It was completely irrational, but she felt that here, in this living room, she was sitting amongst wolves, even if the wolves had human form.

She stayed for less than twenty minutes. George told her more about the history of the Mdewakanton, and how they had lost their land. 'The very name Mdewakanton tells who we are, and where we belong. "Mde" is "lake". "Wakan" is "sacred mystery" and "otonwe" is "village".' Lily looked toward the window. 'Look, it's started snowing again. I'd better go.'

George took her out to her SUV. He opened the door for her, but before she could climb in he took hold of both of her hands. 'I hope you don't feel that I've misled you in any way,' he told her.

'I think you could have explained more clearly that the Wendigo was going to tear people to pieces.'

'Listen to me: if you had died when those men came around to your house, do you think your Jeff would have wept for you?'

Lily pulled a face. 'Probably not. Almost certainly not. But that still doesn't justify killing him.'

'Sometimes people dig their own graves, Lily.'

'Yes, well . . .' she said. She got into the driver's seat and started the engine. George stepped back. As he did so, she saw something in his face that gave her a tingling sensation in her hands. A momentary narrowing of his jaw, a smile that seemed to bare his teeth, and a stare that had no expression at all, the way an animal stares. But then he lifted his hand to wave, and he looked perfectly ordinary.

She watched him in her rear-view mirror as she drove back up the rise. He didn't change. He didn't go down on all fours. *You're spooking yourself. You're letting your imagination run off with your sanity.* But all the same, the Wendigo was still out looking for Jeff and Tasha and Sammy, and now she knew that she had no way of stopping it.

That evening, Bennie came around with a large bunch of lilies wrapped in cellophane. He smelled strongly of Aramis aftershave. 'I thought you might appreciate some company.'

'That's very sweet of you, Bennie, but I'm OK. I'm probably going to have an early night tonight.'

'Have you eaten?' he asked her, taking off his hat. 'You should eat, you know. I thought we could go to Café Twenty-Eight for some of that crawfish tortellini.'

'Sorry, Bennie. I think I'll pass.'

Bennie rocked from one foot to the other, like a small boy who wanted to go to the bathroom but was too embarrassed to ask.

'OK, then,' he said. 'But I still think you need to keep your strength up.'

'Don't worry. I'll probably have a sandwich before I turn in. And – look – thanks for the flowers. They're gorgeous.'

Bennie retrieved his hat. He cleared his throat, and sniffed. 'There's something I need to ask you,' he said.

'What's that, Bennie?'

'I know this is kind of premature. I mean you haven't got Tasha and Sammy back yet. But I'm sure you will.'

'I'm praying I will, Bennie.'

'Well, me too, Lil. Me too. With all of my heart. But what I need to ask you is: do you think there's any place for me in your affections? I mean, do you think there's any possibility of you and me being more than just friends?'

Lily could hardly believe that she had heard him right. She had survived a murderous attempt to burn her alive, her children had been missing for over three months, and still were, and he wanted to know if they could conceivably be lovers.

She was about to snap that he was totally unbelievable, and to get out of her house, and that she wouldn't go back to work for Concord if it was the last real-estate agency on the planet; but then she thought: *Mystery Lake. If I don't get that spit of land at Mystery Lake, I won't be able to pay George for the Wendigo –* and, as George had made clear, a deal is a deal.

She gave Bennie a tight, puckered smile. 'Let's just wait

and see, Bennie, shall we? Until I get Tasha and Sammy back – well, it's hard to make plans.'

'I just wanted you to know that I really care for you,' said Bennie. 'Whatever you want, whenever you want it – you know where I am.'

'Yes, Bennie. I do. That's very kind of you.'

He gave her a clumsy kiss. 'I'll talk to you tomorrow, OK?'

'OK, Bennie. Goodnight. Drive safely.'

She closed the door behind him and stood for a while with her back to it. For the first time in her life she felt as if she were losing faith in the world and everybody in it.

She had another nightmare that night. She was walking through an abandoned house, in midwinter. She went from room to room, and all the rooms were dusty and bare, except for a kitchen chair lying on its back, and a large rocking-horse with no head and a threadbare tail.

Somewhere upstairs she could hear a shutter banging, and hesitating, and banging again. She stopped, and she listened, but all she could hear was the shutter, and the wind. She thought, *There's a storm getting up. I'd better close the windows.* But when she reached the foot of the staircase, she hesitated, though she didn't know why.

On the wall beside her hung a photograph of Jeff. The glass was broken and blood was running from Jeff's left nostril.

'Jeff,' she said. She reached out to touch the photograph but Jeff turned away, and when he turned away she saw that the side of his head had been crushed. She could see brains, and broken fragments of skull, and hair that was matted with blood.

'*Jeff!*' she said, but this time her voice was muffled and deep, like a slowed-down tape-recording. '*Juuurrrfffffff!*'

It was then that she heard claws – or what she thought were claws – softly clattering on the floorboards upstairs.

114

She thought she could hear panting, too. It sounded like dogs, or wolves.

The shutter banged, and hesitated, and banged.

It was then that a shadow fell across her, and a tall figure started to come down the stairs – a figure that was part-man and part-animal, part-wolf and part-deer. It came down awkwardly, with angular legs and arms, leaning against the side of the staircase.

She was too terrified to scream. She was too terrified even to breathe. She turned around and every door in the house slammed shut.

And then the phone rang.

Ten

'Mrs Blake? Lily? It's Special Agent Kellogg.'
'Oh, hi. How are you? Sorry – I was asleep.'
'That's OK. I'm sorry to wake you. Well, I'm not entirely sorry to wake you. We've found Tasha and Sammy.'
Lily sat up in bed. She was so breathless that she could hardly speak. 'You've found them? Oh, my God! Oh, thank God! Are they all right?'
'They're fine, Mrs Blake. They're at Tampa General Hospital, in Florida.'
'They're in *hospital*? Why? What's happened to them?'
'Nothing physically wrong, Mrs Blake, so far as I know. But they've had a pretty bad shock, and we just needed to make sure that they were OK.'
'What kind of a shock?'
'It's your former husband, I'm afraid. He's dead.'
Lily switched on her bedside lamp. 'What happened to him?' she asked, and her voice sounded like somebody else altogether.
'Look – we can come round and pick you up in fifteen minutes. We'll fly you directly down to Tampa and give you all the details on the way. Is that OK with you?'
'Please – I want to know how he died.'
'He was attacked, Mrs Blake, by a person or persons unknown. His injuries were very serious. In fact, you could say that they were catastrophic.'
'Do you have any idea who did it?'
'I haven't had time to speak to the Tampa police yet.

116

So far as I know, though, they don't have anybody in custody.'

'All right,' said Lily. 'I'll get dressed. How long will it take us to get to Tampa?'

'About three and a half hours. We should arrive around two in the morning.'

They left Minneapolis on the last North Western flight of the day. It was snowing heavily, but the flashing lights on the tips of the aircraft's wings made it look as if the snow was suspended motionless in mid-air.

Special Agent Kellogg sat beside her, while Special Agent Rylance sat across the aisle, trying to get some sleep.

'Your ex-husband had rented a beach-house on Crystal Island, just off Clearwater, in the name of Glennan. According to the police, he and the children pretty much kept themselves to themselves.'

'I can't understand why Tasha didn't try to contact me – just to tell me that they were alive and well.'

'People go through a strange psychological change when they're abducted, Mrs Blake, particularly children. Your ex-husband probably persuaded her that she would only upset you, if she called.'

'So what happened? Who found them?'

'It was yesterday evening, round about seven p.m. The old guy who lives next door heard a whole lot of noise like doors being slammed and furniture being thrown around. Then screaming. Tasha and Sammy came running out of the house and according to him they were terrified out of their wits.

'The old guy dialed nine-one-one, and then he went next door. The perpetrator or perpetrators had left the house, although the old guy said that it looked as if a hurricane had been through it. He found the remains of your ex-husband in the den.'

'Remains?'

'I haven't received a full report yet, Mrs Blake. But the detective who called me said that I should try to prepare you for some very unpleasant details.'

'Go on.'

Special Agent Kellogg loosened his necktie. 'Maybe this should wait until we get to Tampa, and I can talk to the medical examiner.'

'No, I want to know now. What did he mean by "very unpleasant"?'

'Your ex-husband was attacked with extreme brutality, Mrs Blake. He was literally torn to shreds. The old guy next door said that the last body he had seen like that was a scuba-diver who had been mangled up by the propeller of a pleasure boat.'

Special Agent Kellogg paused for a moment, and then he said, 'There wasn't very much of him there. One of his arms, and part of his ribcage. That was all.'

He paused again, and then he reached across and took hold of her hand. 'I'm sorry,' he said.

They spoke very little for the rest of the flight. Lily was offered breakfast, but she couldn't have eaten anything. Her stomach had contracted to a small, complicated knot.

She didn't need to hear any more forensic details to know that Jeff had been torn apart by the Wendigo, and that she was directly responsible for his death. Much as she hated him for what he had tried to do to her, she couldn't help thinking about the early days of their marriage, and all the laughter. She had loved Jeff so much. Now that body that used to lie in bed beside her had been ripped apart, and most of it dragged away. She couldn't stop thinking about the pattern of moles on his left shoulder, like a constellation in the sky at night.

'Are you OK?' asked Special Agent Kellogg.

She nodded. She hadn't pulled down the blind over the window, but all she could see was blackness, and her own reflection, like a ghost of herself traveling through the night.

*　　*　　*

Tasha and Sammy were deeply asleep when she arrived at the hospital. They were both on plasma drips to increase their blood volume. A young gray-haired doctor told Lily that he had also given them a mild sedative to calm them down. 'They were both in shock,' he told her. 'Whatever they witnessed, they were simply unable to articulate it. They literally couldn't speak.'

Lily looked down at them. She was desperate to take them into her arms, and hug them, but she knew how much they needed to sleep. They both looked well fed, and suntanned, and Sammy had gingery freckles across the bridge of his nose, just like Jeff used to get in the summer.

'Are they going to be OK?' she asked, touching Tasha's hair.

'It's too early to say,' said the doctor. 'They're likely to experience episodes of panic and insecurity, and they'll probably have nightmares for quite some time. But an experienced therapist should be able to see them through it. We had a boy of seven here who saw his entire family shot dead right in front of him. It took him nearly a year, but he learned to cope with it in the end.'

She was still sitting between the children's beds at seven a.m. when Special Agent Kellogg brought her a cup of coffee and a sugared donut.

'You must be pooped,' he said.

She gave him a smile. 'I want to be here when they wake up, that's all. I don't want them to think that they're all alone.'

'I've been talking to the detective who's running the case,' said Special Agent Kellogg. 'He said that nobody saw anybody enter the house, and nobody saw anybody leave. There were no unfamiliar vehicles parked anywhere nearby, and none of the local stores or bars or gas stations reported any unusual customers.'

He nodded toward Tasha and Sammy. 'It seems like the only witnesses were these two.'

'I don't want them questioned until they're ready,' said Lily.

'Don't worry about it. We have a child-interview specialist flying here from Quantico. She's very, very good. Very sympathetic. She's dealt with scores of investigations involving traumatized kids.'

'I feel so guilty,' Lily told him.

'Why should you feel guilty? None of this was your fault.'

'Maybe if I hadn't been so bitchy and self-righteous . . . Maybe if I had let Jeff see them more often . . .'

'Hey – you told me yourself that he always caused trouble. What else could you do?'

I could have waited for the FBI to find them. It might have taken a whole lot longer, but Jeff was obviously taking good care of them. At least he would still be alive, and Tasha and Sammy wouldn't have had to see him being ripped into pieces.

Special Agent Kellogg got up to leave and, as he did so, Tasha opened her eyes.

'Mom?' she whispered.

Lily stood up and took hold of Tasha's hands. She had promised herself that she wouldn't cry, but her eyes filled up with tears, and her throat was so choked up that she couldn't speak.

'Mom, what happened to your *hair*?'

They were sitting in the day-room overlooking the bright blue water of Tampa Bay when Dr Flaurus came in. Outside, the sun was shining and the yuccas were rustling in the warm Gulf wind. A seagull perched on the balcony rail, and stared at them with one emotionless eye.

Dr Flaurus came straight over to them, holding out her hand. She was tall, with wavy brunette hair and a strong, handsome face. She was wearing a natural-colored linen suit and an emerald-green blouse.

'Jane Flaurus,' she smiled, with scarlet lips.

'Lily Blake,' said Lily. 'This is Tasha and this is Sammy. Say hallo, kids.'

'Hallo,' Tasha whispered. Sammy said nothing at all, but covered his face with his hands and peered out at Dr Flaurus through his fingers.

Dr Flaurus pulled a chair across and sat down, crossing her legs. Out of her purse she produced a small tape-recorder, which she set down on the table next to the *Star Trek* book that Sammy had been reading.

'If you'd rather I didn't record what we talk about – if the tape-recorder makes you feel uncomfortable – then I'll put it away. But if I can listen to our conversation later, that will help me a whole lot.'

'Tasha?' asked Lily. 'Sammy?'

'It's OK,' said Tasha, so quietly that Lily could hardly hear her. Sammy said nothing, and kept his hands in front of his face.

Dr Flaurus said, 'It's beautiful here, isn't it? So warm.'

'We have snow up to our armpits in Minneapolis,' said Lily.

'I love the snow,' said Dr Flaurus. 'How about you, Sammy? Do you like the snow?'

Sammy still didn't answer, but Lily could see him furiously blinking behind his fingers.

Dr Flaurus talked for over fifteen minutes about nothing much at all. She asked Tasha and Sammy what TV shows they liked best, which lessons they enjoyed at school, which games they preferred to play. Lily began to think that she was never going to get around to asking them about Jeff.

'Would you like to live here in Florida, instead of Minnesota?' she said.

'Not now,' said Tasha.

'Not *now*,' Sammy echoed, with even more emphasis.

'But you liked it before?'

Tasha nodded. 'We went swimming every day. We went

to Busch Gardens and saw the animals. We had picnics and we went on all the rides.'

'I couldn't go on the Gwazi,' Sammy put in. 'I wasn't tall enough. But Daddy said I'll be tall enough next year.'

'We won't be here next year,' Tasha retorted. 'I don't want to come back here ever again.'

'I only want to come back here once,' said Sammy. 'Just to go on the Gwazi.'

Dr Flaurus said, 'That person who hurt your daddy – they won't be coming back, I promise you.'

'It wasn't a person,' said Sammy.

'Yes, it was,' said Tasha.

'No, it wasn't. It was nobody.'

'It was a man, stupid. Kind of a man, anyhow.'

'It was nobody. There was nobody there.'

'Yes, there was.'

'Wasn't.'

'Was.'

Dr Flaurus interrupted them. 'Tasha – when you say "kind of a man", what exactly do you mean?'

Tasha looked downwards and sideways, as if she didn't want to face her recollection directly. When she spoke, she shook her fingers as if she were trying to describe something flickery and insubstantial.

'All of a sudden he was just *there*.'

'You mean he came straight into the house without ringing the bell or knocking on the door?'

'No. He was just there, in the middle of the den. He just appeared.'

'*I* didn't see him,' said Sammy.

'Well you're blind.'

'I'm not blind. If I'm blind, where's my dog?'

'OK, OK,' said Dr Flaurus. 'Let's say that he just appeared. What did he look like?'

Tasha was shaking the fingers of both hands now. 'He was black and white, and he was all jumpy and jittery, like those people in those very old Charlie Chaplin movies. I couldn't see him very clearly because he wouldn't keep still.'

'Did you see his face?'

'It kept changing. It was like he had lots of faces.'

'Can you describe any of them?'

'One face looked as if he was shouting, with his mouth wide open. Another face looked really mean, with his eyes all squinched up. I saw another face, too, but that was like an animal. A deer, or a dog – something with a stretched-out head.'

'I didn't see him,' said Sammy. 'Daddy didn't see him, either.'

'How do you know that your daddy didn't see him?'

'Because Daddy walked into the den and said let's all go swimming.'

Dr Flaurus frowned. 'He walked right in and you don't think that he could see this man at all?'

'There wasn't a man. Tasha's making it up.'

Tasha turned on him. 'There was too! If there wasn't a man, who killed Daddy? Who tore his arms and his legs off and pulled off his head?'

Sammy quivered, as if he had wet himself, and didn't answer.

Tasha said, 'I don't think Daddy *did* see him. But I did. When Daddy came into the den the man turned around and took hold of Daddy's neck. He pulled his head off. It was like when you pull the head off a doll except there were strings and tubes and blood. I shut my eyes and I think I screamed but I can't remember.'

Sammy had turned very pale, and he was trembling. Lily put her arm around him and held him very close. 'It's all right,' she said. 'It's all over now. You're safe. Nobody can hurt you now.'

'I didn't see any man,' he insisted. 'Daddy's head came off, but it just jumped up, all by itself. I didn't see any man.'

Lily touched Dr Flaurus's arm. 'I think that's enough for now, don't you?'

'Of course. Yes. There's only one more question I want to ask. Tasha – did you see the man leave?'

Tasha shook her head.

'What I mean is, did you see him physically walk out of the door?'

'No. He turned around, and he disappeared.'

'Just like that? Like a magic trick?'

'Yes.'

Dr Flaurus took Lily into a small office next to the day-room. Special Agents Rylance and Kellogg were there, along with a sunburnt sandy-haired man in an olive-green summer suit. Special Agent Kellogg switched off the loud-speaker that they had been listening to.

'Mrs Blake, this is Detective Nick Moynihan, Tampa PD.'

Lily nodded in acknowledgement.

'Sorry about everything that's happened,' said Detective Moynihan. 'Seems like those kids of yours are pretty shook up.'

'Thank you. Will I be able to take them home today?'

'Maybe tomorrow morning. The doctors want to make sure their blood volume is back up to normal.'

'I'm afraid we'll have to interview them again,' said Special Agent Rylance. 'This story about a man who just appeared – or who *didn't* appear – we really need to get to the bottom of this.'

'There's nothing to get to the bottom of,' Lily protested. 'Those poor children saw their father torn limb from limb, right in front of their eyes. You don't seriously expect them to say anything that makes any sense?'

'Children usually make excellent witnesses,' said Detective Moynihan. 'No prejudice, no assumptions. They see things for what they are.'

'Or what they *aren't*, in this case,' added Special Agent Rylance.

Special Agent Kellogg said, 'I'm sorry, Mrs Blake. We do need to clarify their stories. We can't exactly put out a "most wanted" picture of a black-and-white character from a Charlie Chaplin movie, with three different faces.'

Dr Flaurus took hold of Lily's arm. 'I'll be very gentle with them, I promise. It isn't unusual for witnesses to imagine that they've seen something really strange, especially when they're in shock. It's like looking at a flowery-patterned fabric and seeing faces in it. And it's amazing how many witnesses *don't* see something that happened right in front of them. Did you ever see those experiments they did when they had a man in a gorilla suit walk right through the middle of a basketball game? Dozens of spectators never even noticed him.'

'I don't think we're looking for a guy in a gorilla suit, Doctor,' said Special Agent Rylance. 'More like a real gorilla. I mean – who has the physical strength to tear a man to pieces with his bare hands? And for Christ's sake, what was his *motive*? And why did he take most of Jeff Blake's body away with him?'

Special Agent Kellogg said, 'We also need to check out if this has anything to do with the FLAME homicide in Minneapolis. Very similar MOs, after all. Ripped to pieces, both of them, by an unseen assailant. And they're both linked to Tasha and Sammy's kidnap.'

Lily was strongly tempted to confess: *I asked a Native American medicine woman to conjure up the Wendigo, and the Wendigo kills and eats anybody who gets in its way.* But what was the point? They would simply think she was suffering from stress, and how could she possibly convince them that it was true? John Shooks would deny everything; and so would George Iron Walker and Hazawin.

'I only wish I could help,' she told them. 'Jeff and I – we were always arguing – always at each other's throats. But I would never have wanted him dead.'

'It's OK, Mrs Blake,' said Special Agent Kellogg, laying

a hand on her shoulder. 'You can go back to Tasha and Sammy now. Dr Flaurus will need to talk to them again, but not until tomorrow morning.'

Lily was just about to leave the office when a plump, bespectacled woman came bustling in, wearing a noisy green Tyvek suit. She had tightly curled hair and a large mole on her chin, and she smelled strongly of latex and disinfectant. 'Detective – I just thought you'd like to know that we've discovered some more of Mr Blake's remains.'

Detective Moynihan turned to Lily and said, 'Mrs Blake – you probably don't want to hear this.'

The crime-scene specialist flushed red. 'I'm truly sorry, ma'am. I didn't realize that you were the next of kin.'

'What have you found? Please – I want to know. I was married to him for eleven years.'

'You're sure?'

Lily nodded, so Detective Moynihan turned to the crime-scene specialist and said, 'OK, then, go ahead. But – you know – easy on the graphic details.'

The crime-scene specialist was blowing her nose into a crumpled Kleenex. 'Sorry – allergy,' she sniffed. 'We haven't completed our investigation yet, by any means, but we can tell you that Mr Blake was dismembered with extreme force, judging by the blood spatter, and almost instantaneously. Within seconds, in fact.

'So far we can't even conjecture how this was done. We've never come across a case like this before. But after he was dismembered, his left arm and a portion of his ribcage were left on the floor of the den, while the remainder of his body was carried out of the den, across the breakfast area, and out of the sliding doors at the rear of the house.'

She took out a small notebook and flicked through it. 'We found a pattern of blood spatter leading from the den to the back yard, but the droplets are anything between thirteen and seventeen inches apart and each one struck the floor at an unusually acute angle.'

'From which you conclude what?'

'The perpetrator was carrying what was left of Mr Blake at a considerable lick. He was running. In fact, he was more than running. He was exiting that beach house like a bat out of hell.'

'With three-quarters of a human body in his arms?'

'I can only tell *you*, Detective, what the evidence tells *us*.'

Detective Moynihan glanced at Lily and his expression was distinctly unhappy. Lily looked away. The more she heard, the guiltier she felt, and she was sure that it showed on her face. At least Jeff had died quickly, and he hadn't suffered. But she could still remember the moles on his shoulder. She could still remember the sound of his laugh.

'You, uh – you said that you'd discovered some more remains,' said Detective Moynihan.

'Well, that's right,' said the crime-scene specialist, wiping her nose again. 'I'm afraid there's no delicate way I can put this. We found a length of small intestine approximately eighteen feet long that had caught on the picket fence at the end of the yard. It had obviously been stretched out to the limits of its tolerance and then snapped. It was dangling over the children's swingset next door.'

'Jesus. How high is the swingset?'

'Seven feet six inches. At first we thought that the perpetrator might have *climbed* over the swingset, with the intestine trailing behind him, but there would have been no logical reason for him to do that. He didn't need to go that way. He could have escaped in any direction, without anybody seeing him. Apart from that, there are no scuffs or handprints on the swingset and absolutely no foot impressions on the sand that surrounds it, except for children's feet.'

'So what are you telling me?'

'We were pretty confused at first, I have to admit. But then seven houses away, directly to the north, we found several shreds of the victim's stomach lining, and a section of his trachea – his windpipe – as well as a quantity of fatty tissue.'

Detective Moynihan glanced at Lily again, but Lily said, 'It's all right. Don't worry about me,' even though she was beginning to feel that encroaching darkness that came upon her whenever she was going to faint.

'We found those remains on the *roof*, Detective,' said the crime-scene specialist. 'They were all tangled up in a TV antenna, thirty-five feet off the ground. And of course that explained everything.'

'I see. The perpetrator could fly.'

'Well, obviously not. But we have to assume that – as he exited the sliding doors at the rear of the beach house – he dropped some of the victim's viscera on to the patio. They would have been very slippery, after all – hard to keep hold of.'

'So then what?'

'Seagulls: that's our theory; or maybe pelicans. They're scavengers, after all. After the perpetrator had run away, two or three of them picked up the viscera and flew off with them.'

'You're serious?'

'There's no other explanation. Bird number one made off with the small intestine, but the end got snagged on the fence, and the bird was unable to pull it free. Bird number two made off with the stomach lining and the trachea and the other stuff, but they were too much for it to carry in its beak, or else it was attacked in mid-flight by yet another bird. Whatever it was, it dropped the remains on the roof. Nothing supernatural. Just plain old-fashioned ornithology.'

Detective Moynihan said to Lily, 'I'm sorry, Mrs Blake. You shouldn't have had to hear this.'

Lily raised both hands. 'That's all right. Once we're dead, we're dead, aren't we? I could have been nothing but ashes now, if Jeff had had his way.'

*   *   *

The next morning Dr Flaurus talked to Tasha and Sammy again, but they told her the same story. Tasha had seen a flickering man and Sammy hadn't.

After forty-five minutes Dr Flaurus took Lily aside and said, 'They're still very traumatized. I think they've each invented an imaginary scenario in order to protect themselves from remembering what really happened. I don't think we're going to be able to get at the truth until they've been through therapy.'

'Can I take them home?'

'If the doctors approve, yes. They need familiar surroundings, and security. I haven't talked to my head of department at Quantico yet, but I think she'll want me to interview them three or four more times, if that's OK with you. Believe me, I want them to recover from this experience as much as you do. But I think it will help them tremendously if I can persuade them to tell me what really happened.'

Lily said nothing. She knew that Tasha and Sammy had already described with complete faithfulness how Jeff had been killed. Tasha had seen the Wendigo because it was facing her. Sammy hadn't seen it because it was standing edgewise – *like a sheet of paper.*

Eleven

She didn't really believe that it was all over until they had arrived home, and she had run a deep foamy bath for them, and washed their hair, and dressed them up in their own pajamas, which had been lying neatly folded in their bedroom drawers for so long.

Then they sat around the kitchen table while she made them their favorite supper: Dutch potato scramble, with diced bacon, fried red potatoes, sliced red onions and eggs. As a special treat she allowed Sergeant to come into the kitchen, too. He sat with his head in Tasha's lap, his eyes rolled up in sheer pleasure while Tasha stroked his ears. *Spongebob Squarepants* was showing on the TV, Sammy's favorite, and no evening could have been more normal, or warmer, or felt so complete.

'Mommy – are you going to grow your hair now?' asked Sammy.

'Yes – yes, I am,' said Lily. 'In fact I think I'm going to grow it really long. The last time I grew it really long was at high school. I used to tie it in a pony-tail.'

'I like you bald.'

'Well, I shaved my hair off for a reason. I did it to show people that I was never going to stop looking for you, no matter what.'

'Daddy said you didn't really want us any more. He said you were glad to see the back of us.'

'I know he did. But he wasn't very well. I think we have to forgive him, don't you?'

130

Tasha said, 'Would you forgive him if he was still alive?'

Lily broke four eggs into the skillet, and stirred them around. 'Good question,' she said. She could tell that Tasha was growing up.

'Is there going to be a funeral?' asked Sammy.

'Yes. When the FBI have released Daddy's body.'

'He was all in bits. They'll have to put him back together again before they bury him.'

'Yes, they will. But they have people who are very good at doing that.'

'Do they sew them together, or do they use Crazy Glue?'

Dr Flaurus had warned Lily that the children would want to talk about their experience, and that she shouldn't try to discourage them, no matter how ghoulish it got.

'I guess they probably sew them.'

They sat down to eat. Sammy wolfed down his scramble as if he hadn't been fed in a week, but Tasha only toyed with hers. Lily saw that she had tears in her eyes, and she reached across the table and held her hand.

'You'll get over it, sweetheart. One day you'll go to bed and you'll realize that you haven't thought about it, even once.'

'We had such a good time,' said Tasha, miserably. 'It was almost like being in heaven.'

'I know. Your daddy only wanted to make you happy.'

'But we didn't care about you. We hardly ever talked about you. How could we have been so mean?'

'You weren't being mean. You were enjoying yourselves, that's all. If I was down in Florida, swimming and horse-back riding and going to Busch Gardens all the time, I wouldn't want to think about snow, and school, and tidying my room.'

Tasha wiped her eyes with her fingers. In the short time that she had been away she had started to change, and she was already looking like a young woman rather than a child. She reminded Lily so much of herself at that age, except that Tasha had Jeff's eyes – pale turquoise, and slightly unfocused-looking, as if she were short-sighted, although she wasn't.

They spent the rest of the evening in the living room, sprawled on the couch in front of the fire. Lily had stacked the logs up high, and the fire blazed so fiercely that their faces grew flushed. She told them everything that she had done since Jeff had kidnapped them: how she had spent Christmas with Agnes and Ned, and how Special Agents Rylance and Kellogg had called her almost every day.

At nine thirty she took Sammy up to bed and tucked him in. He looked at her solemnly over his candy-striped sheet and said, 'Goodnight, Mommy. I'm really glad I'm home.'

She smiled and stroked his hair. 'I'm glad you're home, too. And I think the *house* is glad. Can you feel how happy it is? I think it missed you.'

'I was too short to go on the Gwazi. You have to be four feet ten.'

'Never mind. I'll take you snowmobiling next week. You're not too short for that.'

'Cool!'

She kissed him. He smelled like freshly baked short-bread. He wrapped his arms around her neck and held her so tight that he hurt her.

'Mommy?'

'What is it?'

'That nobody who killed Daddy . . . he can't come here, can he?'

'Of course not. You're safe here.'

She left his bedroom door slightly ajar and the landing light on. 'Remember . . . if you have any bad dreams – if you get frightened by anything at all – you just come to my bedroom and wake me up. I won't mind a bit.'

She went back downstairs. Tasha was kneeling in front of the fire, prodding it with the poker, so that sparks flurried up the chimney.

'Do I have to go to Daddy's funeral?' she asked.

'Not if you don't want to.'

'I want to forget about him. I want to forget about everything that happened.'

Lily sat on the hearthrug next to her. 'You shouldn't forget him completely. He was your father, after all. He did love you.' She hadn't yet told Tasha about the men from FLAME, and how they had tried to burn her alive. She didn't know if she ever would. Her last memory of her father was traumatic enough, without thinking that he had wanted to kill her mother too.

Tasha said, 'I still don't understand what killed him. I keep trying to remember what it looked like, but it didn't really look like anything. It didn't look like a man and it didn't look like an animal. And it made this *hissing* noise.'

'You were in shock. People see some very strange things when they're in shock.'

'It had arms like a kind of insect. Daddy came into the den and said did we want to go swimming and I don't think he even saw it. It took hold of his head and pulled it straight up, and there was this horrible tearing sound.'

Tasha stared at Lily and her eyes were filled with desperation. Jeff's death had been horrific, and she should never have had to witness it. But what was obviously disturbing her the most was the fact that she couldn't understand what the Wendigo was, or why it had killed him. Lily put her arm around her, and held her close. *God*, she thought, *I'm her mother and I can't tell her what really happened.*

The next morning both children slept late. At nine fifteen Lily was sitting at the kitchen table drinking coffee and trying to finish the cryptic crossword in the *Star Tribune* when she was startled by a sharp *rappety-rap-rap!* at the window.

She looked up. It was John Shooks, wearing a huge black fur hat, and mirror sunglasses. He was pointing to the back door. Lily got up, unlocked it and let him in. He was accompanied by a north-west wind as sharp as a faceful of box-cutters.

'Unsuccessfully tried to ring your doorbell,' he explained. 'Guess it must have froze.'

'The forecast said twelve below,' said Lily. 'How about a cup of coffee?'

'Never drink coffee – makes me jumpy; but thanks anyhow.'

He took off his hat but left his sunglasses on. Lily said, 'I was going to call you this morning and tell you my news.'

'That's all right. I heard about it already. Nothing much gets past John Shooks.'

'You'll know about my ex-husband then.'

'Yes. Yes, I do.' He wiped his nose on his glove. 'Don't suppose you're grieving about it too much.'

'Oh, you don't think so?'

'Considering what that man tried to have done to you, Mrs Blake . . .'

'That's not really the point. It wasn't up to me to be judge and executioner, was it? It was up to the law. And Jeff *was* the children's father, whatever he was guilty of.'

Shooks raised his eyebrows, so that they appeared over his sunglasses like two rooks, but said nothing.

Lily said, 'I'm upset, as a matter of fact. I'm *very* upset. Jeff was selfish, and pig-headed, and he could be cruel, too. But he still didn't deserve to be killed like that.'

'Well . . . it's a little late to be worrying about that now. What's irrevocably torn to pieces is irrevocably torn to pieces.'

Lily went to the kitchen drawer and took out her checkbook. 'How much do you want, Mr Shooks?'

'Two twenty-five, if that's all right with you.'

'Two twenty-five is fine.'

She sat at the table and began to fill out the check. As she did so, Shooks said, 'I'm going to need the deed for

134

that piece of land, too, so that I can take it to George Iron Walker.'

Lily signed the check, tore it out, and held it out to him. 'I'm sorry. George Iron Walker won't be getting any land. I asked him to find my children, not kill my ex-husband.'

'You're serious?'

'I'm very serious.'

Shooks sucked in his breath. 'This is going to be more than a little difficult, Mrs Blake. See – the deal was, George Iron Walker was to find your children for you, and make sure that they were fetched back to you safe and sound. In return for that service you would hand over the title to that piece of land at Mystery Lake. Whatever the circumstances, you can't deny that George Iron Walker fulfilled his part of the bargain.'

'Mr Shooks, if I had known that the Wendigo was going to slaughter two people, I never would have considered that deal, not for a moment. George Iron Walker misled me, and I told him so right to his face.'

'Yes. He mentioned that you'd paid him a visit.'

'So, that's it. That's the end of it. Take your money, and I hope that I never need your services, ever again.'

Shooks took the check, folded it lengthwise, and tucked it inside his coat. But he made no move to leave.

'Is there anything else?' Lily asked him. Shooks was making her feel breathless and hyped up, as if she had been playing a hard game of raquets. 'Tasha and Sammy will be down in a minute, for their breakfast. I don't really want to have to explain to them who you are.'

'Mrs Blake, this is serious. You promised that piece of land to George Iron Walker, and believe me, he's not going to let you renege on that promise.'

'So what's he going to do? Take me to court? Let him try.'

'He doesn't need to take you to court, Mrs Blake. He has Hazawin.'

'And what can she do?'

'It's more like what she *can't* do. A woman who can raise the Wendigo can turn your whole life into a nightmare.'

Lily said, 'I'm not going to give George Iron Walker that piece of land, Mr Shooks. He made me an unwilling accessory to two violent homicides, and he deprived my children of their father, who they loved. They saw him killed right in front of their eyes. They saw his head torn off his shoulders. How can I reward George Iron Walker for doing a thing like that?'

'Mrs Blake – you listen to me – I'm giving you the gravest of warnings.'

'Well, thank you, Mr Shooks. I appreciate it. But I'm still not going to change my mind. If you want to go back to George Iron Walker and tell him that the deal is well and truly off, that's your prerogative. But I'm not even going to bother. As far as I'm concerned, he deceived me, and I don't think I'm obliged to honor any kind of agreement with a liar.'

From the upstairs landing, Sammy called out, 'Mom! Where did you put my Vikings sweatshirt?'

'Just a minute!' Lily called back. She turned to Shooks and said, 'I think you'd better leave now.'

Shooks looked at Lily for a very long time. She could see herself in duplicate, reflected in his sunglasses.

'OK,' he said at last. 'But I have to tell you this: I'm walking away from here with a heavy heart.'

'Don't worry, Mr Shooks. I think I'm quite capable of taking care of myself.'

John Shooks put on his hat and opened the back door. The wind blew in, and Lily's newspaper flew up off the table like a seagull, or a pelican.

After breakfast Lily drove them over to Wayzata to see Agnes and Ned. Petra and Jamie were at school, but little

William was at home, and Tasha and Sammy took him out into the yard to build a snow house. They laughed and screamed and threw snowballs as if nothing had happened to them.

'We'll still be seeing snow in May,' Ned predicted, watching the children through the living-room window.

'Oh, God, I hope not,' said Lily.

'You only have to look at this season's statistics. Those green people keep yattering on about global warming, but they're talking through their knitted hats. It's all a conspiracy to get government funding.'

'Ned's convinced that we're in for a second Ice Age,' Agnes put in.

They sat down, and Agnes passed around coffee and toll-house cookies.

'Are the kids OK?' asked Ned.

'I think so. They slept all night last night, but of course they were both exhausted. It's the weeks to come that I'm worried about.'

'Are you going to take them to a therapist?'

'They'll probably need it. At the moment they seem so *calm* about it, you know? So matter-of-fact. But seeing Jeff killed like that – I'm sure that it must have caused them some psychological trauma.'

Ned brushed cookie crumbs out of his moustache. 'Any more news on who might have done it?'

'Nothing. Apart from Tasha and Sammy, nobody saw anything.'

'Well, you know that I never liked Jeff much,' said Agnes. 'He was always too darn sorry for himself. But I can't imagine why anybody would have wanted to kill him. I mean – to rip somebody apart like that – you would really have to *hate* them, wouldn't you?'

'Nothing was stolen?' asked Ned.

Lily shook her head.

'Maybe it was something to do with those FLAME people

he was mixed up with. One of them was torn apart, too, wasn't he? Maybe Jeff was threatening to blow the whistle on them, about burning those women.'

'I really don't know,' said Lily.

Ned took a bite of cookie. 'The only other person I can think of who would have had a motive for killing Jeff is *you.*'

Lily managed a tight smile, but Agnes said, '*Ned.* Not funny, Ned. Not funny *at all.*'

As she drove home, her cell phone warbled. It was Bennie.

'Lily! Fiona told me that you got Tasha and Sammy back! Terrific news!'

'Well, it wasn't exactly a picnic. But, yes, they're home. And they're both OK.'

'So who found them? Don't tell me your Native American tracker lucked out?'

'It's kind of complicated. I don't know whether you heard, but Jeff's dead.'

'*Dead*? Are you serious? What happened?'

Lily glanced at Tasha, who was sitting next to her. 'I'll explain it to you later. I'm driving right now.'

'Well, call me later. I can come around to see you, if you like.'

'Maybe we can take a raincheck for a couple of days, Bennie. Tasha and Sammy need a little time to settle.'

'Sure, whatever you say. So – it *wasn't* your Native American tracker who found them?'

'Like I say, it's complicated. But we don't have to give him that spit of land at Mystery Lake.'

'We don't? You really mean that? That's going to make life a whole lot easier. Listen – I'll call you again this evening, if that's OK.'

Lily drew up at the intersection of France and Lake. The sky was a strange purplish color, like a widening bruise.

'How about pizza tonight?' she asked Tasha and Sammy.

Tasha said, 'No – no thanks. Daddy was always bringing home pizza.'

'With pineapple on,' Sammy put in. 'I *hate* pineapple.'

At one fifteen in the morning, Lily heard a piercing scream, and then another. She threw herself out of bed and was halfway across the landing before she was properly awake. 'Sammy! It's OK, honey, Mommy's coming!'

She collided with Tasha, who was just coming out of her room, white-faced. They hurried together into Sammy's room. Sammy was standing on his bed with both hands covering his face. He was juddering and sweating and he had soaked his pajama pants.

'Sammy! It's Mommy! Everything's OK! You had a nasty dream, that's all!'

Sammy took his hands away from his face and stared at her. He looked almost mad. Lily took him tightly in her arms and shushed him.

'You had a nasty dream, baby, that's all. It wasn't real.'

'It – was – nobody,' Sammy quaked. 'He – came – through – the – door – but – he – wasn't –'

'Come on, baby. Everything's going to be fine. Why don't we get you out of these pajamas and change your bed for you?'

'He – came – through – the – door – and – he's – *here!*'

'He's not here, Sammy, I promise you.'

Tasha came up to him, too, and brushed back his wet, tousled hair. 'He's not here, Sammy. He doesn't know where we live, and he's never going to find out.'

But Sammy turned to her, wide-eyed, and screamed, '*He's here!* I know he is! He's come after us! *He's here!*'

Lily picked Sammy up and helped him into a sitting position on the side of the bed. He had stopped screaming now, but he was moaning and muttering, and his eyes kept rolling up into his head, so that Lily could only see the whites.

'Tasha – I think you'd better call nine-one-one. He's having a fit.'

Tasha had only just reached the door, however, when Sammy dropped sideways on to his pillow. Lily said, 'Sammy! *Sammy!* Can you hear me? Sammy!' She pulled back one of his eyelids and his eye was staring back at her, fluttering slightly. She leaned over him. He was breathing evenly and his heartbeat was steady.

'He's asleep.'

She laid a hand on his forehead and although it was sweaty his temperature felt normal.

'Forget about the ambulance. I think he's OK. It was a night terror, that's all. Can you fetch me some clean pajamas out of his drawer? I'll freshen him up and change him and he can come sleep in my bed.'

Tasha said, 'You don't think he really saw something, do you?'

'Of course not. What happened to your daddy, that was all the way down in Florida, and whoever killed him, they're not going to come looking for you. Besides, he said it was nobody. And how can anybody see nobody?'

'I guess,' said Tasha. She gave Lily a kiss on the cheek and went back to her bedroom. But when Lily woke up at seven twenty the following morning, she found Sammy sprawled on one side of her, with his mouth open; and Tasha on the other side, buried deep in the comforter, so that only a few wisps of brunette hair peeped out.

After breakfast they drove down to the Mall of America in Bloomington, so that Lily could buy them both the new coats and sweaters that she had promised them in October, before they were kidnapped. She let Sammy ride on the indoor roller-coaster at Camp Snoopy, and she took Tasha into Bloomingdale's and bought her a new pink corduroy skirt and some jingly silver bracelets.

Afterward they had lunch at Ruby Tuesday's. Tasha said

that she had decided to become a vegetarian, so she asked for the salad plate. Lily didn't argue. Sammy wanted the Ultimate Colossal Burger, but Lily vetoed that. 'You're going to eat a whole pound of beef, with two kinds of cheese? I don't think so.' In the end he chose the hickory chicken breast and Lily ordered crab cakes.

They were still eating when Lily glanced across the restaurant and saw George Iron Walker standing by the door, wearing a short black leather coat, and a black wide-brimmed hat with a braided leather band around it. He was staring at her, stone-faced, his hands forced deep into his pockets. Several people jostled past him, including two of the waitresses, but he didn't move out of the way. He simply stood there, staring.

Lily slowly lowered the forkful of crab cake that she was just about to put in her mouth.

Tasha frowned at her and said, 'Mommy? What is it?'

Lily didn't know if she ought to get up and talk to George Iron Walker, or whether she ought to ignore him.

'Mommy? Are you OK? I was telling you about the time we went to Key West.'

'What?'

'You haven't been listening, have you?'

'Yes, sweetheart, of course I've been listening. You went on a boat and saw dolphins.'

She put down her fork. She stared back at George Iron Walker, challenging him to come over and talk to her. *If you have something to say to me, then say it.* George Iron Walker stayed where he was for another ten seconds or so, and then turned around and walked out of the restaurant. Lily thought she glimpsed Hazawin, too, in her ankle-length sheepskin coat with the beads and the embroidery, but the mall was very crowded and she couldn't be sure.

'Are you all right, Mommy?' asked Sammy. 'Don't you like your crab cakes?'

'No, sweetheart, they're terrific. I suddenly remembered

something I forgot to do, that's all. Come on, eat up. That chicken looks great.'

After lunch they went to Sears so that Lily could buy some new table napkins, and then – as it grew dark, and the temperature began to plummet – they drove home. Sammy fell asleep in the back seat, so that when they arrived outside the house, Lily had to reach around and shake him.

'Come on, Rip van Winkle! Time to wake up!'

As they climbed out of the Rainier, Tasha said, 'What's that *smell*?'

Lily sniffed, and sniffed again, and then looked up. Acrid brown smoke was pouring from the chimney, and swirling around the side of the house. It smelled like burning hair. *Oh God*, she thought. *I hope a spark hasn't jumped out of the fire and set the couch alight.*

'Just wait up,' she told Tasha and Sammy. 'I have to check this out first.'

She pushed her way through the snow-covered privet hedge in front of the living-room window and peered inside. Two of the table lamps were lit, because she kept them connected to a timer, and she could see that the room was hazy with smoke. But she couldn't see any flames, and the fireguard was still in place. Maybe a crow had flown down the chimney and blocked up the flue. It had happened before, only a few days after they had first moved in, and it had cost them nearly $400 to have it cleared.

She unlocked the front door, very cautiously. If there was a fire burning in the living room, she didn't want to feed it with a sudden draft. She slipped through the narrowest gap she could manage and immediately closed the door behind her.

The smell in the hallway was appalling, and she retched. It was much worse than burning hair: it was charred meat. Lily coughed, and coughed, and pulled out her handker-chief to cover her nose and mouth. With her eyes watering, she punched out the alarm code on the panel beside the door, and then she crossed the hallway and hurried into the living room.

She looked around. None of the furniture was smoldering, nor was the hearthrug nor any of the drapes. The smoke was rolling into the room from the fireplace, which appeared to be crowded with many more logs than she had stacked on to it herself. She always left the fire very low whenever she went out – just enough to keep the embers glowing.

She lifted the fireguard away. The logs were burned only on the underside, as if they had been laid on to the fire not much more than a half-hour ago. But there was something on top of them – something black and wedge-shaped, with tiny pinprick sparks glowing all over it. And something was hanging down from the chimney in long festoons – something gray and beige and glistening, like the loops of a fire hose.

Frowning, Lily picked up the poker and prodded the black object two or three times, trying to turn it over to see what it was. One of the logs abruptly dropped, and the object toppled with it. To Lily's horror, she saw a single amber eye staring up at her.

She heard the front door open, and Tasha called out, 'Mom! Mommy! What's happening? We're *freezing* out here!'

Twelve

Special Agent Kellogg said, 'How are the kids taking it?'
Lily shrugged. 'Badly. How do you think? They grew up with Sergeant. They adored him.'

'So what did you tell them?'

'What could I tell them? I could hardly pretend that it was an accident.'

A woman detective came into the kitchen, snapping off her latex gloves. She was mid-thirties, with wiry black hair and bulbous brown eyes. She wore a dark brown duffel-coat and a thickly knitted mustard-colored sweater which made her look as if she didn't have a neck.

'I never saw anything so disgusting,' she said.

'Have the CSU finished up yet?' asked Special Agent Kellogg.

'Well . . .' said the detective, dubiously, looking at Lily.

Special Agent Kellogg said, 'Maybe you should check on the kids.'

'I'm OK. Really.' Lily tried to smile, although she was very far from OK. She felt as if her mind had been smashed like a trodden-on mirror, and she couldn't stop shivering. But she didn't want to go upstairs to see Tasha and Sammy – not just yet, because their distress was more than she could bear. Tasha was almost hysterical, while Sammy was silent and seemed to have forgotten how to blink. Agnes was with them now, trying to comfort them.

The detective said, 'OK . . . we've managed to extricate the dog's insides from out of the flue, poor creature. We found half of its hindquarters up on the roof, protruding from the chimney stack. We're still missing one leg and part of its ribcage.'

Lily pressed her hand against her mouth. She prayed that Sergeant hadn't suffered too much.

'Any idea how the perpetrator did it?' asked Special Agent Kellogg.

'Not yet. It doesn't look like the dog was *pushed* up the chimney, because the perpetrator would have needed some kind of device like a sweep's brush, and there's no trace of soot on the rug in front of the fire.'

'So maybe it was *pulled* up the chimney?'

'With a rope? That's a more practical explanation, but the trouble with *that* scenario is that there are three inches of snow on the roof and no trace of anybody having climbed up there. No ladder-marks, no footprints.'

'So where does that leave us?'

'I honestly can't tell you. Right now, we don't have a suspect, we don't have a logical motive, and we don't have any meaningful forensic evidence whatsoever. One of our guys even suggested that the perpetrator might have been a giant ape, like in *The Murders in the Rue Morgue*. You know, that Edgar Allan Poe story, where the girl's body gets shoved up the chimney.'

'Whoever it was, how the hell did they get in here? There's no sign of forced entry and every door and window is locked and alarmed.'

'Every alarm has a code, Agent Kellogg. Maybe the perpetrator was somebody connected with the security company, or somebody who visited the house recently – a cleaner, or a decorator. Can you think of anybody like that, Mrs Blake?'

Lily whispered, 'No.'

'Well, maybe you could put your mind to it. Meanwhile – is there anyplace else that you can stay tonight? We'll arrange a motel for you and your children if you need it.'

Lily said, 'You don't have to worry about that. We can go to my sister's in Wayzata.'

'OK then. We'll make sure that an officer keeps a watch on you. Until we know why this freak wanted to kill your dog and how he managed to do it, I'm going to make sure that you get round-the-clock protection.'

I wish you could *protect us*, thought Lily. *But there's only one way to stop the Wendigo coming after us, and that's to give George Iron Walker what he wants.*

By the time they reached Agnes and Ned's house, just after ten thirty p.m., Tasha and Sammy were much calmer. Sammy's eyelids kept drooping, and so Lily carried him upstairs to the playroom and tucked him into one of the bunk-beds. When she came back down again, Tasha was sitting by the fire with a mug of warm milk, with Red the cocker spaniel lying close beside her.

'Mommy,' said Tasha, 'everything's going to be all right, isn't it? I mean, nothing bad is going to happen to us, is it?'

'No, sweetheart. I promise.'

She had already called Bennie three times since they had arrived here, and John Shooks twice. Neither of them had picked up. As she went into the kitchen to talk to Agnes, however, her cell warbled and it was Shooks, answering her call.

'Mrs Blake?'

Lily went back to the hallway, where Agnes wouldn't be able to overhear her. 'Mr Shooks, do you know what's happened tonight?'

'I know that George Iron Walker isn't at all happy with you, Mrs Blake.'

'He sent that thing to kill my dog.'

'Yes, Mrs Blake. You can't say that I didn't warn you.'

'Well, tell George Iron Walker from me that I will never forgive him, ever, but he can have his piece of land. I have to get hold of the land title, but as soon as I do, I'll call you, and we can arrange to meet.'

John Shooks cleared his throat with a sharp rattle. 'I think you're taking the most sensible course of action, Mrs Blake. I wouldn't like to see you or your family caused any further distress.'

'Don't threaten me, Mr Shooks.'

'Oh, I'm not. If anything, I'm on your side. I'm only an eighth Native American, remember. The rest of me is pure paleface.'

Lily ended the call and tried Bennie again.

A few minutes before midnight, when Lily had almost given up trying, Bennie at last picked up. 'Lil . . . hi! I'm sorry, I got all of your messages, but I've been running here, there and every darn where. Is anything wrong?'

'I can't tell you the full story, Bennie – not yet, anyhow. But this is urgent. I need the title to that piece of land at Mystery Lake, and I need it first thing tomorrow morning.'

'Uh-*huh*,' said Bennie.

'I can come around to the office and pick it up, if you like.'

Bennie didn't reply. Behind him, Lily could hear people laughing and chattering, and piano music. It sounded as if he were in a bar someplace.

'Bennie? Did you hear what I said?'

'Sure, Lil, I heard you. But I didn't think you needed it any more.'

'I know. But the situation's changed. The tracker wants the land and he's not going to give me any peace until he gets it.'

'I'm sorry, Lil. I don't think it's going to be possible.'

'But . . . hold on a minute. You said that it was all arranged. You said that Philip Kraussman was happy to donate it.'

'It wasn't as simple as that.'

'What do you mean? I thought he was going to use it to show people what a great local hero he is.'

'That was the idea, Lil. But to be honest with you there were complications.'

A woman's voice screamed out, 'Bennie! Bennie! Come over here and show Lizzie your Deputy Dawg impression!'

'What complications, Bennie?' Lily asked him, tersely.

'Well, the truth is, Lil . . . when you told me that you'd hired yourself a Native American tracker . . .'

'What are you trying to say to me? You didn't *believe* me?'

'Of course I believed you. But I didn't believe that this tracker of yours could actually find Jeff for you.'

'But he did, Bennie. And now he wants what I promised him. He wants that piece of land, and if I don't give it to him . . . I don't know what he's going to do. He's killed my dog, Bennie! He's killed Sergeant! He's torn him to pieces and burned him on the fire!'

'What? He's done *what*? You need to call the cops, Lil. You need to have him arrested!'

'I have called them, but they'll never be able to find him. Listen to me, Bennie. I need that land title, as soon as you can get it for me. I'm afraid he's going to come after Tasha and Sammy next.'

'Lil, all I can advise you to do is call the cops. They'll find the son-of-a-bitch. Like, how many Native American trackers can there be in the Twin Cities area?'

'I have to have that land title, Bennie. That's the only way I can ever be sure.'

'Bennie!' screamed the woman. 'Bennie! Come over here, will you?'

Bennie said, 'I'm sorry, Lil, you know how much you mean to me. I'm so fond of you, I really am. I guess I just wanted to impress you. How else can a guy like me hope to get close to a woman like you? You're beautiful, Lil. I'd do anything.'

Lily turned around. Agnes was standing in the kitchen doorway, with a questioning look on her face. She came and stood a little way away, waiting for Lily to finish on the phone.

Lily said, 'There *is* no land title, is there, Bennie?'

'Not exactly.'

'Did you even raise the subject with Philip Kraussman? Did you even *ask* him?'

'Not exactly, no. You know what Philip Kraussman's like. He wouldn't donate a bottle of sour milk to a starving baby.'

Lily was so angry that she couldn't speak. She had to breathe deeply to keep herself under control.

'Lil?' asked Bennie. 'Lil, are you still there, Lil?'

'Let me tell you something, Bennie: if anything happens to Tasha and Sammy, or to me, then you'll know that it's your fault.'

'Lil, I can get on to Philip Kraussman first thing tomorrow morning! I can try to swing it!'

'Oh, you think? Jesus, Bennie – how could I have been so gullible?'

'Lil, listen to me – please—'

'It's too late, Bennie. I'm too upset.'

Lily switched him off.

Agnes came up to her and took hold of both of her hands. 'What's happened, Lily?'

'I can't tell you. But I know who killed Sergeant, and I know why he killed him.'

'You know who it was? My God, you need to tell the police!'

'I can't tell them, either. They just won't believe me.'

'Lily, this is crazy!'

'I know it is. But I've gotten myself involved in something I shouldn't have even thought about.'

'Lily, please – *tell* me!'

'I will, Agnes, I promise. But I have to get Tasha and Sammy away from here, tomorrow morning, as early as possible.'

'What? Where are you going to go?'

'Anyplace at all. Someplace where this person can't find us. Europe.'

'*Europe?* What are you *thinking* about?'

'Agnes, this person doesn't let anybody get away from him, ever. Wherever they go, he can find them. Please don't ask me any more.'

'Lily, this is madness! You're shocked, you're upset, that's all!'

'Yes, I am. But I know that we have to get as far away from here as we possibly can. Can I use your computer? I need to book a flight.'

The alarm buzzed at seven a.m. Lily opened her eyes. At first she couldn't remember where she was – but then, next to the alarm clock, she saw the familiar silver-framed photograph of herself and Agnes when they were at school.

She switched on the bedside lamp. In the photograph, Agnes was dressed as Father Louis Hennepin, the Franciscan adventurer who had been the first European to set foot in Minneapolis. Lily wore a blanket and a beaded headband, to play the part of Father Hennepin's Dakota guide.

Both girls were laughing, although she couldn't remember what they were laughing at. In the background stood the huge oak tree that they used to climb up, so that they could sit astride one of the branches and read *Archie* comics.

She looked more closely. She had never noticed before that there was a figure standing beside the oak tree, partly sunlit and partly in shadow. It looked like a tall, thin man, yet its face was unusually long, almost like a dog or a deer, and its arms were bent.

You're allowing your imagination to play tricks on you again, she thought, and when she looked again she saw that the figure was nothing more than another tree, and a section of fence, and a bend in the sunlit path.

She climbed out of bed and took down the floral-print bathrobe that was hanging on the back of the bedroom door. Downstairs, Tasha and Sammy were already sitting around the kitchen table, eating Cheerios, while little William was making a happy mess with a bowl of apricot purée. Agnes said, 'Hi, Lily. Sleep well?'

'Yes – surprisingly. Like a log. How about you, kids?'

'I had a dream about Sergeant,' said Sammy. 'But it was a nice dream. He was running and fetching sticks.'

'Coffee?' asked Agnes. 'How about some eggs?'

'No eggs, thanks. Maybe some toast.'

'Ned had to go into the office, but he'll be back before nine. That's unless you've changed your mind.'

'Changed your mind about what, Mommy?' asked Tasha.

Lily sat down, and Agnes gave her a large cup of black coffee. 'I was thinking that we ought to take a vacation,' she said. 'We deserve one, after all the horrible things that have happened.'

'But I want to go back to school,' said Tasha. 'I want to see all my friends again.'

'*I* don't want to go back to school,' Sammy put in. 'I don't want to go back to school *ever*.'

Lily held Tasha's hand. 'You will go back to school, Tasha, I promise. But we need to go away for a while. What happened to Daddy – what happened to Sergeant – I can't explain it yet, but they're kind of connected. Somebody wants to hurt us and we have to make sure that they don't know where we are.'

'Somebody wants to hurt us? Who?'

'It's really better that you don't know.'

'Why would *anybody* want to hurt us?' asked Sammy. '*We* haven't done anything.'

'Well, you remember the poem about the Pied Piper? How he got rid of all the rats, but once they were gone, the people in Hamelin wouldn't pay him?'

'I don't understand,' said Tasha.

'This is the same, in a way. I said that I would pay somebody for something that they did for me, but I can't. So that's why he wants to hurt us.'

'Can't you *borrow* the money?'

'It's not money he wants,' said Lily. 'Please – don't ask

me any more, sweetheart, not at the moment. I'm going to try to find a way to pay him, but I need some time.'

American Airlines flight 1437 was scheduled to leave Minneapolis at twelve thirty-five that afternoon, heading for Paris, France, with a stopover in Chicago.

'What are we going to do about clothes?' asked Tasha. 'We only have this one overnight bag.'

'I'll buy you more clothes when we get to Paris. New jeans, new sweaters – everything.'

'Really?' Tasha was beginning to look more cheerful now.

'Where's Paris?' Sammy wanted to know.

Tasha said, 'It's the capital of France, stupid.'

'Where's France?'

'It's a country where they speak French all the time and eat very long bread and snails.'

'Urgh! Snails are even worse than pineapple! I don't want to go *there*!'

Ned arrived. He bustled into the house in his padded windbreaker, chafing his hands together. 'Think we're in for another snowstorm. Sooner we get you to MNP, the better. We can swing by your place and collect your passports on the way.'

They left the house. While Agnes and Ned helped the children into their Explorer, Lily crossed over the road and went up to the two police officers sitting in a radio car. They were drinking coffee and they had the engine running to keep themselves warm. The driver put down his window and said, 'Everything OK, ma'am? You going out for a while?'

'We're going to do some shopping at Calhoun Square, if you want to take some time out. We'll be back around four o'clock this afternoon.'

'You want us to come with you?'

'I don't think that's going to be necessary, thanks. We'll be walking around the mall the whole time.'

'All the same, I'd better check.'

The officer called headquarters, and then said, 'OK. That's

fine. But call us immediately if there's any sign of trouble, or you notice anybody acting suspicious. See you back here at four.'

Lily came back and climbed into the back seat of Agnes and Ned's Explorer. 'I hope the police don't give you a hard time, when you come back without us.'

'I doubt it, if we tell them that you've flown to France. It'll save them from sitting out in the cold all night, freezing their butts off.'

They drove to Lily's house first. Lily peeled the bright-yellow crime-scene tape away from the front door and opened it up. Quickly, she crossed into the living room and took their passports out of her bureau. The house was chilly and dark, and there was still a lingering stench of burned dog hair. She wondered if they would ever be able to come back to live here again.

As they drove south on I-35W toward the airport, the sun disappeared behind a dark bank of orange-tinted snow cloud, and the day began to grow gloomier and gloomier.

'You'll call us when you get to Chicago?' asked Agnes.

'Of course. *And* when we get to Paris.'

'I can't believe we're really going to France,' said Tasha. 'It's like a dream.'

'I'm still not going to eat snails,' said Sammy, emphatically.

Little William, sitting in his car seat between Sammy and Tasha, said, 'Nails! Nails!'

As they neared the intersection with I-62, a fierce snow shower blew across the highway, and Ned had to switch on his windshield wipers. 'What did I tell you? I sure hope your flight isn't delayed.'

The snow began to fall even more thickly, and Lily could hear the wind gusting underneath the Explorer with a hollow sound like a huge slide-whistle.

'*Whoooo!*' said little William, with his eyes wide.

Lily laughed. But at that moment, Ned shouted, '*Jesus!*' and jammed on the Explorer's brakes. As the SUV slewed to one side, Lily could see that there was a figure standing in the middle of the highway, only twenty yards in front of them. It looked like a man, but it was taller than a man, and it juddered and jumped like an image from an old black-and-white movie. Lily glimpsed a stretched-open mouth, and sightless black eyes, and arms that looked jointed in all the wrong ways, but then it turned away and disappeared altogether.

The Explorer's tires slithered on the road surface as Ned tried to bring it under control. Tasha was screaming and Agnes was twisting around in her seat, trying to make sure that little William was firmly buckled up. They spun round almost 360 degrees before Ned managed to bring the Explorer to a stop. They were overtaken by a huge truck, its headlights ablaze and its klaxon blaring like a passing train.

'Did you see that?' said Ned. 'Did you see that guy? Right in the middle of the goddamn highway like he had a goddamn death-wish or something.'

Lily tugged at the shoulder of his windbreaker. 'Ned, let's get out of here, right now.'

Ned looked around, increasingly frantic. 'Did I hit him? I didn't feel anything, did you? I don't think I hit him. Where the hell is he? He was standing right in the middle of the goddamn highway.'

'Ned – let's go! I don't think there was anybody there! It was like a mirage!'

'But what if I hit him? I can't just leave him lying in the road!'

Another car came to a halt behind them, flashing its lights and sounding its horn. Then another, and another, and another.

'Please, Ned, let's get moving,' Lily urged him. 'It's really dangerous, stopping on the highway like this. There was nobody there, I promise you. It was just your headlights, shining on the snow.'

Ned switched on his emergency flashers. 'I'll pull over. I need to get out and take a look.'

'Honey,' said Agnes, 'I think that Lily's right, and we should go. I didn't feel you hit anything.'

'I saw the guy, hon. Don't tell me you didn't.'

'*Ned!*' Lily shouted at him. '*Will you please just hit the gas and get us the fuck out of here!*'

Ned turned around, blinking in surprise. 'Come on, Lily. We got young kids with us here. No need to use language like that.'

Lily was about to shout at him again when they were deafened by a sharp, explosive blast, like escaping steam. The Explorer began to vibrate, as if they were driving at high speed over a plank road, and then it started to shake wildly from side to side, until it was thumping and banging on its suspension. Agnes and Tasha and Sammy all shrieked in terror. Ned let out a deep, frightened, 'Whoa!'

'*Make it stop!*' Tasha cried out. '*Make it stop!*'

'What's happening?' said Agnes. 'Ned – what's happening?'

Ned was grappling with the gearshift. 'I don't know! I don't know! I can't make it—!'

But the hissing was so intense now that his words were swallowed, and it kept on growing louder and louder until Lily found it almost impossible to think.

'*Ned!*' she shouted, but he couldn't hear her. '*Ned!*'

Through the undersides of the doors, lights began to stream in – narrow, criss-crossing lights, which shifted and altered, forming themselves into all kinds of distorted shapes. Even though she was being shaken so violently from side to side, Lily could see strange attenuated faces sliding diagonally across the Explorer's floor, and up the back of the seats in front of her – faces, and slowly opening limbs, and what could have been branches, or antlers. She tried to lean forward and shout at Ned again, but she was slammed back so hard that her neck was whiplashed.

'*Ned! The doors! Unlock the doors!*'

Still Ned didn't hear her. She had to grip the grab-handle with both hands to stop herself from being jolted against

155

the door on one side and William's baby seat on the other. All she could think was: *Please don't hurt my children. Please don't hurt my family.*

'*Stop!*' Lily screamed out. '*Wendigo! Stop!*'

But if the apparition could hear her, or understand her, it showed no signs of it.

'*Stop! I'll stay here! I'll do whatever George wants me to do!*'

A rhomboid-shaped light shuddered across the glove-box, and then rose up in front of Agnes like a hologram, reassembling itself into a canine head. Two long arms unfolded themselves on either side of it, and then the head began to rise higher and higher, leaning over Agnes at an angle. At the same time it changed itself into a human face, which stared at Agnes with a terrible expressionless detachment.

'*Stop! I'll get the land for him! I promise!*'

Agnes shrank down in her seat, raising her hand to protect herself. But the scissor-like arms caught her around the neck, and yanked her straight up again. She turned toward Ned with her eyes bulging.

Ned shouted something that Lily couldn't hear. He pulled at one of the arms and tried to twist Agnes free. But then the figure somersaulted backward, straight through the Explorer's windshield, which exploded into thousands of sparkling fragments. Agnes was wrenched out of her seat and into the snowstorm. She literally flew away into the air, as if she had been shot from a cannon. At least half of her did. Her seatbelt kept her hips and her legs firmly in place, and only her head and her arms and her torso disappeared, with long strings of bloody intestines unraveling behind her.

Immediately the Explorer stopped bucking up and down, and the hissing died away. The only sounds were William sobbing and the impatient beeping of car horns. Ned turned around to Lily and his face was gray with shock.

'Ned, get us out of here!' Lily begged him.

'Agnes . . .' said Ned. 'Oh my God. *Agnes!*'

'Ned, for Christ's sake, put your foot down and *go!*'

But Ned started to unfasten his seatbelt. 'She's out there, Lily! I can't just leave her!'

'She's dead, Ned! You have to go!'

Ned opened his door, but as he did so, something landed on the Explorer's hood, with a resonant thump.

Tasha screamed.

Lily saw a creature on the hood that could have been a giant spider if it hadn't been made of nothing but light and shadow and optical illusions. It had a huge head, with an oversized human face, but the head peeled open to reveal a smaller face, more like a slippery, hairless dog. Ned tried to scramble out of his seat, but two arms jabbed in through the shattered windshield and seized him by the shoulders. He was dragged out of the Explorer with such force that one of his boots caught in the steering-wheel. There was a crackling noise like a turkey-leg being twisted and his foot was pulled off at the ankle joint.

With his arms and legs tumbling across the hood, Ned was pulled up into the air. Lily heard him screaming, but then there was another explosive hiss, and he vanished into the whirling snow, in the same way that Agnes had vanished. It happened so fast that Lily was left with her hand still raised to shake Ned's shoulder, and her mouth still open.

She turned to the children. Tasha and Sammy were staring at her in disbelief, both of them stunned into silence. William was still crying, his cheeks bright red and his little face bewildered.

'We have to get out of here,' said Lily.

'What was that?' Tasha asked her, and her voice was quaking with absolute dread. 'Mommy – what *was* that?'

Lily unfastened her seatbelt, reached over to the driver's seat and pressed the central-locking switch. 'Come on, we're going! And when you get outside, *run!*'

Tasha and Sammy opened the Explorer's door and almost fell out on to the highway. A long line of traffic had been

building up behind them, and there was an irritable chorus
of horns, but so far nobody had climbed out of their vehicle
to find out what was wrong. Lily was finding it almost
impossible to extricate William from his car seat. He was
wearing a thick corduroy romper suit and his straps were
held in place by four fiddly buckles.

She turned around to see where Tasha and Sammy were.
They had run a short distance away, but now they had stopped
and were waiting for her. She opened her door and called
out, '*Run!* But watch out for the traffic!' William's seatbelt
buckles had jammed solid and she was jiggling them in frus-
tration. 'Come on, you stupid damn car seat!' William started
to cry even louder, a high distressed piping that made Lily
feel even more panicky.

She was still struggling when there was a thunderous
bang on the Explorer's roof, and the whole vehicle shook.

'*No!*' she shouted. '*I'll give him the land! I swear it!*'

But the roof began to buckle, and slowly come downward. With a whole cacophony of bangs and groans and
warping noises, the entire vehicle started to crumple. Lily
was forced to slide off her seat and kneel on the floor. She
took hold of the sides of William's car seat and tried to
shake it free from its mountings, but it wouldn't budge.
With another groan, the Explorer's roof came down as far
as the headrests, and the sides started to fold in too.

Lily was forced to crouch down in the foot-well, but still
she couldn't get William free. The roof pressed down on
the top of his car seat and started to tilt it forward. William
was crying so hysterically that he could hardly breathe.

It was then that Lily realized that she couldn't save him,
and that the frame of the open door had been pressed down
so far that she only had a few seconds to crawl out of the
last remaining space.

She heard somebody shout, 'Come on, lady; you have to
get yourself out of there!'

She managed to twist herself around, and two buckskin-gloved hands reached into the Explorer and firmly grasped her wrists.

'There's a baby in here!' she screamed. 'There's a baby in here! You have to save him!'

But there was nothing she could do. She was dragged out into the snow, and helped up on to her feet, just as the Explorer was crushed up into a tangled sculpture of twisted doors and distorted seats. The noise of protesting metal was deafening, like a car crash in slow motion.

Six or seven men had left their cars to see what was happening, and more were approaching through the snow. The man who had rescued Lily was a tall, rangy truck-driver in a thick plaid jacket. 'Anybody called nine-one-one?' he called out. 'Listen – there's a kid inside. Go get a couple of jacks . . . maybe we can lift the roof up.'

'Damndest thing I ever saw in my life,' said another man. 'How the hell does a vehicle get itself all scrunched up like that?'

Lily begged, 'Please, see if you can get William out of there. I can't hear him crying. Can anybody hear him crying?'

She leaned against the crumpled-up side of the Explorer and shouted, 'William! *William!*' But she couldn't hear anything except the *swish-swish-swish* of passing traffic and the sporadic blaring of horns. She stood up straight again and looked around, and she felt as if she were going mad with grief. There was no sign of the Wendigo anywhere, no dimly shifting light, no shapes, no faces. She didn't even have a mirage to scream at.

Tasha and Sammy came up to her, accompanied by a gray-haired couple in matching green padded coats. Both children looked stricken.

'Mommy?' said Tasha. 'Is William dead, too?'

'I don't know. I don't know. These men are going to try to get him out.'

'Anything we can do?' asked the gray-haired man.

'Did you *crash* or something?' asked the gray-haired woman, looking at the crushed Explorer in disbelief.

The man said, 'Your kids came running up to us and said that you was attacked by some kind of animal. Never saw no animal that could do nothing like *that*. Not even your full-grown moose.'

'I don't know,' said Lily. She couldn't think what else to say. She could hear sirens warbling and honking in the near-distance. 'Please . . . I think I have to sit down.'

She was still sitting in the back of the gray-haired couple's Buick when two Highway Patrol officers came up to her, a man and a woman.

The woman climbed into the car beside her. She had orange-tinted glasses and she smelled of breath-mints. 'How are you feeling?' she asked. 'We'll have the paramedics take you and your children to the hospital in a couple of minutes.'

'We're fine. The three of us – we didn't get hurt. It was only my sister and my brother-in-law, and my little nephew.'

'Well, that's what I need to ask you about. You said your nephew was in the vehicle, but all we could find was a child's car seat.'

'What? What do you mean?'

'There was a child's car seat in the vehicle but there was no child in it.'

'I don't understand. I was trying to get him out, but I couldn't. The buckles were stuck fast.'

'Are you absolutely sure about that?'

'Of course I'm sure! How can he not be there?'

'Well, ma'am, we've searched the whole area and there's no trace of him anywhere.'

'Oh, God,' said Lily. 'What about the others? What about my sister and my brother-in-law?'

The male Highway Patrol officer said, 'We've found some remains, ma'am. Looks like they both went clear through the windshield when you crashed.' He paused, and then he said, 'What we can't work out, though, is what the heck you guys hit.'

Thirteen

They returned home late in the afternoon, as it was growing dark. Tasha ran straight up to her bedroom and closed the door, but Sammy tagged around after Lily wherever she went – from the kitchen to the living room and back again – sucking his thumb like he used to when he was three years old, and saying nothing.

Lily was relieved to find that the crime-scene investigators had swept all of the ashes out of the living-room grate. She laid a new fire with crumpled-up copies of the *Star Tribune* and a little tepee of dry pine kindling, and soon had it crackling into life.

'Are you hungry?' she asked Sammy. He shook his head, but she went into the kitchen anyway and opened up a can of tomato soup.

She was pretty sure that there was no hope of them flying to France now. The Wendigo wouldn't let them go. George Iron Walker wouldn't let them go. He wanted his land and he was obviously going to pursue her until she gave it to him.

She called John Shooks' number. He didn't answer, but she left him a message: 'Tell George Iron Walker to call it off. I'll get his land for him, one way or another, I promise. Meet me at my house tomorrow, around three.'

She was shaking, but she managed to restrain herself from telling Shooks how she really felt. She was so grief-stricken for Agnes and Ned and little William that she felt as if somebody had their hands around her throat and was trying to choke her. She was terrified, too, that the Wendigo might come after them here. But more than that she felt deeply burning fury, like nothing she had ever experienced before. She was determined to show George Iron Walker that she was not going to allow him to massacre her family and escape without being punished for it.

She called Ned's parents, John and Matilda. Two women from the children's welfare services had picked up Petra and Jamie from school and driven them to Shingle Creek, so that their grandpa and their grandma could take care of them. Matilda said, 'Poor kids . . . they've been sobbing their hearts out ever since they got here.' All that Petra and Jamie had been told so far was that their parents had died in a highway accident, and that their little brother was missing – although they had to be prepared for the probability that he was dead too.

As Lily was stirring the soup, a picture of the crushed Explorer was flashed up on the local TV news, but Sammy was sitting with his head resting listlessly on the table, and she was able to reach the remote and switch channels before he saw it.

She had taken the phone off the hook, too, because she guessed that reporters would be calling, as well as friends and well-wishers. This evening they needed nothing but warmth, togetherness and peace.

Tasha appeared in the kitchen doorway. Her cheeks were still blotchy with tears.

'Tasha?'

When she spoke, Tasha's voice was trembly but accusing. 'You know what it was, don't you, Mommy? That thing that killed Aunt Agnes and Uncle Ned.'

Sammy took his thumb out of his mouth. 'I saw its face. It had *two* faces. It was like a dog. Then it was like a horrible man.'

Lily switched off the soup. 'I *do* know what it was, yes. It was trying to stop us from reaching the airport.'

'Is it a ghost?' asked Sammy.

'In a way, yes. A kind of a ghost. When your daddy took you away, we couldn't find you anywhere, so I asked this ghost to go looking for you.'

'You did *what?*'

As simply as she could, she told them about John Shooks and George Iron Walker and Hazawin, and how she had asked them to summon up the Wendigo.

'I don't believe you,' said Tasha. 'There's no such thing as a Wendigo. How can there be?'

'Yes, there is, Tasha. You saw it for yourself. You saw what it can do. I'm so sorry for what's happened, you don't have any idea. I wish to the bottom of my heart that I'd never heard about it. Even if I had never been able to find you again, at least your father would still be alive, and so would Aunt Agnes and Uncle Ned and little William.'

'But if it's true – why haven't you told the police?'

'I could. But do you think that they'd believe me? George Iron Walker would say that I was making it all up, and he'd *still* send the Wendigo after us. There's only one way out of this, sweetheart, and that's for me to give him his piece of land.'

Tasha sat down next to Sammy. 'It's like having a nightmare,' she said. 'I keep thinking that I'm going to wake up and none of it ever happened.'

Sammy declared, 'I'm never going to go to sleep, ever again.'

As it was, they all slept until well past eight the next morning. During the night it had been snowing again, and the neighborhood was eerily muffled.

'I'm going to see Philip Kraussman this morning,' said Lily, as she poured out their Lucky Charms. 'Bennie might have been too scared to ask him for that land, but I'm not.'

'You're not going to leave us here alone?' asked Tasha.

'I'm not going to leave you alone for a single *second*, sweetheart – not until this is all over.'

Tasha and Sammy were still eating their cereal when the doorbell chimed. Standing on the doorstep stamping their feet were Special Agents Rylance and Kellogg, and Dr Flaurus, too.

'Oh my God,' she said. 'Have you found William?'

'Not yet, I'm afraid,' said Special Agent Rylance. 'But the police have more than a hundred officers and deputies out looking for him, as well as who knows how many volunteers. Is it OK if we come in? We asked Dr Flaurus to come along, in case we need to talk to the kids.'

'OK. Can I offer you some coffee?'

'No – no, thanks. We really need to discuss one or two things with you. We have to get some kind of perspective on this.'

Lily took them into the living room. 'I hope you're not going to take long. Tasha and Sammy are very upset.'

'Well, that's understandable,' said Special Agent Rylance. 'But the thing of it is, there have now been four or possibly five deaths associated with you and your children, not to mention the killing of your dog. All of these deaths have been brutal in the extreme, involving violent dismemberment and the disappearance of body parts. Not only that: all of them have occurred in circumstances that are not only inexplicable but – at first sight – downright impossible.'

Special Agent Kellogg tugged off his black knitted hat. 'We've had a preliminary report from the State Highway Patrol technicians, and they're of the opinion that the vehicle you were traveling in yesterday was not involved in any kind of moving collision – either with another vehicle, or an animal, or any roadside structure or traffic sign. They said that the damage could only have been caused by something similar to an automobile crusher of the type used in commercial scrapyards.

'Except that your brother-in-law's vehicle was right

slapbang in the middle of I-35W, and the nearest commercial scrapyards are in Frogtown, in St Paul.'

'I don't know what happened,' said Lily. 'The vehicle just collapsed.'

'But then there's also the question of the human remains,' said Special Agent Rylance. Lily thought that he was looking very old today, and very tired, with flat, papery wrinkles under his eyes. 'I don't want to disturb you by going into too much detail, but your sister and your brother-in-law were taken apart in much the same way as your late husband and the man who was killed at the FLAME office. What little we found of them was strewn along the highway and across nearby fields. We found your sister's left hand caught on a razor-wire fence more than two miles away.'

Lily slowly sat down on the couch. She felt as if she were someone else altogether. 'They went through the windshield,' she said, so quietly that Special Agent Rylance had to lean forward and say, 'Excuse me?'

'They went through the windshield. That's all I saw.'

'But you'd agree that the way they died bears remarkable similarities to the way your former husband died? And this time we can't even blame seagulls or pelicans for carrying their remains away. Something flew off with them, and I mean *flew* because we found no footprints in the snow around your brother-in-law's vehicle and no footprints or snowmobile tracks across the fields.

'Whatever took 'em, Mrs Blake, it must have carried them through the air.'

'I can't think what it could have been. A crow, of some kind? I just don't know.'

'A crow,' repeated Special Agent Rylance, clearly unconvinced.

Special Agent Kellogg sat down beside her. 'You told the officers on protection duty that you were going shopping to Calhoun Square. Can you explain what you were doing heading southward on I-35W, in the opposite direction?'

'We changed our minds. We decided to go to the Mall of America instead.'

'OK . . . then there's one only more thing we want to ask you about. You know that old barn you took us to, at Sibley's End?'

Lily looked at him warily.

'That barn fell down about a week ago. Well – "fell down" isn't quite accurate. At first the city council thought it was simply the weight of snow on the roof. But a local conservationist who examined the site said that the building had been literally ripped apart – forcibly disassembled, joint by joint. Said he'd never seen anything like it. There was an article about it in the paper.'

'I don't know what you want me to say.'

Special Agent Rylance said, 'All I want to know is: can you think of any way in which these events might be connected? I strongly believe that there *is* a connection. I believe that there's an explanation, too. But right now I'm darned if I know what it could possibly be.'

'I wish I could help you.'

'Yes, Mrs Blake. I wish you could, too.'

Dr Flaurus went into the kitchen and spent a few minutes with Tasha and Sammy, but when she came out again she shook her head. 'I don't want to push them any further. They've seen more horrible things than most people see in a lifetime. Maybe I can come back in a few days' time.'

'Sure,' said Lily.

The agents left. They said nothing more, but Lily had the uncomfortable feeling that they suspected her of knowing much more than she had been prepared to tell them – which, of course, was true.

She told Tasha and Sammy to put on their sweaters and their coats, and they left the house. The sun had come out, and the snow was so bright that Lily had to put on her sunglasses. She went across the road to tell the protection officers where they were going, and then she climbed into her Rainier and they headed for Edina.

'That woman asked her if we'd seen anything strange,' said Tasha.

'So what did you tell her?'

'I said no, we were too frightened to look.'

'You could have told her the truth.'

'No. She wouldn't have believed us, would she?'

Lily drove through the slushy streets to West Seventy-Seventh and parked outside the maroon brick offices of Kraussman Developments, which stood on the curving corner with Park Lawn Avenue. Inside the reception area, with its glossy marble-effect floor and its potted yuccas, she went up to the receptionist and asked to see Philip Kraussman. 'Tell him it's Lily Blake, from Concord Realty. Just a social call, really.'

They sat and waited for twenty minutes on a curvy maroon couch, flicking through magazines and listening to syrupy interpretations of Frank Sinatra hits, until Philip Kraussman came bustling down the stainless-steel staircase. He was a short, bull-headed man with cropped silver hair, a bulbous nose, and a very deep suntan. He was wearing a shiny gray shirt with a shiny red necktie, and gray pants that were two sizes too tight for him.

'Lily! Good to see you! Sorry I kept you waiting!' He grasped her hand and gave her a kiss on both cheeks. 'These are your kids?'

'Tasha, Sammy – say hallo to Mr Kraussman.'

'Hi, Tasha! Hi, Sammy! They're great kids! You must be so pleased to have gotten them back.' He took hold of Lily's arm and lowered his voice. 'I heard about the circumstances, and you have my condolences for that. Are the FBI any closer to finding out who did it?'

'Not yet. They're not even sure if it was a who or a *what*.'

'You mean some kind of an *animal* attack? Like an alligator?'

'They don't know yet.'

'Well, I'm still very sorry. Listen, I'm so glad you dropped by! But was there anything special you wanted to talk about? I'm pretty pushed for time right now.'

'As a matter of fact, yes. Can you give me just two or three minutes?'

'OK . . . Do you want some coffee? Kids – how about a soda? Nancy – would you bring these two lovely young people a Dr Pepper or something?'

Philip Kraussman steered Lily to a couch underneath the staircase. 'So . . . what can I do for you?'

'It's Mystery Lake . . .'

'Mystery Lake! You bet! Mystery Lake! That whole development is going to make us a small fortune, believe me. My planners told me this morning that we can probably fit in at least three more units without in any way compromising that "superior abode" feeling – subtly raise a couple of sightlines, trim a few inches off a driveway here and there.'

'Well, that's terrific news,' said Lily. 'But I've been doing some background research on Mystery Lake.'

'Background research? Meaning what, exactly? Hey – you haven't found any soil pollution, have you? I don't want a repetititon of that Boulder Bridge fiasco.'

'No, no. I'm talking about *history*. I wanted to give our potential buyers a feeling of time and heritage . . . I don't know – a feeling of continuity with the past. So many of these prestige communities feel the same, don't they? They're beautifully landscaped, they're very high-quality build; but they're isolated from their surroundings – not so much geographically as socially.'

'Lily – that's why people buy these properties. They *want* to be isolated from their surroundings. *Socially*, most of all.'

'But Mystery Lake used to be a Sioux encampment before they were all driven south of the river, and it was a very sacred place.'

Philip Kraussman let out a sharp bark of amusement. 'Don't tell me it's going to turn out like that *Poltergeist* movie, and all the houses are going to collapse into some ancient Indian burial pit.'

'No – nothing like that. But that spit of land on the western side of the boat marina, where you're going to be constructing the jetty – that was the place where a great Native American god made his appearance and told the Mdewakanton that they would soon lose their lands to the white man. I was thinking that if Kraussman Developments were to donate that spit of land to the Native American community, as a kind of memorial – maybe if you put up some kind of plaque or statue or piece of sculpture – that would give Mystery Lake a real sense of magic.'

'Magic?' Philip Kraussman frowned at Lily as if the word completely baffled him. '*Magic?*'

'Absolutely. It would create a fascinating feature on the lake shore, a real talking-point. But more than that, it would make you look like a developer who cares about local people and local culture.'

Philip Kraussman thoughtfully squeezed his nose between finger and thumb.

'No,' he said, at last.

'It would make a really memorable promotion.'

'No, you're wrong. It wouldn't. The kind of people who are going to buy property at Mystery Lake are not at all sympathetic to Native Americans. They associate them with alcoholism, drugs, gaming and all kinds of anti-social behavior. Apart from that, why should anyone who's just paid two-point-six million dollars want a constant reminder that the original owners of the land on which they're now sitting were forcibly dispossessed, without any compensation, and even *killed* for it? You see, Lily – I *do* know a little local history.'

'But surely—'

'I'm sorry, Lily. The whole idea is very bad psychology.

169

Apart from which, Kraussman Developments do not as a matter of principle make donations of any kind to anybody. The only charity which Kraussman Developments supports is Kraussman Developments – i.e., me.'

'Philip – I believe that this could do you so much good. You've been thinking of standing for the city council, haven't you?'

Philip Kraussman shook his head. 'You can't change my mind, Lily. The answer is no.'

She had promised Tasha and Sammy that she wouldn't leave them, but now she had no choice. She dropped them off three streets away, at the home of one of Tasha's schoolfriends, Maris Halverson, promising to pick them up again by seven p.m.

John Shooks was waiting outside her house in his old black Buick, wearing his fur hat and his sunglasses. As she turned into the driveway, he climbed out and approached her.

'Mr Shooks,' she said.

'Oh . . . I think you can start calling me John, don't you?'

'All right, then.' She glanced across the street at the protection officers. One of them was reading a newspaper and the other was asleep with his cap over his face.

'Did you get it?' asked Shooks, as she unlocked her front door.

'No. Philip Kraussman is adamant about it. He doesn't make philanthropic donations of any kind and in particular he refuses to give that piece of land to the Mdewakanton.'

'In that case, Lily, you're in very deep shit.'

She closed the door, went straight through to the living room and opened the whiskey decanter on the bureau. 'Do you want one?' she asked him.

'I've never been known to decline a drink. And you know why? Because there's no sure way of telling if it's going to be my last.'

She poured a large tumbler of Jack Daniel's for each of

them, and sat in the button-back armchair close to the fire.
'So what can I do now?'

Shooks knocked back his whiskey in one. 'OK if I help
myself to another? That might be my last, too.'

'Help yourself.' She leaned forward and gave the fire a
prod with the poker. 'What do you think would happen if
I killed him?'

Shooks stopped in mid-pour. 'You mean *George*?'

'Yes. Supposing I went after him and shot him?'

'Jesus. I don't know. I guess you'd end up in Shakopee
Women's Prison. At least it doesn't have a fence around it,
and the food's supposed to be pretty good.'

'I'm asking you if the Wendigo would still come after me.'

'Oh, for sure. You see, George has already honored his
promise to the Wendigo by giving him a human sacrifice
or three; and so the Wendigo will make darn sure that you
honor your promise to George, even if you've blown
George's brains out. And if you *don't* honor it, or *can't*,
then you'll have to pay the price. It's a blood thing. A Native
American thing. If you say you're going to give something
to somebody, then you give it to them, no matter what, even
if it's the most precious thing that you possess.'

'Maybe I could offer him an alternative piece of land.'

'Do you have one?'

'Not right now. But my friend Joan Sapke works part-
time for the Minnesota Indian Affairs Council. She might
be able to suggest someplace else . . . someplace that still
has some sacred connotations for the Mdewakanton but
doesn't happen to be right in the middle of a multi-million-
dollar residential development.'

'I guess you could try. I can't think of anyplace offhand,
but you could always suggest it.'

'You mean I should go *talk* to George?'

Shooks gave a one-shouldered shrug. 'What other way
is there?'

'That man slaughtered my sister and my brother-in-law

and my fifteen-month-old nephew. It's as much as I can bear knowing that he's still living and breathing. How can I talk to him?'

'Because you have to.'

There was a very long silence between them. Then Shooks said, 'Truly, Lily, you don't have any choice. The Wendigo will come for you, sooner or later, and it'll find you, no matter where you try to run.'

Lily looked up at him. 'So – will you come with me?'

'I don't know, Lily. I don't want George to start thinking that I'm a white woman's pet poodle. There's a good chance that I'll need his help again in the future.'

'You'd ask him to raise up the Wendigo again, after everything that's happened?'

'Lily – I'm not a judge and I'm not a jury. I'm simply a guy who facilitates the finding of people that nobody else can find. Everything in life has to be paid for, one way or another.'

'But when you go to George Iron Walker, you know that people are going to get killed! – innocent people, some of them! How can you *live* with yourself?'

'It isn't easy, Lily, believe me. But don't forget how you felt when Jeff took your kids away from you, and those loony tunes from FLAME almost burned you to death. What I do – there's kind of a sort of justice to it, albeit a justice of the tooth-and-claw variety.'

'Oh God,' said Lily. 'I really don't know what to do.'

John Shooks looked toward the window. 'Snow's stopped. Sun's still shining. I don't mind driving you to Black Crow Valley. That's if you're game to do a deal with the devil.'

When they arrived at George Iron Walker's house, however, there was no sign of him, nor of Hazawin. George's Subaru Forester was parked outside, and its hood was covered in snow, so it obviously hadn't been driven anywhere recently. But when Shooks rapped at the door, there was no reply.

'George! It's John Shooks! Anybody home?'

Still no answer. Shooks turned to Lily and said, 'Maybe they're sleeping. Or high. Sometimes they smoke this blood root, so that they can converse with the spirits or something. Makes you kind of horny, too.'

'George!'

Shooks tried the doorhandle, and the door was unlocked. He stepped inside and Lily cautiously followed him. The log fire was still smoldering in the hearth, and there were two half-empty coffee mugs on the table, so wherever George and Hazawin had gone to, they couldn't have been gone for very long.

Shooks went into the kitchen, and then he looked into the bathroom and the bedroom. Then he went back out on to the verandah and hoarsely shouted, 'George! Hazawin!' But there was no reply, not even an echo. Only the faintest rustling of the wind among the pine trees, and the furtive dropping of little clumps of snow.

'This is strange,' said Lily. 'Where do you think they are?'

'Went for a walk, maybe,' said Shooks.

'A *walk*?'

'Well, you know what George is like. He enjoys, like, communing with nature.'

'Doesn't he have a cell phone?'

'Sure, but I've never known him to answer it.'

They went back inside. 'So what do we do now?' asked Lily.

Shooks picked up a half-empty bottle of whiskey from the bureau and read the label. 'We could wait, I guess. Or leave him a note, and ask him to contact you.'

'I can't stay too long. Tasha and Sammy are expecting me home.'

'OK, then. We'll give him thirty minutes, and if he doesn't show by then, we'll head back to the city.' He lifted the whiskey bottle. 'Did you ever hear of Old Zebulon bourbon? No, neither did I. Do you want some?'

173

He went into the kitchen to find himself a glass. As he was coming back, however, Lily thought she heard something: a distant, high-pitched wailing. It was coming from outside somewhere, but the wind was blowing it down the chimney.

'I can never get the measure of that George Iron Walker,' Shooks was saying. 'I can't decide if he's slicker than any white man, or more native than any native.'

'Ssh!' said Lily, raising her hand. 'Listen!'

Shooks stopped talking and listened, cocking his head to one side. 'Sorry . . . I don't hear nothing.'

'No . . . there it is again. Like a small child crying.'

She opened the front door and went out on to the verandah. Although the wind was beginning to rise, she could hear it much more distinctly out here. It was definitely a child. She had the impression that it was coming from the forest off to their right, up the slope where Hazawin had summoned the Wendigo.

'Yeah, I hear it now,' said Shooks, swallowing whiskey. 'Mind you – it could be nothing but a raccoon caught in a trap. Raccoons can sound a whole lot like babies, when they're distressed.'

Lily said, 'Ssh.' The crying went on and on, with occasional pauses for breath. 'That's not a raccoon. That's a child. Not too far away, either.'

Shooks stared at her. 'What are you thinking, Lily? You're not thinking the same as *I'm* thinking, are you?'

'*William*,' said Lily.

Fourteen

John Shooks said, 'If the Highway Patrol couldn't find your sister's baby in the truck, or anywheres in the vicinity, then I guess it's *possible* the Wendigo took him.'

They were only halfway up the slope toward the forest but already he was seriously out of breath. Lily was ten yards ahead of him, bounding through the knee-deep snow with her arms flailing to keep her balance.

'Question is,' John Shooks panted, '*why* did it take him?'

'To put more pressure on me – that's my guess. George Iron Walker must have known that I'd come back here, if I couldn't give him the land at Mystery Lake.'

They had reached the tree-line now. Lily stopped again, and listened, and now there was no question that a child was crying somewhere in the forest, less than a hundred yards away. The crying was quavering and hysterical, interspersed with agonized gasps for breath. Lily was sure it was William.

'William!' she shouted out. '*William!*'

'Not too sure it's advisable for us to advertise our presence,' said Shooks, catching up with her.

'He wants that land,' said Lily. 'He may put pressure on me, but I don't think he'll hurt me while he still believes I can get it for him.'

'Hmm – glad *you're* so confident about it.'

The crying seemed to be coming from the clearing where Hazawin had laid out her bones and her mirror. Lily pushed her way through the briars and the tangled branches until

175

she came out in the open. The huge rock in the center of the clearing was covered in snow, and there was no sign of a child anywhere. Lily looked up. Above the tops of the pine trees the sky was so intensely blue that it was almost purple.

John Shooks joined her, tugging at a briar that had snagged his sleeve. He circled around the rock, and then he said, 'It's stopped.'

He was right. The forest was quiet again.

Lily crossed over to the other side of the clearing and shouted, 'William! Can you hear me? It's Lily! Call out if you can hear me!'

Nothing. Only the wind, and the nervous rattling of the branches.

Shooks said, 'Could have been a ghost voice. Hazawin can do stuff like that – make you hear things that ain't really there. Kind of like ventriloquistics.'

'William!' Lily persisted. 'It's Aunt Lily! Where are you, William?'

Still nothing. Shooks said, 'Maybe we'd best get back to the house.'

'*William!*'

Shooks took hold of her elbow. 'Come on, Lily. I don't like this one iota.'

'But we heard him! We both heard him! He must be here!'

'I know we both heard him. But like I say, Hazawin can do things that'll make you believe that day is night or your dead grandpa's talking to you from inside your closet.'

Lily stayed where she was, straining to hear that crying again. She felt desperate. She knew that Shooks was probably right, and that George Iron Walker was tricking her, but she felt so guilty about what had happened to William that she couldn't bear to abandon him a second time, if there was any chance at all that he were here.

'Come on, Lily,' said Shooks, more gently this time.

'All right,' she agreed, and allowed him to take hold of her arm and lead her back around the rock.

As they reached the trees, however, she heard a sharp rustling noise, and then a quick pattering of feet. She turned around, and Shooks turned around, too. There was another rustle, and the crackling of broken branches.

Out of the trees, an enormous brindled wolf appeared, with shaggy fur and luminous yellow eyes. Its long gray tongue was lolling between its teeth, and its breath was smoking. It stood less than thirty feet away from them, staring at them.

'Oh . . . shit,' said Shooks.

Lily heard more branches breaking, off to her right. Another wolf appeared, long and gray; and then another, and another. They came through the trees and stood in a circle, like a gathering of ghosts. Lily guessed that there were more than a dozen of them.

'This is seriously fucking awkward,' Shooks told her.

'You said that wolves didn't attack people.'

'Not so far as anybody knows.'

'What makes you think that these wolves are any different?'

'These wolves set a trap for us, didn't they? What kind of a wolf can do that?'

They waited. Lily's heart was thumping underneath her fur coat. She looked from one wolf to the other, trying to decide if they were going to go for them or not. The wolves kept their distance, endlessly panting, *huh-huh-huh-huh*, but not showing any signs of going away.

'Let's try edging back toward the trees,' Lily suggested.

'Edging?'

'A couple of steps at a time. No sudden moves. If wolves are frightened of humans, if they *really* don't attack people, then we should be OK.'

Shooks pulled a face. 'OK. I guess we can't stay here for the rest of the day.'

Lily took a cautious step to the left, and then another, and Shooks followed her. She reached the trees and pushed aside a branch with her upraised elbow. The branch snapped sharply, and instantly the brindled wolf trotted forward two or three paces, and all of the other wolves came nearer too.

'Jesus,' said Shooks.

'Let's keep going,' Lily urged him. 'It looks like they're curious, more than anything else. I mean, they would have gone for us by now, couldn't they, if they really wanted to kill us?'

'Don't ask me. I'm not a wolf expert. Maybe they're just playing with their food.'

'I'll tell you what,' said Lily, 'we won't edge any more; we'll simply start walking, as fast as we can. We don't want to show them we're afraid.'

Shooks looked around them. The wolves were everywhere, their yellow eyes unblinking, long strings of saliva swinging from their jaws. 'You're right,' he said. 'We might be filling our shorts in sheer terror but we don't want to give them the satisfaction of knowing it, do we?'

'OK then, let's go.'

Lily took the first step, and then they began to walk away from the clearing, as briskly as the briars would allow. Immediately the wolves began to follow them. On either side Lily could see their long gray shapes flowing between the silver birches. Somehow they didn't seem like real wolves – more like the wolves that you would see in nightmares, weirdly misshapen.

Shooks turned his head. 'They're right behind us,' he said, between clenched teeth. 'That big black-and-brown bastard – he's almost close enough to take a bite out of my ankle.'

Lily didn't look back. She was trying hard not panic. She knew that fear was infectious, especially amongst animals. Dogs often attacked people because they could sense they were frightened of them. She had seen horses go berserk, when they smelled human fear, and cattle collide with barbed-wire fences.

'Come on, John,' she urged him.

They started almost power-walking, and then they started jogging. The wolves kept up with them, loping faster and faster. Lily glanced to her left, and she was sure that she glimpsed one of the wolves rise up on to its hind legs and start running like a man. It was then that she lost any sense of control, and started to sprint.

'Lily!' shouted Shooks. 'For Christ's sake!'

But now terror had taken over, and adrenaline was surging through her body, and all she wanted to do was get out of there alive. The wolves were chasing close behind her. She could hear their claws clattering over the briars. Shooks was yelling, 'Lily! *Lily!*' but she knew what would happen if she stopped and turned back.

She caught her ankle on a root, and fell heavily sideways, jarring her shoulder against a rock. Shooks shouted, 'Lily!' again. She looked up and saw the trees spinning. Then a huge furry body jumped on top of her, heavy and rancid and snarling, and she felt claws scrabbling against her right cheek. They tore right into her skin, just beneath her eye, wrenching the flesh away from her cheekbone.

She screamed, but she didn't know if she was screaming out loud. Her right cheek was clawed away from her face, and thrown aside, like a bloody piece of rag. Then a mouthful of crowded, razor-sharp teeth bit into the bridge of her nose, with a crunch that penetrated her whole being. She couldn't breathe. She couldn't even shout out, because it hurt so much. She could hear Shooks still screaming out, 'Lily! Lily!' but there was nothing she could do to save him, because the gray wolves were already ripping at her clothes, tearing off her coat and reducing her sweater to multi-colored rags.

The gray wolves worried the muscles from her thigh-bones, tearing them downward with a crackling noise, and she experienced an agony so intense that she prayed that she would die, then and there. Then they clawed their way into her stomach, tearing open the skin and the muscle, and thrusting their snouts into her intestines. She could actually feel them doing it, gnawing at her ribs, and it made her jump, and jump, because her nerves were so sensitive. With horrified disbelief, she saw one of the wolves dragging out her intestines, across the snow. They looked like red-and-yellow hosepipes. She could see blood everywhere, hers and John Shooks', although Shooks had been silent for a long time now, and she could only suppose that he was already dead.

She let her head drop back on to the snow. The sky above her was still so blue. She realized that she was dead, too, or as close to death as it was possible to be. The wolves had torn her to pieces, pulled her apart, and she was nothing more than the dying remnants of Lily Blake, the last dwindling spark of a woman who had once loved her family, and her husband, and who now lay flat on her back in a forest in Minnesota, breathing her last few bubbling breaths.

She reached across with her left hand, and she could feel her exposed ribcage, and her lungs, slippery and bloody, but still inflating.

'I should pray,' she whispered.

'*Why?*' said a man's voice.

'I'm dying. I should say the Lord's Prayer, at least.'

'You're not dying.'

Lily opened her eyes. The sun was still shining between the trees. The birds were still twittering, and somebody was making a staccato tapping noise that sounded like a coded message.

George Iron Walker was kneeling beside her, in his black leather coat. He wore a single silver earring that flashed in the sunlight.

'You're not dying,' he repeated.

Lily lifted her head and looked down at her body. Her

fur coat was still intact. She felt her face. Her face was still intact, too.

'What happened?'

George Iron Walker held out his hand. 'Let me help you up.'

'I can get up myself, thank you. What the hell happened? Where are the wolves?'

'Wolves?'

She stood up, though she tilted sideways and nearly lost her balance. She felt bruised and winded, as if she had been jostled and trampled by a panicking crowd. About thirty feet away, John Shooks was kneeling upright in the snow, angrily brushing his sleeves.

'*John!*' called Lily. 'Are you OK?'

Shooks staggered to his feet, and then took two hops toward her. 'Me? I'm fucking terrific. I have a ton of snow all down the back of my neck, and I've twisted my goddamned ankle. You can't see my Ray-Bans anywhere, can you? Lost my fucking Ray-Bans.'

Lily looked around. It was only then that she saw Hazawin, half-camouflaged by patches of shadow and sunlight. She was standing between the silver birches, holding a collection of birch twigs in one hand, and two human thighbones in the other, decorated with feathers and beads.

'You saw wolves?' said George.

Lily turned to him. He was standing uncomfortably close. 'I'm not sure *what* I saw. I thought . . .'

George gave her a strangely humorless smile. 'The forests are full of dreams, Lily, but you know what dreams are like. Some of them come true, but most of them don't.'

'This wasn't any dream, George. This was a nightmare.' She looked around again, and then she said, 'I heard a young child crying. I thought it might be my nephew William.'

'We need to talk,' said George. 'That was why you came here, wasn't it?' He held her with a steady gaze, as if he

181

were daring her to look away. It had only been a few days since she had seen him last, but she had forgotten how handsome he was. It was almost impossible to believe that a man so good-looking could be so ruthless.

'You're telling me that *was* William?'

'Yes, Lily, it almost certainly was.'

'Is he all right? Tell me! He's not hurt, is he?'

'For the time being, he's fine.'

'What do you mean "for the time being"? Where is he? You can't keep him! That's kidnap!'

'You can call it whatever you like. Personally, I call it insurance. We made a bargain, you and I, and I need to know that you're going to keep your side of it.'

'You killed my sister! You killed my brother-in-law! You killed my ex-husband! You killed them! You had them torn to pieces, you bastard! You're nothing but a *savage*!'

John Shooks had been hopping toward them, but when he heard Lily say that, he stopped, and held back, with a wary expression on his face.

But George kept up that humorless smile. 'I don't mind if you call me a savage, Lily. Savage means fierce and it also means untamed – and that, to a Sioux, is a high compliment. Not only that, "savage" comes from the Latin word *silva* – "of the woods". And right here – in the woods – this is where my heart is, and my spirit. So – yes – you're right. I *am* a savage.'

'Where is he?' said Lily. 'Where's little William? You haven't left him out here on his own?'

'Oh, he's safe enough. But you could search through the forest for months and you'd never find him.'

Shooks said, 'The Wendigo has him, doesn't he?'

George didn't answer, but Lily demanded, 'Is that true?'

'You've seen the Wendigo,' Shooks told her, '– partly here, partly someplace else. If you ask me, that's where it's taken your nephew, and that's why you'll never be able to find him.'

'This is madness,' said Lily. 'What are you talking about, "someplace else"?'

'You believe in God, don't you?' asked George. 'You believe in heaven?'

'I don't think so. Not any more.'

'Well, let's just say that there are places which exist, but which can't be seen. Your William is in a place like that.'

'Then I want him back, and I want him back *now*.'

'You can have him back, Lily, I promise you. Give me the title to the land at Mystery Lake, and I will lift him into your arms myself. But let me warn you – I can't wait too much longer. I have to have that title by sundown, day after tomorrow.'

'And what if I can't get it for you?'

'Then the Wendigo will live up to its name.'

'You're crazy!' Lily screamed at him. 'You're crazy and you're totally sick! If you so much as touch one hair on that little boy's head, I'll kill you myself!'

George raised his hand. 'Yelling at me won't change anything. *You* set all of this in motion, not me. You were the one who wanted her children back. You were the one who promised to give me the land.'

'Well, I can't,' said Lily. She was so furious that her eyes were filled with tears. 'That's why I came here today. I can't get the title. I thought I could, but I can't.'

She took off her glove and wiped her eyes with her fingers. 'I came to ask you if you could accept someplace else instead. Someplace just as sacred, or meaningful, if you know of one. But just not *that* particular place.'

Hazawin approached them, and she looked almost as if she were gliding across the snow. Shooks hobbled two or three steps away from her.

'I'm sorry, Lily, it has to be Mystery Lake. Nowhere else will do. It was there that Haokah appeared to Little Crow, and there was a reason for that.'

'Aren't you *listening*?' Lily retorted. 'Philip Kraussman

simply won't give it to me. He won't even consider *selling* it. He says the people who are going to buy properties there – they won't want a constant reminder that Mystery Lake was stolen from the Sioux.'

'Of course they won't,' said George. 'Imagine how *uncomfortable* they would feel, sipping their margaritas in their back yards – knowing that the soil beneath their sundecks was still soaked with the blood of hundreds of Native Americans – men, women and little children.'

'Are you looking for some kind of *revenge*?' Lily challenged him. 'Is that why you're insisting on this particular piece of land?'

'Revenge? You really underestimate me, don't you, Lily? There is no act of revenge you can possibly think of that could compensate for what the white man did to the Mdewakanton. I want this particular piece of land because it's *unique*. There is no other location in the whole of Minnesota which has the same mystical and geographical qualities.'

'So I can't change your mind?'

'No.'

'What if I call in the FBI, and have you arrested for kidnap, and for tearing people apart, and extortion, and fraud, and deception?'

'But you won't. You will bring me the title to Mystery Lake, before sundown the day after tomorrow. And then we'll be quits.'

Lily didn't know what more to say. John Shooks limped up to her and took hold of her hand, and said, 'Come on, Lily. We can find a way.'

Lily hesitated for a moment, and then she said, 'OK.'

Without saying another word to George Iron Walker or Hazawin, she turned and made her way back down the slope, with Shooks following close behind her. The sun was burning the tops of the fir trees now, and it was beginning to grow darker, and chillier. Lily looked back just once, and saw George and Hazawin still standing by the tree-line, watching them. Shooks opened the creaky passenger door of his Buick for her, and she climbed in, but almost immediately she tried to get out again.

'Try to keep it together,' Shooks urged her. 'We'll get this sorted, one way or another.'

'But how can I just drive off and leave little William in the hands of people like that? He must be terrified! And this "someplace else" – this "other existence"– I don't understand that at all. Where actually *is* he?'

Shooks started the engine. 'The Sioux believe that everything that you see in the real world is reflected in the spirit world, like a mirror. Underneath the soles of our feet, there's a whole other Minnesota, upside-down, except that this Minnesota is the way that it used to be, before the white devils came. And there's a *sideways* world, too, right next to us – kind of like *Alice Through the Looking Glass*. There's another Lily, sitting right next to you, and another me. That's the world that the Wendigo lives in – well, *half* lives in. And that's where your nephew will be right now.'

'Isn't there any way of rescuing him? I mean – if the Wendigo could take him into this sideways world, what's to stop us from going after him?'

'Excuse me – but do you happen to know *how* to get through to the spirit world? Because I sure don't – sideways world, upside-down world, or any-which-way world: I wouldn't know where to start.'

They drove along the bumpy track in silence for a while. But then Lily said, 'There's only one thing we can do, isn't there?'

'What's that?'

'We're like cornered animals, aren't we? And what do animals do, when they're cornered?'

'They crap themselves.'

'No, they don't. Whatever's chasing them, however

much more powerful it is, they turn around and they attack it.'

'Meaning?'

'If the Wendigo's hunting for us, we'll have to find it first – go after it, and kill it.'

Shooks stared at her for such a long time that he almost drove into a tree beside the road. Eventually, he said, '*We'll* have to hunt down the Wendigo?'

When they arrived back at Lily's house, they found Special Agent Kellogg waiting for them. He climbed out of his car and came over to them, blowing on his hands to warm them up.

'I'm sorry,' said Lily. 'I had my cell switched off. You haven't been waiting too long, have you?'

'Ten minutes, that's all. Mind if I come in?'

'Sure. Oh – by the way, this is John Shooks. John, this is Special Agent Kellogg from the FBI.'

'Our paths have crossed from time to time,' said Shooks, dryly. 'How's life with you, Nathan?'

'Fine, thanks, John. Be interested to know what you're doing here?'

'Friend of the family, Nathan, that's all.'

'Wasn't aware that you *had* any friends.'

Lily opened the front door. Shooks said, 'Listen, Lily, I have some people to see regarding that little bit of business of ours. I'll check with you later.'

'OK, John. Thanks for the ride.'

She led Special Agent Kellogg into the living room. 'Take off your coat,' she said. 'I'll have this fire burning up in a minute.'

Special Agent Kellogg unwound his scarf. 'You've been doing business with John Shooks? What kind of business, if you don't mind me asking?'

'Nothing much. He's helping me to trace a long-lost uncle of mine. You know – so that I can tell him about Agnes.'

'Oh, yes? He's a hoser, that guy, believe me.'

Lily shrugged. She hated to lie to him, but what else could she say?

Special Agent Kellogg took off his coat and draped it over the back of a chair. 'I wanted to talk to you off the record,' he said.

'About anything special?'

He closed his eyes for a moment, as if he were trying to remember something. Then he said, 'This is real difficult. You've been the victim here. But Agent Rylance and myself . . . we can't help but think that we're missing something.'

'I don't know what you mean.'

'Lily – you don't mind if I call you Lily?'

'Of course not, so long as I can call you Nathan.'

'Sure. But the thing is – what's really going on here, Lily?'

'What do you mean?'

'I mean that we have a jigsaw here and there's a big piece of sky missing and we have the feeling that you may know where it is – wittingly or unwittingly. I'm not suggesting that you're deliberately holding out on us. But four people have died during the course of this investigation, and they've all been killed in pretty much the same way: torn to pieces, and their bodies strewn for thousands of yards.

'Like we told you before, we don't have any idea who killed them, or *what* killed them, or how. A giant eagle? A flying bear? But I've searched through the FBI database and I've discovered that seventeen other people have also been killed like that, over the past twenty-three years. None of them was related to any of the others, and they were all killed in different parts of the country.

'But thirteen of them were involved in kidnap or abduction cases, and the other four were listed as missing persons. And all of them originally came from southern Minnesota or northern Iowa or western Wisconsin – none of them further than two-hundred-fifty miles from Minneapolis.

'So there are strong similarities between each killing, and those similarities apply in your case, too.'

Lily said, 'I honestly don't know what I can tell you.'

'Well, for beginners, you could tell me what you've really been doing with John Shooks. Come on, Lily, you must know what kind of a guy he is. He's the living definition of a Shady Character.'

Lily took a deep breath. 'All right,' she said. 'My boss at Concord Realty put me in touch with him, when Tasha and Sammy first went missing. He helped my boss's brother to get *his* children back, when their mother abducted them.'

'But you have Tasha and Sammy back now. Why is Shooks still hanging around?'

'He's been very supportive – that's all I can say.'

'John Shooks? Supportive? Now I've heard everything.'

Lily sat down by the fire, and Special Agent Kellogg came and sat down opposite her. He looked at her appealingly, and for the first time she noticed that one of his eyes was gray and the other green.

'I'm going to be open with you, Lily. The rules say that agents should never get themselves emotionally involved. Total detachment from fellow agents, perpetrators, witnesses and victims – the bureau insists on it. But ever since I first walked into this house and saw you . . . well, I've been finding it real hard not to tell you how special you are.'

'*What?*' She had always thought that Special Agent Kellogg was good-looking, in a sharp-faced, loose-wristed way, like a young Clint Eastwood, and he had always been very attentive, but she had been far too stressed to notice that he might have found her attractive. She didn't *feel* attractive. Her hair was still as fuzzy as thistledown and she hadn't slept more than a few hours since Agnes and Ned had been killed, so she now had plum-colored circles under her eyes.

'I think you're special,' Special Agent Kellogg repeated. 'It's just the way you look. Vulnerable, I guess, but tough with it. And very pretty.'

'Well, I might be vulnerable. But as for *pretty* – I think you need to go back to FBI headquarters and take an eye test.'

'Look,' said Special Agent Kellogg, 'I'm not trying to come on to you. I only want you to understand that I really care about you, and I don't want to see anything bad happening to you.'

'Is this your way of getting me to confess?'

'Lily – what the hell is going on? If you can tell us *anything* that helps us to fit this thing together . . .'

God, she was so tempted to tell him. At least it would take some of the burden off her. But she knew that telling him wouldn't change anything, and it would probably make her situation even more dangerous. The FBI might be able to arrest George Iron Walker and Hazawin, but they would never be able to find the Wendigo, even if she could persuade Special Agent Kellogg that it really existed. Little William would be ripped apart and eaten, and then the Wendigo would come after *her*.

'Nathan,' she said, and reached out to take hold of his hands. 'You've done my confidence a whole lot of good. Thank you.'

He shook his head in exasperation. 'Take my advice, Lily. Even if you can't tell me what's happening, stay well away from John Shooks. He's trouble.'

Lily thought, that's exactly what I'm looking for: *trouble*.

Fifteen

The next morning, Special Agent Rylance phoned Lily just after nine a.m. to tell her that the Minneapolis coroner had released Agnes and Ned's remains, and asked her if she had chosen a funeral home.

Remains. The word made her feel as if she had stepped up to her chest in icy-cold water, and she couldn't answer him for almost fifteen seconds. In spite of that, Special Agent Rylance waited patiently on the other end of the line while she tried to pull herself together.

'I'll get back to you,' she said. 'I really hadn't thought about a funeral.'

'You've seen their kids? How are they coping?'

'Not too bad, I suppose, but I don't think it's really sunk in yet.'

'OK. By the way – I asked the St Petersburg police about your ex. They're holding on to *his* remains for the time being, pending some further investigation.'

'Thanks.'

There was a long pause, and then Special Agent Rylance said, 'We're here to help you, Mrs Blake. You do understand that? It's our job.'

'I know,' Lily told him. 'One day – well, I hope one day that I can show you how much I appreciate the way that you and Agent Kellogg have helped me to cope with all of this.'

'Like I say, Mrs Blake, it's all in a day's work. Call us –

you know – if you need us. Or if you think of anything that might help us. You know what I'm saying?'

She was beating up Aunt Jemima's pancake mix when the doorbell chimed. It was John Shooks. He was shivering and sniffing and chafing his hands together, and there was a drip on the end of his nose.

'Why the freak do I live in Minnesota?' he demanded. 'I must be some kind of freaking masochist! I could just as easy be a private eye in California, or Florida. I could run my business from a sun-lounger, with some babe in a bikini for a secretary. A very, very small bikini.'

'Here – come into the kitchen. Did you have any luck last night?'

He dragged off his scarf but kept his overcoat on. 'Yes, and no. I talked to some of my Native American relatives. Jesus, what a crew! Most of them sound like Tonto on speed. They all knew about the Wendigo. Like, find me a Native American who *doesn't* know about the Wendigo. But what they knew was all mythical stuff, like how it chases you and never lets you get away and how it comes right up behind you but when you spin around it's *still* right behind you. Nothing *practical* – like how to track one down and annulify it.'

'So none of them could help us?'

'Not definitely sure yet. My second cousin Kenneth Return-From-Scout said I should visit my great-uncle in Como – Thomas Bear Robe. Apparently he used to teach Native American Studies at the U, and he's written books about Native American legends. So that's what I'm going to do, as soon as I've had a leak and a cup of coffee and . . . Are those pancakes you're whipping up there?'

He was still eating when Tasha and Sammy came downstairs for their breakfast. Sammy promptly sat down on his usual stool but Tasha stayed close to Lily, frowning at Shooks with deep suspicion.

'These are great pancakes,' said Shooks, waving his fork. 'I haven't had pancakes in a coon's age.'

Lily put her arm around Tasha's shoulders. 'This is my friend John Shooks, sweetheart. John is a private detective. He's helping me to find out what happened to Aunt Agnes and Uncle Ned, and little William too.'

'OK,' said Tasha, reluctantly. She sat as far away from Shooks as she could, while Lily served her pancakes and poured on maple syrup for her.

'You mustn't mind me,' Shooks told her. 'I know I look like I've slept in a dumpster, but I've been working all night on behalf of your mom, and all I'm interested in doing is arranging for you and your mom to have the happiest ending possible.'

'Mom?' said Tasha.

Lily smiled at her. 'It's true, sweetheart. John's here to help us.'

Tasha drew her very close. 'But he *smells*,' she whispered. 'He smells like old carrots.'

'That's OK. I'll make sure that he takes a shower. You want to take a shower, John?'

Shooks wiped his mouth with a paper napkin, and burped. 'Sure, I'd love one. Don't want to go around smelling like old carrots, now do I?'

He laughed, and then Sammy laughed, and Tasha looked up at Lily, and Tasha smiled too.

Thomas Bear Robe sat in the far corner of his yellow-leather couch, his bulky legs crossed, his stomach bulging over his silver-buffalo-head belt.

'The *Wendigo*?' he said, in a deep, chocolatey voice. 'Hell of a long time since anybody asked me anything about the Wendigo.'

He was a big, broad-shouldered man, at least seventy-five years old, with long steel-gray hair that was tied in a pony-tail. His eyes were so pouchy that they were half-closed and he had a prominent bump on the bridge of his nose. He looked like one of those old sepia photographs of Indian chiefs like Sitting Bull or Crazy Horse.

They had driven up to the university suburb of Como under a sky that was growing grimmer and grimmer, and Lily began to feel that something terrible was about to happen. The wind was rising, too, so that snow-devils whirled across the highway.

Thomas Bear Robe lived in a dilapidated bungalow on a sloping triangular plot, surrounded by seventy-five-foot pines. It looked as if the bungalow's cladding hadn't had its pale-green paint refreshed since the 1960s, and there was a rusting old truck parked outside the garage, draped in a snow-covered tarpaulin.

The inside of the bungalow was gloomy and smelled of stale cigarette smoke and the roast-chicken pie that Thomas Bear Robe must have made himself for lunch, because the dirty plate was still on the dining table, along with heaps of newspapers and magazines and books.

Thomas Bear Robe said, 'My father would never say the name "Wendigo" out loud because he believed that the Wendigo would prick up its ears and hear it, carried on the wind, and was likely to come after him. He always called it "That Forest Thing".'

'We need to know if anybody ever caught one,' said Shooks.

'*Caught* one? Why would you want to know that?'

'Because *we* need to catch one,' Lily explained. 'We need to catch it, and we need to kill it . . . or send it back to wherever it comes from – or whatever you have to do to rid yourself of a Wendigo.'

'You're a woman and you're white. Catching Wendigos – that's not something that you should be getting yourself involved in.'

'I don't have a choice. If I don't kill the Wendigo first, then the Wendigo is going to kill me – and my children, and my parents, and maybe my friends, too.'

Shooks said, 'Lily made a deal with George Iron Walker . . . he raised the Wendigo to help find her children when her ex-husband took them away.'

'George Iron Walker? There's a man I'd keep a good distance away from. What happened?'

'I couldn't keep my side of the bargain,' said Lily. 'I promised him a piece of land at Mystery Lake, but I couldn't get the title to it. I offered him anything else instead – money, another piece of land – but he insisted. He's given me till sundown tomorrow.'

Thomas Bear Robe took a crumpled pack of Camels out of his shirt pocket, shook one out, and lit it with a trembling hand. 'George Iron Walker isn't everything that he appears to be. Talks like a modern entre-prenewer, when you first meet him. Very smooth, very friendly, all charm and white teeth. But he has a dark side to him, that one. An *old* side. His family goes back a long, long way, to the days when men and animals could talk to each other, and whole forests could move overnight.'

'We still have to catch and kill the Wendigo,' said Lily. 'I tried to leave the country . . . I was going to take my children to Europe. But it wouldn't let us. It came after us when we were driving to the airport.'

'It'll come after you no matter where you go,' said Thomas Bear Robe. He sounded completely unsurprised. 'Once a Wendigo's looking for you, there's no escaping it, ever.'

He blew smoke out of his nostrils, and then he said, 'There are so many different stories about the Wendigo, and most of them are not true – or only half-true. But let me tell you something for certain: the Wendigo is a spirit of the woods. And anything that lives in the woods, or is *of* the woods – whether it's a man or an animal or a spirit or a tree, or any mixture of any of those four – has one common enemy. One thing that terrifies them above all things. *Fire.*'

'But I thought that the Wendigo were actually supposed to *cause* fires,' said Lily. 'Don't they swoop down and snatch hold of people and make them run so fast that their feet burst into flame?'

'That's right,' said Shooks. 'It's all in that Algernon Blackwood story, isn't it? *"Oh, my poor feet of fire!"* And they leave a trail of burning grass and trees, all the way through the forest, for miles.'

'That's where Algernon Blackwood got it ass-about-face,' said Thomas Bear Robe. 'When he was researching that story, he talked to some senile old Ojibwe up at Mille Lacs, who couldn't remember half of the tribal legends, and the ones that he could remember he was too drunk to remember straight. Apart from which, he talked to Blackwood in Ojibwe, which was translated for him by some nine-year-old kid.

'Like I told you, the Wendigo is afraid of fire. About the only thing it *is* frightened of. Not only is it a tree spirit, with a close physical kinship to wood and leaves, it exists in a highly volatile state between this world and the world beside us. Two dimensions *here*, a third dimension *there* . . . so it's almost like a vapor. That's how it can slide into your house without even opening the door.

'But if you can catch hold of the Wendigo, and hogtie it, and drag it along the ground, it'll catch alight eventually, and burn, and it won't stop burning, and all the water in all Minnesota's ten thousand lakes won't put it out.'

Shooks thought about this, and sniffed. 'So . . . what you're telling us is, that's the mistake that Algernon Blackwood made. It wouldn't have been the *guide*, burning like that. It would have been a Wendigo.'

'That's right.'

'And you know this for sure? I mean, there are reliable eyewitness accounts of Wendigos being offed like that?'

'No. But a chief called Red Thunder, who lived around the late 1660s, claimed he killed a Wendigo up near Fond du Lac someplace, and his account of that was written down by a French fur trader. And the story goes that a Wendigo was caught and killed in the Koochiching Forest in the 1880s.'

'Oh, yes? What happened then?'

'Well, it seems that there were two trappers, one by the name of Renville and the other by the name of Giddings. They were deep in the forest when they accidentally shot an Ojibwe boy mistaking him for a deer. The boy's father was so angry that he went to the tribal medicine-woman and had her send a Wendigo after them.

'Renville and Giddings were tracked down by the Wendigo and it attacked them when they were sitting by their campfire. Of course it approached them edgewise and they couldn't see it coming. Giddings was torn open on the spot, clear back to his spine – but Renville held the Wendigo off with a burning brand, and managed to get a rope around it, and bring it down to the ground, and lash its arms. Then he got on his horse and rode through the forest dragging the Wendigo behind him.

'Now a Wendigo can run as fast as the fastest man, and when it isn't tethered it can fly above the treetops, but Renville rode that horse flat out and the Wendigo couldn't keep up with him. After three or four miles the Wendigo's feet caught fire, and it started to blaze, and there was Renville riding hell-for-leather through the forest with this fiery apparition running after him.

'Then the Wendigo fell apart, and lay there burning, until there was nothing left but silvery ash. And that is the only known account of a Wendigo being caught and destroyed in what you might call modern times.'

'This Renville got a rope around it, and tied its arms?' asked Lily. 'How on earth did he manage to do that?'

'That's one of the questions that I was asking myself, too,' said Shooks. 'All the Wendigo had to do was turn sideways, and he wouldn't have been able to *see* it, let alone tie it up. And I was also saying to myself, if *I* was deep in the forest and I had a drunken dispute with my companion and accidentally or purposefully killed him, how would I explain it? Nothing like blaming a Native American forest demon, wouldn't you say, of which there is now no trace, except for some ash?'

Thomas Bear Robe shrugged. 'You can either believe it or not believe it.'

'Are these the only accounts you know of?' Lily asked him.

'Of course not. Many tribal legends tell of similar encounters with Wendigos, but they were passed down by word of mouth, and all of them fancifully elaborated with each telling, the way these legends are.

'All I can tell you is that every legend and every story is in agreement when it comes to *how* to kill a Wendigo. You tie it up, you drag it behind your horse, and you keep going until it bursts into flame – praying all the time that it doesn't catch up with you before it does.'

They drove back to Lily's house. Tasha and Sammy had gone out snowboarding with their friends the Lutmeyers from across the street, and so Lily and Shooks had some time to themselves.

Lily poured Shooks a whiskey. He knocked it back, and then he shook his head. 'I'm too damned old for this, Lily. Too damned tired and too damned drunk.'

She poured him another one. He looked into the glass and said, 'All the same, I'm going to do it. I got you into this fuck-up. It's my duty to get you out.'

They sat down together at the kitchen table. 'How do you suggest we go about it?' Lily asked him.

'Well . . . you have a power winch on the back of your SUV, don't you? We can pay some wire out, and make a loop of it on the ground, and hide it with snow. Then we set fire to the woods. When the Wendigo comes out, one of us is going to have to stand there and act as bait. A Judas goat.

'As soon as the Wendigo steps into the loop, you put your foot down and drive like hell.'

'That sounds to me like *you're* volunteering to act as bait.'

'I'm a lot older than you, Lily – a whole lot more wore out. And I don't have two kids to take care of.'

He leaned back in his chair. 'All the same, I won't pretend that this won't be highly goddamned risky for you too. Anything goes wrong – you hit a tree or something – and you're royally screwed. And who knows? – the Wendigo might run faster'n that truck of yours can travel, and catch up with you. Those stories that Thomas Bear Robe told us . . . they were passed on by people who survived. How many others *didn't*?'

Lily looked around the kitchen. On the dresser stood a large color photograph of the three of them – Tasha and Sammy and her – all dressed up in their best clothes for Tasha's last birthday. Shooks saw where she was looking, and reached across the table and laid his hand on top of hers. He had a heavy silver ring on his wedding finger, with a human skull on it.

'Let's do it,' said Lily. 'I'll go over to Marjorie Lutmeyer's and see if she can look after Tasha and Sammy for a few hours longer.'

'You're sure?'

'I don't have any alternative, do I?'

'You realize – if something goes wrong – those kids might never see you again?'

Lily looked at him for a long moment, saying nothing. Then she nodded, and whispered, 'Yes.'

They both dressed up warmly. Lily put on her thick black padded jacket with the nylon fur hood, and she gave Shooks an old windbreaker that Jeff used to wear when he went snowmobiling, and a green woolly hat.

They went outside and checked the Warn power winch in the back of Lily's Rainier. It was installed under the rear bumper, with a wire cable that could pull 2,500 pounds without breaking. Most of her friends and neighbors had one, to rescue anybody who might have skidded off the highway in the middle of winter.

She opened up the garage and Shooks carried out a five-gallon can of gasoline, which he loaded into the back of the SUV. At about four fifteen they were ready to leave.

'Do you have a gun?' Lily asked Shooks as she steered out of the driveway.

'Sure I do. But I can't say that I'm America's greatest shot. And what good is a gun going to do us against the Wendigo?'

'I wasn't thinking about the Wendigo.'

'Oh . . . you were thinking about George.'

'When we've gotten rid of the Wendigo, I want George and Hazawin to help me find little William for me, wherever he is. I just wanted to make sure that we had the wherewithal to persuade them, if we need to.'

'You bet. When I point my gun at people – believe me, they're persuaded. I think it's the wildly shaking barrel that does it.'

The sky was so dark that it could have been midnight. As they drove south-westward out of the suburbs, however, a diagonal streak of reddish light appeared over Black Crow Valley, almost as if a wound had opened up, and the clouds had started to bleed.

'Red sky at night . . . Isn't there a saying about that?' said Lily.

'Sure. Something to do with staying at home, burying yourself under the bedcovers, and not annoying Native American spirits with a penchant for tearing people open.'

They turned off on to the track that led past the forest toward George Iron Walker's house. They jolted and bumped through the crimson-tinted gloom, with Shooks softly whistling 'Hotel California' between his teeth: '*You can check in any time you like . . . but you can never leave . . .*'

At last they saw the lights of George Iron Walker's house over the ridge. Shooks said, 'Turn off here, up the hill a ways. We don't want him to know that we're here. Not yet, anyhow. He's going to, soon enough, when we start our little bonfire.'

Lily drove the Rainier up the slope at a sharp angle, as near to the trees as she could. Then she made a three-point turn, so that the SUV was facing back the way they had come. Even though she had snow-chains on her tires, they whirred and slithered on the snowy ground, but at last she managed it.

John Shooks climbed out and walked around to the back of the vehicle while Lily pressed the button that paid out the winch cable. He laid the cable in a ten-foot circle on the ground – fastening it with a running cleat so that when it was sharply pulled, it would tighten up like a slip-knot. Then he took out Lily's shovel and carefully covered it with snow.

Lily got out of the Rainier and went up to him.

'Listen,' he said. 'They say that it's silent in the woods. But just listen.'

Lily could hear the soft rattling of branches, and the fluttering of birds, and all kinds of crackling and pattering noises. And, very faintly, she could hear music from George Iron Walker's house – a samba, which was so incongruous that it made her shiver.

'Want to dance?' asked Shooks, though he wasn't smiling.

'I think we'd better just get on with it,' said Lily.

'OK . . . you get back in the truck. Keep the motor running. I'll torch the woods, and then all we can do is wait for the Wendigo to show up. That's if it *does* show up, but I got a feeling in my water about this. This is where it lives . . . this is where it hangs out. If we threaten its natural habitat, it's going to come after us.'

'I'm really worried about little William. The Wendigo has him here someplace. I don't want him to get hurt.'

'Lily, I really don't know. I don't understand this other-reality stuff any more than you do.' He hefted the gasoline can out of the back of the SUV and levered open the cap.

'John,' said Lily, 'you'll be careful, won't you?'

'Of course I'll be careful. I may be reckless, but I'm not stupid. How do you think I've survived for all of these years? You be careful, too. When I tell you to, you drive twice as fast as you've ever driven in your entire darned life, and don't stop until that thing is totally incinerated. You can come back for me later.'

Lily climbed back into the driving seat. In the rear-view mirror, she could see Shooks tramping this way and that, sloshing gasoline all over the trees. When he had finished, he came back and stowed the empty can in the back of the SUV.

'Just remember,' he told her. 'As soon as I give you the word, you go like a bat out of hell.' Then he slammed the rear door shut.

Lily sat waiting, with the window open. The wind blew a soft coda to 'Hotel California', as if it had picked it up from Shooks and couldn't stop whistling it.

She looked at her eyes in the mirror. *This is all madness*, she thought. But at the same time she felt a determination far stronger than any emotion she had ever felt before. She was going to finish this thing for good. She was going to protect herself, and protect her children, and she was going to have her revenge on the Wendigo for Agnes and Ned.

The sudden explosion of fire caught her by surprise, and gave her a sick little jolt in her stomach. The chair, the kitchen, the men in masks. Within seconds, at least fifteen pine trees were blazing – the flames rippling up their trunks and shriveling their branches.

Shooks shouted out, 'Woo-hooo! Woo-hooo! Come on, Wendigo, your woods are on fire! Come on out, you two-dimensional piece of crap! You want to see your whole forest burn down? Wind's in the right direction, feller! Come on out!'

He was right about the wind. It was blowing sharply from the north-west, and it had been rising ever since they had arrived here. The fire turned tree after tree into a hundred-foot torch, and as it reached the upper branches, it seemed to run from one branch to another, like hordes of blazing squirrels.

The air was becoming thick with the aromatic smell of pine smoke, and the popping and snapping of burning twigs was almost deafening.

'Wooo-hooo! Come on, Wendigo! Come on out!'

Lily looked down toward George Iron Walker's house. As she did so, the front door opened, and she could see light shining on to the porch. She just hoped that the Wendigo appeared before George Iron Walker could get up here and discover what they were trying to do.

As the pines burned more fiercely, the wind seemed to blow more strongly too, as if it were eager to feed them with oxygen. After only a few minutes, all that Lily could see behind her was fire, and John Shooks' silhouette dancing in front of it, waving his arms.

'Come on, Wendigo! Come on out of there!'

She glanced back down the hill. George Iron Walker's house was too far away to see him clearly, but the brake-lights of his Subaru Forester suddenly lit up, and the vehicle began to back up and turn in a circle.

'John!' she shouted. 'John! George is coming up here! John, can you hear me?'

'What?'

'George is coming up here! George!'

Shooks cupped his hand to his ear to show her that he couldn't hear her. Lily could see George Iron Walker's head-lights now, and he was definitely headed this way. Every pine tree along the top of the ridge was burning now, and the flames were jumping fifty and sixty feet into the air. In spite of the snow and the coldness of the wind, the blasts of heat were enormous, almost enough to take your eyebrows off.

Lily didn't know what to do. If the Wendigo failed to appear before George Iron Walker reached them, he would probably try to stop them – or Hazawin would, if she were with him, and God alone knew what *she* would do. After the wolf-pack hallucination, Lily was seriously frightened of her.

'*John!*' she shouted, but he still couldn't hear her.

She started to climb out of the SUV. Shooks momentarily disappeared in a great swirl of smoke and sparks.

'*John! George is coming!*'

Shooks reappeared. This time he heard her shouting, and he turned around. As he did so, however, Lily saw a flicker of silvery light through the smoke. It vanished again before she could be sure what it was.

'What's wrong?' Shooks called out.

Lily stared into the smoke. She glimpsed another flicker of light, and then – over the rifle-fire crackling of the burning trees – she heard that distinctive *hissing* noise.

'*Wendigo!*' she screamed, pointing.

'What?'

'John, it's the Wendigo! It's there! It's right there beside you!'

Shooks spun around. For a split second Lily saw a tall figure approaching him – a figure with antlers and a long, animal-like face – yet with arms that appeared to be jointed all the wrong way. It was no more than a glimpse, and then the figure turned sideways and vanished.

'It's there! John – it's there!'

'*Back in the truck, Lily! Get ready to go!*'

Lily scrambled back into the driver's seat, slammed the door and gunned the engine. She looked frantically into her rear-view mirror, and she could see Shooks ducking first to the right and then to the left, and then back again. She twisted around, trying to see if there was any sign of where the Wendigo might be, but the flames were too bright and she had to shield her eyes with her hand.

Shooks was jinking around behind her like a football player trying to find a way through a tight defense. He jabbed out his right hand, and then his left, and it was obvious that he had no idea where the Wendigo was, or how close.

Lily looked into her rear-view mirror again, and this time she saw to her horror that the figure was only two or three feet away from him. *She* could see it, because it was face on to her, but it was edgewise to Shooks, and invisible.

'*John!*' she screamed, banging at her horn. '*John, get out of there!*'

Shooks turned toward her. He was shouting something but she couldn't hear what it was. He looked excited rather than afraid. But the figure made the quickest of moves, and seized him by the front of his jacket. It tore the nylon fabric apart, ripped through the kapok quilting, and then it must have gripped his ribcage and wrenched it wide open, because all Lily could see was three or four spectacular jets of blood, followed by a slippery cascade of stomach and liver and intestines.

John Shooks was hauled up into the air, completely out of her sight, leaving behind him an unraveling trail of viscera. It had taken only seconds. Seized, torn open, gone.

Breathless with shock, Lily stamped her foot on the Rainier's gas pedal. The engine bellowed but the vehicle spun its wheels for five heart-stopping seconds before it abruptly lurched forward. Lily was half-blinded by the smoke from the burning trees, but she kept her foot right down to the floor and careered down the snowy slope at nearly sixty miles per hour. The Rainier bounced and jarred and jolted, but still she didn't slow down, even when it flew over the drainage ditch at the side of the road with all four wheels off the ground.

Bang – she hit the road, and as she did so, George Iron Walker's Subaru appeared out of the smoke and she slammed into the side of it. There was a loud collision and the Subaru was spun off the road and into a fence.

That was all Lily saw. She was too busy grappling with the wheel to stop her SUV from skidding out of control, and when she had straightened it up she jammed her foot down and kept on driving as fast as she dared, and then some. She veered from one side of the track to the other, her snow-chains rippling on the ice.

About two miles down the road she slowed down and looked back. The forest was burning like a fiery flag, waving in the dark. There was no sign of George Iron Walker's Subaru, and so with any luck he wasn't following her. Her heart was palpitating, rapidly and painfully, and it took six or seven deep breaths before it started to slow down.

Oh, John. He must have known that their plan had hardly any chance of success. But it was obvious that even *he* hadn't realized how quick and elusive the Wendigo was, and how easily it could pull a human being wide open.

She didn't have any idea what she was going to do now. She carried on driving, more slowly now, but her mind was a kaleidoscope of fire, and trees, and running wolves, and George Iron Walker grinning at her, and the Wendigo, the spirit of the woods.

As she turned on to Route 169, heading back toward the Twin Cities, she heard a scraping, whirring sound. After a half-mile she pulled over and went around to the back of the SUV. The winch-cable was still extended, and it was dragging along the blacktop behind her. She went back and pressed the button to wind it back in again. Hanging from the cleat that Shooks had used to make a loop was something that looked like a man's pink-and-beige necktie. It was only when she tried to tug it free that she understood that it was a torn strip of John Shooks' bowels.

She bent over by the side of the highway and brought up a bitter tide of coffee and pancakes.

Sixteen

That night she went into the children's bedrooms, one after the other, to kiss them goodnight.

'Where did you go today?' Tasha asked her.

'Well . . . we went to see somebody who might know where William was taken, and how to get him back.'

'And *did* they know?'

'It's more complicated than that, sweetheart.'

'The Wendigo's not going to come after us, is it?'

Lily sat down on the side of her bed. 'Try not to worry. I know that everything's been really frightening. But I'm going to make sure that the Wendigo goes away and doesn't hurt anybody any more.'

'How?'

She smiled, and leaned forward, and kissed Tasha on the forehead. 'I'll think of a way.'

If only I could, she thought, as she closed the bedroom door.

When she went to Sammy's room he was already fast asleep. Since they had witnessed Agnes and Ned being killed, both children had been prescribed Ambien tablets, and they always knocked Sammy out within a few minutes of him swallowing them.

These nights, though, he never sprawled across the top of his comforter the way he used to: he bundled himself up tight, as if he didn't want to leave a single gap for the Wendigo to slide into.

Lily went slowly downstairs, crossed into the living room

and poured herself a glass of red wine. She had never felt so shattered and alone. So far, she had heard no local news bulletins about a forest fire out at Black Crow Valley, nor any reports of a man's body being found in the woods. But it couldn't be long before somebody missed John Shooks. He had scores of relatives, after all, both Native American and white, and it would soon come out that the last person to be seen with him was *her*.

She felt as if she were a Jonah – as if every person she touched was immediately cursed, and that she brought death and pain and disaster to everybody around her, especially Tasha and Sammy. Those were her own two children, upstairs in bed, both of them traumatized and terrified and only able to sleep because she had drugged them. And it was all her fault.

The long-case clock in the hallway struck ten. Almost as soon as the last chime had reverberated, the phone rang, making her jump.

'Lily?'

'Yes? Who is this?'

'Lily . . . this is George.' He sounded very calm, but in a way that was much more threatening than if he had shouted at her.

Lily didn't say anything. She didn't know what she *could* say.

'You still there, Lily? Fine mess you made of my SUV today. Fine mess you made altogether, you and John Shooks. Good thing for you those trees burned themselves out. The Minnesota Department of Natural Resources takes a pretty dim view of arsonists.'

'John Shooks is dead,' said Lily, her voice shaking with distress. 'That thing of yours ripped him to pieces in front of my eyes.'

'The Wendigo? The Wendigo isn't *my* thing, Lily. The Wendigo is *your* thing. You wanted it raised. Everything that's happened subsequent to that is down to you.'

Lily swallowed, and took a deep breath, and then she said, 'Is it any use begging you?'

'Begging me for what? More time? I'm sorry, Lily, but tomorrow is the last night of the Moon of the Snowblind, and that's a very significant date for the Mdewakanton. I have to take possession of that land before the Moon of the Red Grass Appearing.'

'I don't understand what you're talking about.'

'I didn't expect you to. But there are only two days in every year when the hunting god Haokah can appear in the mortal world – the first day of the Moon of the Falling Leaves, and the last day of the Moon of the Snowblind. These days are the beginning and the end of winter, after Haokah lays down his hunting spear, and before he picks it up again.

'Haokah appeared to Little Crow on the first day of the Moon of the Falling Leaves and told him that our lands would be lost, when he laid his hunting spear down, and we lost them. Tomorrow is the last day of the Moon of the Snowblind. If we get the land back on the day that Haokah picks up his hunting spear, the legend says that we shall never lose it again, for all time.'

'George! This is the twenty-first century! All of this is mumbo-jumbo! People have been killed!'

'*My* people were killed, back in the 1850s – not three or four, but hundreds of them! *My* people! My flesh and blood! They were deceived into giving up their own land and then they were starved and they were hung and they were shot! Just because it happened all those years ago, do you think we've forgotten, or forgiven?'

'George, please. I can't get the land. It's impossible.'

'Nothing is impossible, Lily. Not in this world.'

He hung up. Lily tried to call his number back, but the line was busy. In any case, what was the point? He wasn't going to listen to reason. He wasn't going to listen to begging. He wasn't going to listen to anything. Thomas

Bear Robe had been right: George Iron Walker had a dark side to him. An *old* side.

She dropped another two logs on the fire. She was exhausted, but she wasn't ready to go to bed yet. She hadn't asked the doctor for any sleeping pills for herself because she didn't want to fall into a deep sleep and leave Tasha and Sammy unprotected. Not that she had any illusions that she was capable of fighting off the Wendigo.

The phone rang again.

'George,' she said. 'Listen—'

'Lil? Didn't wake you, did I?'

It was Bennie. He sounded drunk, and there was Frank Sinatra singing in the background: '*Come fly with me – let's fly – let's fly away –*'

'Oh, Bennie, it's you. I thought you were somebody else. No, you didn't wake me. The truth is, I haven't slept much at all, in the past few days.'

'I'm a little inebriated, Lil. But I just wanted to apologize for the Mystery Lake thing. I was trying to impress you and I made a fool of myself. I'm sorry. I hope we can still be friends.'

'You caused me a whole lot of grief, Bennie – more than you know.'

'I didn't mean any harm, Lil. Honest I didn't.'

'OK, Bennie. What's done is done.'

'Maybe I can buy you lunch. How about that?'

'I don't think so. But thanks for the offer.'

Bennie was silent for a moment. She could almost hear him swaying.

'I think I'm going to hang up now, Bennie. Goodnight.'

'Do you know something?' said Bennie. 'I was looking through the files on Mystery Lake this afternoon . . . and there it was, the title to that little spit of land you wanted. Well, a copy of it. Kraussman had to buy it separately from the rest of the development, because it was Federal land.

Damn shame Kraussman got there first. If it had still been Federal land . . .'

'Yes,' said Lily. 'But he did, and he refuses to part with it, and there's nothing more that I can do about it.'

'He's an asshole.'

'I know, Bennie. Goodnight.'

'I always said that about Philip Kraussman. He's a prime-grade USDA-certified asshole.'

'*Goodnight*, Bennie.'

She finished her glass of wine and then decided that she would try to get some sleep. The house seemed unusually quiet tonight, although she could hear the oak tree scratching at the weatherboards. She was about to go upstairs, however, when she thought she heard the softest of hissing noises. She stopped and listened, one hand on the banister rail. Silence. Only the *tap-tap-tap* of the tree. But when she started to climb the stairs, she heard the hissing again.

It wasn't a loud hiss. Not like the air-brake hissing that the Wendigo had made when it attacked them on the way to the airport. It was a sliding, sibilant hissing, as if some-body were pouring very fine sand down the stairs.

She looked around. She could feel a shrinking sensation all the way down her back, and a tingling in the palms of her hands. There was nobody there, and no sand pouring down the stairs. But the hissing went on, and she had a sudden strong feeling that she wasn't alone.

She made a determined effort not to run up the stairs, though she found herself climbing them stiffly and quickly. She crossed the landing and went into her bedroom and closed the door, and locked it. She could see herself in the mirrored doors of her closet, and she was surprised how white her face was, and how fixedly she was staring at herself. She thought she looked like a madwoman.

She listened. The hissing had died away. Maybe she had imagined it. Maybe it had been nothing more than her own blood rushing through her ears.

She waited for over a minute. Then she sat on the bed and waited a few minutes longer. After a while she decided that even if she *hadn't* imagined it, whatever it was, it had gone.

Tiredly she stood up and tugged off her thick cream cable-knit sweater. Then she unbuttoned her black denim jeans and stepped out of them. She went through to her shower room, switched on the light and reached into the shower to start the water running. In this house, it always took an age for the hot water to reach the bathrooms, especially in the winter.

She took off her bra and her big warm brushed-cotton pants and put on her tartan bathrobe. She squinted at herself in the medicine cabinet over the washbasin. *God, Lily, you look tired.* Her hair had grown over an inch now, although it seemed to be much finer than it had been before she had shaved it all off, and it seemed to stick up more. What had Bennie called her? *An elf.*

She was just about to take off her robe and step into the shower when she thought she glimpsed a flash of light from her bedroom. It was so quick that she thought she might simply have blinked. But then it flashed again, and again, like a quick, quivering, will-o'-the-wisp.

She listened. She couldn't hear the hissing sound, but then the shower was clattering too loudly. Very slowly she reached up and opened the door of the medicine cabinet, so that its mirror was angled toward the mirrors on her closet.

She almost shouted in fright, but she clamped her hand over her mouth to stop herself. Clearly reflected in the medicine cabinet, she could see a tall figure standing in the corner of her bedroom, beside her bed. It was hard to see exactly what it was, because it constantly shifted and changed. In many ways it was like a man. It had a human face, although its features were long and angular, and its upper lip seemed to be cleft, although that could have been the shadow under its nose. It had glittering black eyes that rapidly darted from side to side, but it didn't seem to be focusing on anything in particular. It stood upright like a man, yet it had an arrangement of horns on its head that resembled antlers, and a deep, narrow chest that resembled a deer's chest rather than a man's.

Its image wavered and jumped, so that it looked to Lily like a weak TV signal, struggling to resolve itself into a recognizable picture. And – yes – she could hear the hissing sound now, like static – not much louder than before, but highly distinctive.

So this is how my life ends, she thought. *Torn apart by a mythical creature in my own house, and nobody will ever know what really happened to me.* She just prayed that the Wendigo wouldn't go for Tasha and Sammy too.

The Wendigo turned sideways and vanished from her medicine-cabinet mirror as if it wasn't there at all. But when she looked around, into her closet mirror, she could still see it. Its face appeared to be re-assembling itself, and its body went through one metamorphosis after another. As she watched it, she began in a curiously oblique way to understand what it actually was: it was everything that made up the spirit of the woods – the men, the animals, the insects, and the flickering light that came down through the branches. The Wendigo wasn't just *of* the woods, as Thomas Bear Robe had described it. The Wendigo *was* the woods.

It turned sideways again, and re-appeared in her medicine-cabinet mirror. It was staring directly at her, and she realized that it must have seen her. *Please let it be quick. Please don't let it hurt too much. Agnes was killed so fast she probably didn't know what hit her. Please let it be the same for me.*

But the Wendigo made no move toward her. Instead, it continued to stare at her, and the longer it stared at her, the more she felt an overwhelming sense of panic. The Greeks had invented the word 'panic', after Pan, the wood-god. Panic was the dread of lonely places, like forests – the feeling of being hopelessly lost.

Lily started to hyperventilate. She pressed her hand against her chest to try to control her breathing. She could feel that darkness closing in again – the darkness that came before a faint.

But the Wendigo turned away again and disappeared from her medicine-cabinet mirror. Lily looked quickly around at her closet mirror, but she was only just in time to see the Wendigo folding itself up like origami – except that it was made of thin rays of light rather than paper. It became nothing but a geometric pattern of light on the carpet, and then it slid beneath her door and vanished.

Immediately, Lily ran across her bedroom, opened the door and ran to Sammy and Tasha's rooms. They were both asleep, untouched and undisturbed.

She went back to her shower room and stood in front of the medicine cabinet for a long time, trying to read the expression on her own face. She felt an extraordinary mixture of shock and relief, but the beginnings of something else, too: a new understanding of what America must have been, before white men arrived; a new understanding of why George Iron Walker wanted that land at Mystery Lake so much. It was only a vaguely formed grasp of Native American feelings, and she couldn't find any sympathy for them, after everything that had happened in the past few days, but it moved her, and disturbed her. She felt as if the ground had moved beneath her feet.

After a while she took off her robe and stepped into the shower. She wondered if the Wendigo had come of its own volition, to warn her, or if George Iron Walker and Hazawin had sent it, as a threat.

There was one thing she had learned, though. With *two* mirrors, placed at angles to each other, the Wendigo remained visible even when it turned edgewise. With three, or four, it wouldn't be able to vanish at all.

She toweled herself, pulled on a warm pink nightdress and went to bed, though she couldn't sleep for hours. When she did, she dreamed that she had woken up, and that patterns of antlers were moving across her bedroom ceiling.

'*They're outside, Lil,*' said Bennie. '*They're outside, and they're coming for you. I just want to apologize.*'

When she woke up it was seven twenty a.m. She looked in on Tasha and Sammy before she went downstairs. Sammy was still asleep but Tasha was already tugging her jeans on.

'Sleep all right?' Lily asked her.

Tasha nodded. 'I didn't have any nightmares, anyhow.'

Lily went downstairs and filled the percolator with coffee. The morning sunlight was so cold and brittle that it leached all of the color out of the kitchen, like a 1950s photograph. She looked out into the back yard. The snow was beginning to thaw, and where the sun was shining on their upper branches, the trees were dripping.

There were paw-prints criss-crossing the yard in all directions. Stray dogs, probably, looking for scraps. She looked up at the kitchen clock and thought to herself: *Only eleven hours to go before sunset. How am I going to catch the Wendigo before then?*

She knew now that if she had enough mirrors, she could *see* it, whether it turned itself edgewise or not. But the mirrors had to be set up in exactly the right places, and how could she make sure that the Wendigo walked into her line of sight? Even if it did, what was she going to do then? How was she going to snare it with her tow-cable? Supposing the loop didn't catch around its ankles? The Wendigo would be on her before she knew it.

She kept playing the scenario over and over in her mind, trying to work out a way in which she could lure the Wendigo into the precise location where she could see it, and then catch it, and then drive off with it.

But – single-handed – she could see that there was no way. She just couldn't do it on her own.

Tasha came up behind her and put her arms around her waist. 'Mom . . . everything's going to be all right, isn't it?'

'Sure it is. You'll see. '

'Maybe you should call those FBI men to help you. Like, even if they don't believe you, at least they can make sure that nothing happens to us.'

'We'll be OK. The police are right outside, aren't they?'

'I guess. But the Wendigo . . . supposing it gets in here without them even seeing it?'

'Tasha – I promise you, we're going to be OK.'

She had never knowingly tried to deceive her children, not even when she was going through the worst of her divorce with Jeff; but this morning she simply couldn't find the words to tell Tasha how terrified she was. The minute hand on the kitchen clock kept moving on, minute by minute, and each time it moved she shuddered.

She poured herself a cup of coffee, although she felt much more like a double shot of Jack Daniel's. What the hell was she going to do? There was no point in locking the doors. There was no point in trying to run away. The future was coming for her, and there was no way to avoid it and no way to escape it.

She thought: *Condemned criminals must feel like this, when the day of their execution dawns.*

She watched Tasha eating her cereal, and it almost broke her heart. Tasha and Sammy relied on her so much, but she had allowed her own selfishness to jeopardize their lives. They would have been better off without her, spending the rest of their lives with Jeff, playing in the sunshine and forgetting all about her.

If only there was somebody she could turn to. Somebody strong. Somebody who could protect her. Maybe Tasha was right. Maybe those FBI agents *could* help her. Or one of them, at least.

Special Agent Kellogg arrived at the house shortly after eleven a.m. He looked pale and pinched, as if he had been awake all night, and the cold morning air had given him a hard, barking cough.

'What's up?' he asked her, doing a quick Ali shuffle on the doormat to get the snow off his shoes.

'Would you like some coffee?'

'Sure, but you didn't ask me here for a social visit, did you?'

'It was that obvious?'

'I've been a special agent for fifteen years, Lily. When you called me, I recognized that tone of voice right off.'

'What tone of voice?'

'It's a very particular tone of voice that suspects use when they've decided that they need to make a clean breast of things. Don't get me wrong. I'm not saying that that you're a suspect. But you do have something to tell me, don't you?'

She led him into the kitchen and took a blue china mug from the dresser. 'I need your help, Nathan.'

He stood in the doorway. He still hadn't taken off his long gray overcoat. 'OK,' he said.

'What I'm going to tell you now – you probably won't believe a word of it; but then again you might, because it makes sense of everything that's happened, even if it doesn't make sense in itself.'

Special Agent Kellogg waited and said nothing.

Lily said, 'I thought maybe I could deal with this myself, but I can't, and I'm scared out of my mind.' She started to pour coffee out of the percolator, but then her eyes filled up with tears and her hand started to shake and she had to put the percolator down on the table. *Stop*, she told herself. *Just stop it.*

Special Agent Kellogg came around and laid his hand on her shoulder. 'Think you'd better sit down, Lily, and tell me all about it.' He pulled out a chair for her and she sat down.

'I'm so stupid. I'm so damned stupid. And crying's not going to make things any better.'

'Come on, Lily. Get it off your chest. What's been going on?'

She told him, haltingly, about the Wendigo. She told him everything. He sat next to her, holding one of her hands, but he didn't nod and he didn't interrupt and he didn't ask her any questions until she had finished.

'That's it,' she said. 'I have about ten hours left to find the land title, or else find a way to destroy the Wendigo. One or the other. And I don't think I can do either.'

Special Agent Kellogg said, 'That was you, then, last night, that forest fire out at Black Crow Valley? You and John Shooks?'

'I feel terrible. I feel like I killed him myself.'

'Well, yes. But I wouldn't shed too many tears for good old John Shooks. In aggregate, I would say that more people in the Twin Cities wanted Shooks dead than wanted him alive.'

'Do you believe me?' asked Lily.

'What – about the Wendigo? Like you said, it makes sense of everything that's happened even if *it* doesn't make any sense. I don't know. I don't believe in spirits and ghosts, but then again, what else could possibly rip people to pieces and fly through the air with their guts trailing behind them? And what else could squash an SUV like a Coke can, right in the middle of the highway?'

'I feel so guilty,' said Lily. 'If it hadn't been for me, none of those people would have died. And I still don't know what's happened to poor little William.'

Special Agent Kellogg finished the last cold dregs of his coffee. Then he leaned back in his chair and said, 'Let's suppose, for the sake of argument, that I *do* believe you.'

'It's all true, Nathan. I swear it. Unless I'm going stark staring mad and I've been hallucinating.'

'Well – I saw the bodies for myself, Lily. I saw your sister's SUV. Those weren't hallucinations. Those were real. Now – maybe there's an alternative explanation as to how those people were killed, and how that vehicle was crushed, but right now we don't have one. So until somebody can prove different, I'm prepared to work on the assumption that there really *is* a Wendigo.'

Lily was so relieved that she didn't know what to say to him.

Special Agent Kellogg squeezed her arm. 'I'll help you. OK?'

'Thank you. Really, Nathan, you don't know what this means to me.'

'Hey, I've always tried to keep an open mind. Dick Rylance says I should have been assigned to the *X-Files*. I warn you, though: I'll have to fly solo on this one. Dick's a skeptic, to say the least. He won't even believe that a fire's hot until he's shoved his hand in it to make sure, so I don't think he'd be too willing to go looking for Native American forest spirits – not until he's been shown some concrete evidence.

'As for my division chief – he'd send me straight off for a psych-evaluation.' He paused, and then he added, 'Maybe he'd be doing the right thing, too. Maybe you and I, we're both nuts.'

'Nathan, that thing was in my bedroom last night and it was real.'

'OK, don't get upset. Like I say, I'm prepared to accept for the time being that you're telling me the truth. What we have to do as a matter of urgency is devise a plan for getting you out of this bind – whether we persuade George Iron Walker to relinquish his claim to that piece of land, or we zap the Wendigo, or whether we think up some other way.'

'Bennie told me that he had a copy of the land-title certificate. Apparently the land used to belong to the Federal government. Maybe we could persuade somebody in the government to put a block on planning approval, so that Philip Kraussman wouldn't want it any more.'

'I don't know . . . It could work, but you've only got ten hours, right? And you know how long it takes to get a response out of any government department. Months, usually.'

'Then we'll have to destroy the Wendigo, won't we?'

'It looks like it. But if we're going to do that, we need to *find* it first – or lure it out of hiding, the way that John Shooks lured it out. And we need a really effective way of catching it when we do. That wasn't a bad idea, laying a loop of towing-cable under the snow, but from what you've told me, the Wendigo is super-quick. If we don't manage to lasso it the first time, you and me are going to be Wendigo chow.'

'Can you think of any other ways of catching it?'

Special Agent Kellogg gave another cough, and nodded. 'Back at division we have hand-held catching nets. They use compressed gas to shoot out a net which entraps a suspect completely.'

'A *net*? Is that going to be strong enough?'

'I should think so. They're made of high-molecule fiber. You can't even cut your way out of them with a knife.'

He checked his watch, even though the kitchen clock was right in front of him. 'Listen – I'll go back to Washington Avenue and pick a couple up. I'll requisition some high-powered ordnance too.'

'So what can I do?'

'You stay here and try to think of a way to bring the Wendigo out of the woods, so that we can snag it.' He stood up, and coughed again.

Lily said, 'You don't know how much I appreciate this. I was so scared that you weren't going to believe me.'

'It's a riff on the old Sherlock Holmes thing, isn't it? "When you've eliminated the impossible, whatever remains must be the truth – even if that's damn near impossible, too."'

Lily almost managed a smile. She was still deeply frightened, but at least she felt that she wasn't alone any more.

Seventeen

A round twelve thirty p.m. she made Tasha and Sammy some peanut-butter-and-jelly sandwiches, and poured them two glasses of milk. Tasha was upstairs reading, but Sammy was out in the front of the house, sliding on the snowmobile trail with his friend Josh from across the street.

Except that, when Lily opened the front door, she couldn't see Sammy or Josh anywhere. She shielded her eyes against the glare from the ice and looked up the street, but, apart from old Mr Harkins clearing his driveway, it was deserted.

She tippy-toed in her slippers as far as the sidewalk, so that she could see the other way. And it was then that she felt the salty taste of shock in her mouth.

Sammy was standing about twenty-five yards away, in his bright-blue windbreaker and his purple woolly hat. He was talking to a tall man in a black-leather jacket – a man with dark sunglasses and silver chains and feathers around his neck: George Iron Walker.

She stalked up to them. 'What the hell are *you* doing here?' she demanded.

'I'm talking to your boy,' said George Iron Walker. 'Where's the harm in that?'

'Sammy – go indoors,' said Lily.

'But, Mom—'

'I said go indoors, this instant!'

Sammy reluctantly walked back to the house, and went inside.

'I was only passing the time of day, Lily,' said George

Iron Walker, taking off his sunglasses. His eyes were like stones.

'You stay away from my children. Haven't you caused my family enough grief already?'

'I'm sorry, Lily – but, like I said before: you were the one who set these events in motion.'

'So what are you doing here?'

'I came to pay you a visit, to see how things were progressing. Do you have the land title yet? No? Are you likely to lay your hands on it before sundown?'

'Look,' Lily began. But then she suddenly thought: *The land title. Bennie has a copy of it, in his office.* And she thought something else, too: if the Mdewakanton had been tricked out of their land once, maybe they could be tricked out of it again. Long enough to buy her a few moments of vaulable time, anyhow.

'Yes,' she said. 'Yes, I'll have it.'

'You don't sound too sure of that.'

'Don't you worry. I'm going to collect it this afternoon.'

George Iron Walker looked impressed. 'That's wonderful. I don't know how you managed it, but I'm very pleased. I didn't want this business to end badly, you know. I never did.'

'It's already ended badly. Will I get little William back?'

'I promise you. And when I make a promise, Lily, I keep it.'

'Is he safe?'

'Oh, he's safe. Where he is, he's doing nothing but dreaming.'

'You're a bastard, George.'

'No, Lily, I'm not. I'm only trying to make things right.'

'Turning back the clock two hundred years: that doesn't make things right. Killing innocent people: that doesn't make things right.'

'Tell that to the thirty-eight Mdewakanton men who were hanged at Mankato. Tell that to the fifty-five women and children who were shot down like dogs at Blood Hill.'

It was then that she glimpsed a silvery flicker of light on the opposite side of the street. If she hadn't known about the Wendigo, she would have thought it was nothing more than a chance reflection from a passing automobile. But she saw the snow flurry up, as if a sudden wind had caught it, and she heard the faintest hissing sound.

'It's here, isn't it?' she said.

George Iron Walker turned to look across the street, and then he said, 'Yes. It just wants to make sure that everything's settled the way it should be.'

'Where do you want me to meet you?' Lily asked him.

'Mystery Lake – where else? Any time before sundown. I'll be there.'

'And the Wendigo?'

'Like I said, it just wants to make sure that everything's settled the way it should be.'

Lily turned her back on him and walked back to the house without saying anything more. Her heart was thumping, but she was beginning to work out the rudiments of a plan. The most important thing she had learned from George Iron Walker was that the Wendigo was going to be there, at Mystery Lake, when she was supposed to hand over the land title. The spit of land was very narrow – only a few yards wide – which meant that she and Nathan Kellogg would have a fair chance of setting up their mirrors in such a way that they would catch the Wendigo's image, no matter if it turned edgewise or not.

Everything was going to depend on timing, and speed, and more luck than it took to win the lottery six weeks running. But at least she didn't feel so helpless any more.

Back in the kitchen, Tasha and Sammy were eating their sandwiches.

'Who was that man?' asked Sammy. 'He's nice.'

'He's not nice at all. He's the man who raised up the Wendigo for me. He's the man who wants that piece of land.'

'He was nice to *me*. He asked me if I knew who used to live here, before they built all these houses.'

'Oh, yes? And who did live here?'

'The Beaver People. He said it was a long, long time ago, when beavers could talk and people could understand them. They all lived together and everybody was happy.'

'It's just a story, Sammy.'

'How do you know?'

Lily hesitated. Then she said, 'As a matter of fact, I *don't* know. Maybe he's right. Maybe beavers *could* talk. Maybe there really *was* a time when everybody was happy.'

Bennie swung around in his revolving chair and said, 'Lil! This is a surprise!'

'I was passing – thought I'd call in to see you.'

'You're looking good. In fact you're looking terrific. Your hair's growing, huh?'

Lily ran her hand through the soft blonde down on top of her head. 'Nowhere near fast enough. I can't wait for it to grow long enough to curl it.'

'How about a coffee, or a drink, maybe? I was going to lunch in about ten minutes; do you want to join me?'

'Tempting, but I don't really have the time. I wanted to talk to you about that Mystery Lake thing, that's all.'

'Lil – you don't know how sorry I am about that. I didn't think you would ever speak to me again.'

Lily sat down on the opposite side of his desk. 'Don't be silly, Bennie. We're friends, aren't we? We'll always be friends.'

'A little more than friends, I like to hope. You can't blame a fellow for wishful thinking, can you?'

'Of course not. That little spit of land – you said that used to belong to the Federal government.'

'That's right. It was kind of complicated. Something to do with the Cession Treaty of 1863 . . . For some reason the land on the north-west side of Mystery Lake stayed in Federal ownership, and nobody realized it until Kraussman

Developments came to buy it up. Are you sure you don't have time for lunch? I was going to Ping's for Szechuan.'

'I'm really sorry, Bennie. I have so much to do. But do you think I could see that land title? I think it might be worth mentioning in our promotional material.'

Bennie stood up and went across to his filing cabinet. 'You know that we really miss you here at Capitol, don't you, Lil? As soon as you've managed to put all of your family tragedies behind you . . . you're more than welcome to come back.'

'That's good of you, Bennie.'

'I didn't really want to lay you off – you know that. But with all that negative feedback I was getting from the clients, what could I do? People are so lacking in human understanding, don't you think?'

'Oh, people are unbelievably callous.'

He lifted out a folder marked 'Mystery Lake Legalistics', opened it, and took out a copy of the land title. 'There . . . there's nothing very special about it. It's just a plain old land-title certificate.'

'Still, I'd like to include some mention of it. I think people like to know the history of the property they've bought. OK if I make a copy?'

'Sure.' He leaned over and clicked his intercom. 'Janice – do you want to come in here and make me a copy for Mrs Blake? Thanks.'

While his secretary was copying the land title, Bennie came and sat on his desk, very close to Lily. 'How are you really, Lil? You're as beautiful as ever, but I have to say that you're looking a little *strained*.'

'Well – as you can imagine, things haven't been very easy.'

'Why don't you and me start over? I'd love to take you out to dinner. Then maybe we could go to the Fine Line Café for some folk music. I'm really into folk music. Bet you didn't know that.'

'No, Bennie. Can't say that I did.'

He bent forward and awkwardly kissed her on the forehead. 'You do things to me, Mrs Blake,' he whispered, hoarsely, and managed to spit on her left cheek as he did so.

She returned home just before two p.m., and less than five minutes later Special Agent Kellogg arrived, driving a black Jeep with dark-tinted windows and no license plate.

He came into the house carrying what looked like a very large black flashlight.

'Is that it?' asked Lily.

'This is it. Made by GaGa Security of Korea, believe it or not. You hold it up like this, twist the safety ring in the middle, then press the butt. The net comes flying out, spread by weights. I've used it twice, and both times it was amazing. Stopped one suspect who was six-five and three hundred pounds and going totally berserk.'

Lily held up a manila envelope. 'And this is a copy of the land title, courtesy of Bennie Burgenheim at Capitol Realty. Creep.'

Lily had asked her friend Ettie Lindborg to take care of Tasha and Sammy for the rest of the day, which Tasha and Sammy didn't mind at all, because the Lindborgs owned two ponies and five dogs.

She drove them to the Lindborg house, which was a sprawling ranch-style property overlooking the lake, with white-painted stables and a barn.

'What time are you going to pick us up?' asked Tasha.

'I'm not sure. Not too late, I promise.'

Sammy said, 'Make sure it's after supper. Mr and Mrs Lindborg always have fried chicken for supper and it's scrumptious.'

'I don't think they *always* have fried chicken for supper. But – OK, then. After supper. Just don't blame me if they have tuna bake.'

She held them close – Sammy first, and then Tasha –

and she breathed in the smell of them. She might never see them again, and the thought of that was almost more than she could bear.

They walked up the curving driveway toward the house, and Ettie opened the front door and waved to her.

''Bye, Mommy!' called Sammy. 'See you later!'

Tasha turned around, too, but didn't say anything. Tasha knew that this was no ordinary afternoon. Lily blew her a kiss, and then climbed back into her SUV with tears in her eyes.

Lily and Special Agent Kellogg spent the rest of the day preparing themselves. Lily scanned the land title on her computer, and altered the name on it from 'Kraussman Developments, Inc.', to 'George Iron Walker', as well as changing the dates. The finished title wouldn't have deceived a lawyer, but that wasn't what she was trying to do. She was simply trying to buy them two or three minutes of time, so that they could trap the Wendigo.

Special Agent Kellogg took down the large mirror from the hallway and stowed it in the back of Lily's Rainier. He fastened two wires to the eyelets on either side of the frame, so that when she opened the Rainier's rear door, the mirror would be hoisted up into a vertical position. He went upstairs to her bedroom and took her cheval-mirror off its stand, wedging it into the back of his Jeep.

He tested the mirrors by parking his Jeep at right-angles to Lily's Rainier. Lily came out to watch.

'Perfect,' he said, peering at himself in both mirrors. 'Whichever way the Wendigo turns, we'll still be able to see it. Then – *pow*! – I'll net it, and – *varoom*! – you'll drive off with it.'

Lily took hold of his arm. 'Do you think this is crazy?' she asked him.

'Of course it's crazy. But how else do you deal with a spirit that's half in one world and half in another?'

226

'You don't have to do this, Nathan. I don't want to be responsible for anything happening to you.'

'Lily,' said Special Agent Kellogg, looking at her with his different-colored eyes, 'I've been shot at; I've been stabbed; I've been beaten half to death with a scaffolding-pole. This kind of thing – it's what I've been trained for. It's what I do.'

A large grayish-green cloud began to slide slowly over the sun, like glaucoma, and the afternoon grew gloomy and chill. Special Agent Kellogg said, 'Four o'clock. What time do you want to go to Mystery Lake?'

'Soon. It takes at least forty minutes to get there.'

'OK. Guess this is it, then.'

'Nathan . . .'

'No need to say anything, Lily. Not until it's all over.'

They drove due westward on the Olson Memorial Highway, Lily in front and Special Agent Kellogg close behind. The sky became darker and darker, and a fine snowy rain began to fall. By the time they reached the turn-off for Mystery Lake, the rain was so heavy that Lily could hardly make out the sign.

The road led uphill, past a series of smaller lakes, and into the forest. It had been a logger's road originally, and it ran almost completely straight for over seven miles, with dense pines on either side. In some places the trees over-shadowed the road so much that the asphalt was still dry.

Lily's cell phone warbled. 'You'll be able to build up a fair lick of speed along here,' said Special Agent Kellogg.

Lily was so nervous that she had to clear her throat before she spoke. 'Let's hope so.'

At last the road rose higher, and they were clear of the trees. Below them, and off to their left, lay the steel-gray water of Mystery Lake. The snow-filled rain was blowing diagonally across it, ruffling the surface, and small breakers were nagging at the rocks.

Lily could see the natural inlet where the marina was

going to be built – and, on the far side of it, the narrow hook of land where Haokah had appeared to Little Crow. George Iron Walker's Subaru Forester was parked on the very end of the spit, with its amber marker lights on. Lily followed the road around the inlet, and then turned around and backed up her SUV on to the spit, so that it was facing inland. Special Agent Kellogg turned around, too, so that his Jeep was parked at right-angles to her.

'That's it,' said Special Agent Kellogg, on his cell phone. 'Perfect positioning. Don't forget to leave your engine running.'

Lily climbed down from the driver's seat, but left the door open so that the 'headlights-on' reminder kept up a monotonous chiming. She raised the hood of her dark-blue duffel-coat and buttoned it up to the neck. Special Agent Kellogg got out of his vehicle, too, and gave her a thumb's-up signal.

At the far end of the spit George Iron Walker appeared from one side of the Subaru, and Hazawin from the other. George Iron Walker was wearing a black ankle-length oilskin coat, which flapped noisily in the wind. Hazawin was dressed in her usual embroidered sheepskin.

Lily walked four or five paces toward them, and then stopped. George Iron Walker waited for a few moments, and then approached her, with Hazawin following him closely.

'Who is this man?' he asked her, pointing toward Special Agent Kellogg.

'A friend, that's all. I didn't want to come out here all on my own.'

'Very well. I hope he realizes what an historic moment this is.'

As George Iron Walker spoke, lightning flickered on the far side of the lake, and there was a low grumble of thunder.

He looked up. 'Portentous weather for portentous times. You do have the land title?'

'Yes.'

He held out his hand, but Lily said, 'William first. I'm not giving you anything until I know that he's safe.'

'You don't trust me? I gave you my word, didn't I? I gave you my solemn promise as a Mdewakanton.'

'William first. Then you get the title.'

George Iron Walker turned to Hazawin. 'All right. Let's have the child back.'

Hazawin reached into her bag and took out her two human thighbones. She lifted them up, one in each hand, and tilted her head back. Lightning crackled again, much nearer this time, and a drum-roll of thunder followed almost at once.

Hazawin called out in a monotonous, sing-song voice, 'Wendigo, I ask you to bring us the child that you have hidden. Honor is satisfied. The promise has been kept.'

She tapped the bones together in a series of complicated staccatos. 'Wendigo – fold back the tepee of time and space. Bring us the child that you took to the other side. Wake him, lift him out of his dream, and bring him to us.'

For nearly half a minute there was no response. But gradually Lily became aware of a high-pitched hissing. Then she saw a nervous shuddering of silvery light close to Hazawin's right shoulder. First of all it formed diamond patterns, which danced and jumped and lit up the thickly falling snowflakes. But as the hissing grew louder, she gradually began to distinguish the outline of the Wendigo, with its long distorted face and its gargoyle-like shoulders. She stepped back – first one pace, then another, and another.

'You don't have to be afraid, Lily,' said George Iron Walker, raising his hand. 'You've settled your account. The Wendigo won't hurt you now.'

For a split second she saw the Wendigo clearly and brightly, face-on. It had a human head, but highly distorted, with a wide jaw and a tapered forehead, as if she was lying on the ground and it was staring down at her. When she looked at it, she felt a sudden surge of dread in its purest form. She felt all the wildness and desolation of the north woods, where animals spoke and trails disappeared and nothing was ever what it appeared to be. She felt the terror of being human, in a world teeming with spirits and illusions.

'Wendigo,' said Hazawin, rapping her bones yet again. 'Bring us the child, Wendigo. Honor is satisfied. The deal has been done.'

The Wendigo turned sideways, and instantly vanished. Lily couldn't see anything where it had been standing except the lake and the snow. Lightning flickered yet again, and this time the thunder burst right over their heads – so loud that Lily instinctively ducked.

'Wendigo!' Hazawin repeated. '*Wendigo!*'

The Wendigo turned back to face them again, and this time, to Lily's astonishment, it was holding little William in its arms, as if it had simply brought him in from another room. William was still dressed in the same corduroy romper suit that he had been wearing when Lily had been struggling to release him from his car seat. He looked very pale. His eyes were closed, and his arms and legs were dangling limply.

'William!' said Lily. 'You *bastard*, George, what have you done to him?'

But George Iron Walker said, 'Nothing at all, Lily. He's been asleep, that's all.' He went across and lifted William out of the Wendigo's shimmering arms, and as he did so, William opened his eyes and looked around him, and kicked his legs.

'Here,' said George Iron Walker, bringing him over.

'My God,' said Lily. She took William and held him up in front of her. William frowned at her but he didn't cry. He was still too sleepy.

'Is he OK?' called out Special Agent Kellogg.

'He's fine. He seems to be fine. Let me just put him in the truck.'

She carried William back to her Rainier, opened the door

and sat him on the back seat. He promptly lay down sideways and put his thumb in his mouth. He still didn't cry, though Lily thought that he would have done if he had known what had happened to his daddy and mommy.

'Now – please – the title,' said George Iron Walker, holding out his hand.

Lily took the manila envelope out of her coat and handed it to him. As she did so, she glanced quickly to his right, where she had last seen the Wendigo. It was standing edgewise now, but she could still see a faint ripple of light. She glanced back at Special Agent Kellogg, too, and tilted her head to indicate that the Wendigo was still there, and that she knew roughly where it was. Special Agent Kellogg gave her an almost imperceptible nod.

George Iron Walker opened the envelope and drew out the land title. He looked at it briefly and then said, 'Yes . . . this is the right title. Is the transfer all legal?'

'Completely. This piece of land belongs to you now. I hope it brings you much joy.'

'There's no need to be bitter, Lily. It doesn't suit you.'

'You expect me to be happy? Anyhow – we're going now. Let's hope we never have to meet again.'

While they were talking, Hazawin had taken a small iron bowl out of her bag and set it down on the rocks. Now she produced a leather pouch fastened with a drawstring, which she opened up – tipping the contents into the bowl. They looked to Lily like small lumps of dark-green wax.

'You can stay and watch if you want to,' said George Iron Walker.

'Stay and watch what?'

George Iron Walker held up the land title, so that it fluttered in the wind. 'Don't you understand? I needed this title by tonight so that I could call Haokah. I couldn't have summoned him here if the land hadn't been given back to the Mdewakanton.'

'I don't understand. You're going to summon Haokah?'

'We're going to bring him back from his exile. No god can pass from the world of gods into the world of men unless the place where he passes through is owned by those who believe in him. When white men came here, they took possession of so much land that scores of our gods were sealed away from us for ever. Haokah was one of them, even though Haokah is so powerful. But you, Lily – you have made it possible for him to return.'

After four or five attempts, Hazawin had set fire to the dark-green lumps of wax in the bowl. They gave off thick, pungent smoke that smelled like pine. She stood up, taking out her bones again, and rapping them briskly together.

'Haokah, god of blood, god of the hunt, hear us calling you!'

Special Agent Kellogg stepped forward. 'Who's Haokah?' he asked George Iron Walker.

'As Hazawin has said, he is the god of the hunt, the god of pursuit, and the god of righteous slaughter. He is the god of opposites. He feels cold in summer and warm in the winter. Mdewakanton braves used to plunge their fists into boiling water so that they could feel how cold it was, the way that Haokah felt it.'

'And what exactly do you hope to achieve by calling on him?'

'I thought that would have been obvious, my friend.'

'Well, maybe I'm slow on the uptake, but it's not so obvious to me.'

George Iron Walker's face seemed to be transfigured. He was still handsome, but there was something feral about his eyes and his nostrils flared as if he could smell blood.

'We are calling on Haokah to revenge all of those Mdewakanton who were killed or starved by the white men – every one of them: every warrior, every hunter, every woman, every child. Tonight will be the night of the greatest reckoning in Sioux history. Haokah will sweep through your cities and there is nothing that you can do to stop him. It will be like a terrible wind, which smashes down your buildings and uproots your roads and breaks hundreds of your people into pieces.'

Special Agent Kellogg turned to Lily. 'Is this guy nuts?' Lily shook her head. 'I wish he was. But I don't think so. My God, you've seen the Wendigo for yourself.'

Hazawin rattled her bones again, and began to circle the iron bowl. 'Haokah, god of blood, god of the hunt, we have opened the way for you! Haokah, O great one, hear us calling you!'

'You really think this is serious?' asked Special Agent Kellogg.

There was another crackle of lightning, and thunder bellowed behind the trees. But almost immediately the wind began to die down and the snowy rain began to thin out. Lily looked around. The trees had stopped thrashing so wildly and the surface of the lake was no longer broken with spray. She felt as if Mystery Lake were quietening itself down, in anticipation of some momentous arrival.

'Haokah! Haokah! Hear us, Haokah! Appear to us now and give us the revenge we have been waiting for!'

Lily said, 'Nathan – I think we need to get out of here. Really.'

But she had taken only two steps back toward her SUV when the ground beneath their feet gave a huge shudder, as if it had been struck from underneath by a massive hammer. This was followed by another shudder, and another. Small rocks jumped up into the air, and larger rocks cracked in half with a noise like rifle-fire.

'Haokah!' screamed Hazawin, whirling around and around. 'Haokah! He who weeps when he is happy and laughs when he is sad! He who feels hot in winter and cold in the summer sun! He who boils ice-water and freezes steam! Haokah! Hear us!'

There were three more devastating shudders. The first one threw Lily off balance, and she was just picking herself up when there was another, and another. She stayed where she was, on her hands and knees, waiting for a fourth. But a fourth never came.

'*Haokah! Hear us, Haokah!*' Hazawin shrieked out. But George Iron Walker grabbed hold of her sleeve.

'Stop!' he shouted. 'It's futile! Haokah cannot get through! He beats on the door between the worlds but he cannot get through!'

He lifted up the land title in his fist. 'Lily! You told me that this was legal! You said that this land belonged to me! But if Haokah cannot get through, you were lying to me!'

Hazawin wrenched her sleeve free. She stared blindly at Lily and Special Agent Kellogg and her face was distorted with fury. '*Now it's too late!*' she screamed. '*This moon will pass and Haokah will still be trapped!*'

She started to climb over the rocks toward them. She was so quick and agile that it was hard to believe that she couldn't see. She held out her bones in front of her and knocked them together again and again.

'You will die for this! You will be my sacrifice to Haokah! The Wendigo will tear you to pieces and devour your body and your spirit will go to Haokah and serve him for ever!'

Close beside her, Lily saw a brief flicker of light.

'Nathan!' she warned him.

Special Agent Kellogg reached inside his coat and hauled out a massive Desert Eagle .50-caliber automatic. 'Hold it!' he ordered. 'I have a very large gun here, lady, and it's pointing directly at your head.'

'You think that a *gun* can stop the Wendigo?' said Hazawin, and spat on to the rocks in contempt. 'Even if it could, how can you shoot something which you cannot see?'

George Iron Walker started to approach them too. 'Lily,' he said, shaking his head, 'you don't know what you've done.'

'Oh I do, George, and believe me, I feel as guilty as all

hell. But that doesn't mean that you're not going to be punished for what *you've* done.'

'I liked you, Lily. I liked you from the very first day that we met. But now I have to watch you being torn apart. You – and your friend here – and your children. The Wendigo will hunt down your entire family and it will eat them all.'

'Wendigo!' called out Hazawin. 'Wen-*dee*-go!' She came nearer and nearer, clattering her bones, and her purple eyes staring at nothing at all. Lily backed toward her Rainier, and Special Agent Kellogg backed toward his Jeep.

Hazawin threw her head back and let out a long ululation that made Lily's skin prickle. Then she cried, 'Wendigo, you can take these people! You can drag them up into the sky and feed off their flesh! The promise has been broken, and they must pay for their trickery!'

Lily could hear the Wendigo softly hissing but she couldn't see it. Now and again she thought she glimpsed a dancing pattern of light, but when she looked again it had vanished. She started to breathe faster and faster, which made her feel light-headed and giddy. She knew that the Wendigo must be very close now, but she was terrified that when the moment came for her to act, her arms and legs simply wouldn't obey her.

The day went completely still. Except for the hissing of the Wendigo there was no sound at all. No wind blowing, no lake rippling. A crow flew over them, but it flew silently, not even a fluttering of wing feathers.

'*Wendigo! Take them!*' Hazawin screamed, in a voice so high that it sounded more like an animal howling than a woman.

'Lily!' shouted Special Agent Kellogg. '*Now!*'

Eighteen

L ily released the catch and the Rainier's rear door sprang upward, lifting the mirror upright on its wires. Special Agent Kellogg opened up his Jeep, too, revealing the mirror that he had wedged into the luggage space at the back. Both mirrors showed all four of them on the lake shore, like characters seen through two different windows.

In *her* mirror Lily could see Hazawin screaming at her, and George Iron Walker a little way behind her in his long black oilskin, and the lake. But when she looked at the double reflection in Special Agent Kellogg's mirror, she could clearly see the Wendigo – a stretched-out creature made of restless lights and complicated shadows, with a rack of upcurving antlers and a narrow, insect-like skull. It was already raising its arms to seize her, and its glistening white lips were peeling away from its teeth in anticipation of biting into her head.

Lily jerked backward, jarring her hip against the side of her SUV. *It's all gone wrong. I'm going to be torn to pieces, and die.* Her dread was so intense that all she could do was make a hopeless barking sound, like a clubbed seal.

She felt something like a huge serrated lobster claw tear into the shoulder of her coat, and another claw seize her left arm just above the elbow. At that moment, though, she heard Special Agent Kellogg yell out, '*Lily!*' and a sharp, pressurized crack.

A fine mesh net billowed in the air above her, and the next thing she knew the net was full of lights and antlers and pincers, struggling wildly on the ground in front of her. It

236

was the Wendigo, completely entangled. It hissed so loudly that Lily couldn't even hear Kellogg shouting at her, but she knew what she had to do. She limped to the open door of her Rainier and climbed into the driver's seat.

Special Agent Kellogg ran over to the back of her vehicle. He looped the strings of the net around the tow-hook, using its heavy black handle like a tourniquet to pull them tight. As he did so, the Wendigo was hissing and screaming and thrashing furiously from side to side. Parts of it appeared and disappeared as it twisted around in the net, and every few seconds its face changed, from human to animal to insect, as if it were trying every possible manifestation in its fight to get free.

Hazawin and George Iron Walker were already hurrying toward them, but in her rear-view mirror Lily saw Special Agent Kellogg lift his Desert Eagle. George Iron Walker stopped, and held on to the strap of Hazawin's shoulder-bag to stop her too. Kellogg banged the back of Lily's SUV with his fist and Lily slammed her foot on the gas-pedal. The Rainier took off in a shower of dirt and stones, dragging the hissing, battling Wendigo behind it.

Lily drove as fast as she could back up the hill toward the logging road. For a two-dimensional creature made of light and shadows the Wendigo felt impossibly heavy. The SUV's transmission whined in protest as Lily neared the crest of the hill, and it was all she could do to keep her speed up to thirty-five m.p.h. In her mirrors she could see the net slewing wildly from side to side, and now and then she saw a claw emerge from the mesh as the Wendigo tried to tear its way free.

In the back seat little William suddenly started to cry. 'I want my mommy! I want my mommy!'

'William – we're going to see mommy now! But sit down, darling, please! Just sit down and I'll take you home as fast as I can!'

But William continued to cry, louder and more desperately. 'I want my *mommy*! I want my *mommy*!'

237

Lily had reached the logging road now, and she jammed her foot right down to the floor. She had seven miles of dead straight driving ahead of her, and she prayed that it would be enough to burn up the Wendigo. The Rainier's speedometer needle gradually wavered up through forty – fifty – sixty – until she managed to get it up to seventy-five.

After only a mile, though, she was jolted so hard that she nearly hit the windshield, and the SUV slowed down to fifty-five. She looked in her mirror and saw that the net appeared to be much closer to the rear of the vehicle than it had been before. The Wendigo must have managed to get a grip on the lines that fastened the net to the tow-hook, and it was gradually pulling itself nearer and nearer.

Oh Jesus, she thought. *What if it pulls itself right up to the rear of the SUV, so that it can untie the net, and get itself out?*

There was another jolt, even harder this time, and the Rainier swerved from one side of the road to the other, so that pine branches rattled against the windows. William was sobbing so hysterically now that he was almost choking, but there was nothing that Lily could do to help him.

Two miles . . . three miles. The Wendigo pulled at the SUV again and again, and Lily had to struggle to keep it on the road. The pine trees seemed to be crowding her on both sides, as if they were deliberately trying to catch hold of her bumper-grille and snatch at her side-mirrors and slow her down. Maybe they were. After all, the Wendigo was the spirit of the forest. The Wendigo *was* the forest.

Four miles. Four and a half miles. In spite of the Wendigo's constant jolting, and the branches flailing and clattering against the SUV's sides, she was managing to keep her speed between fifty-five and sixty, and when she looked in her mirror again she thought she saw smoke. Just a brief blurt of it to start with, but as she passed the fifth mile, it started to pour out more and more thickly – brown smoke, tinged red from her tail-lights.

'Come on, you bastard,' she whispered to herself. *'Burn!'*

She sped through the forest, with the Wendigo tumbling behind her in its net, a kaleidoscope of lights, with smoke billowing out of it. Even before she reached the sixth mile she saw flames. The Wendigo was ablaze now, leaving a long trail of fire behind it, and setting alight the branches of the trees on either side of the road.

But, even though it was burning, the Wendigo kept on jolting her. It couldn't be dead yet. And inch by inch it still seemed to be hauling itself closer to the back of her SUV. Almost all she could see in the rear window now was fire, and in the fire she could briefly see antlers and claws – all burning, but still inching toward her.

She didn't know what to do, except to keep going as fast as she could. John Shooks had told her that Wendigos eventually burned into nothing but ash, but how long did that take?

She was approaching the end of the logging road now. Only a half-mile to go before she hit the main highway. She kept her foot down, but she could feel the Wendigo dragging itself right up to her back bumper.

She glanced around, to make sure that William wasn't choking. As she did so, she became aware that something was running alongside her. At first she thought it was just a shadow, or the reflection of her sleeve in the window. But when she looked again, she realized that it was an animal – a great brindled wolf – and it was running so fast that it was keeping up with her.

She turned to the other window. Another wolf was running on the right-hand side of her, a lean gray wolf with eyes that were shining yellow. And in the darkness of the pine trees more wolves were running, most of them on all fours, but some of them upright.

She slewed the Rainier to the left and then to the right. The brindled wolf leapt up at her. She saw its eyes blazing yellow and its teeth bared, and its claws scrabbled against her door. The gray wolf leapt up too, on the other side, and its body thumped against the paintwork.

Now the whole vehicle shook and she heard squeaking, grating noises. The Wendigo had reached the rear bumper and was pulling itself up on to the tailgate. It was hissing like a steam boiler that was just about to explode, and she could hear the flames roaring, too, as they were fanned by the wind.

The Wendigo might be burning, but if it could still crush this SUV, the way that it had crushed Agnes and Ned's Explorer; then she and little William would not only be mangled but incinerated too. Lily began to hyperventilate again – each breath whining as if she were suffering an asthma attack.

The Rainier shook again, so that its suspension bucked and its tires howled on the blacktop. The Wendigo had clawed its way up the tailgate now, and she could see its fiery pincers trying to get a grip on the roof rails. On either side the wolves were running in closer, and still keeping up with her. She couldn't see how many, but there must have been scores of them. *Wolves, or witches.*

She passed the seven-mile mark and she could see lights up ahead. Maybe the wolves wouldn't chase her along the highway. She kept her foot hard down and screamed, 'Come on! Come on!' And William started to scream too.

Almost too late she realized that the lights weren't highway lights at all. A huge Winnebago was blocking the entire road ahead of her, with its emergency lights flashing. She blasted her horn but she knew that it wasn't going to get out of her way. She saw a startled man kneeling in the road, changing a tire. She saw a woman lifting her hand up to shield her eyes.

She jammed her foot on the parking brake and spun the wheel all the way round. The Rainier slewed around 180 degrees, its tires all screaming in hysterical chorus. Lily heard a sickening, tumbling noise above her. The blazing Wendigo had fallen from the roof and dropped back on to the road. But almost at once, she felt it tugging at the net again.

She didn't hesitate. She slammed the gearshift into reverse, gunned the engine, and backed up at high speed, with the transmission whinnying like a disobedient horse. She hit the Wendigo with a sharp crunch and pushed it along the road, its fiery claws flailing and its body sliding noisily on the asphalt, until she collided at nearly twenty miles per hour with the rear end of the Winnebago.

She heard the man and the woman shouting at her, but she didn't care. She shifted into drive and sped forward again – but only thirty or forty yards. Then she jerked to a halt, changed into reverse, and backed up again, smashing the Wendigo into the back of the Winnebago for a second time.

She drove forward, and twisted around in her seat, and now she could see that there were pieces of burning Wendigo all across the road, and underneath the Winnebago, too.

The man was screaming, 'What the *fuck*! What the *fuck*! What the fuck did I ever do to you, lady?'

Then the wolves started to gather around the Rainier and jump up on either side, and Lily saw the man and the woman turn and run into the darkness.

The wolves jumped up again and again, and some of them remained standing on their hind legs, stalking around the SUV with a strange, ungainly gait. The large brindled wolf came right up to Lily's window and bared its teeth at her, fogging up the glass. Then she heard their claws tugging at the doorhandles, and she knew that she had to get away from them, fast.

She put her foot on the gas and the Rainier sped back the way she had come, back toward Mystery Lake. Without the Wendigo trailing behind her she could drive much faster, and when she looked from one side of the vehicle to the other, she could see that the wolves were having trouble keeping pace with her. After two or three miles, only the brindled wolf was still running beside her, and then even he dropped back. For about a half-mile she could still see his yellow eyes shining in her rear-view mirror, and then he was swallowed by the darkness.

She drove another mile or so, but little William was sobbing so pitifully that she drew over to the side of the road and pulled up. She lifted him over from the back seat and held him tight, shushing him. She could feel that he had wet his romper suit and he was shaking with distress.

'There, there,' she said. 'Everything's going to be OK now. Everything's going to be fine. You can come live with me now, and we'll all be happy ever after. How would you like to live with your Aunt Lily, and Tasha, and Sammy? That would be fun, wouldn't it?'

She felt exhausted, and bruised, but at least she knew that she had succeeded in saving her family from the Wendigo. It was probably nothing but ashes now, and those poor people with the Winnebago would never understand what hit them, or why.

After a while, William began to settle down, and she buckled him up in the lap-belt next to her. She tried to call Special Agent Kellogg on her cell, but there was no signal. She needed to drive back to Mystery Lake to find out what had happened to him. She prayed to God that George Iron Walker hadn't hurt him. He might have had a .50-caliber Desert Eagle, but Hazawin had all the powers of the forest, and the spirits that lived in it.

She started the engine again. 'Come on, little William. Let's go find Nathan, shall we?'

But as soon as she pulled away, she saw a black shape rushing at her out of the darkness. With a hideous bang, and a flurry of scratching noises, the huge brindled wolf leapt on to the Rainier's sloping hood.

Lily swung the Rainier from one side of the road to the other, trying to shake the wolf off. If it had been a real wolf, it couldn't have clung on. But it was gripping the lip of the hood with human hands, and it had found itself a foothold on the bull-bars on the front of the Rainier with human feet, and when it stared at Lily through the windshield with an expression of utter fury, she saw that it had a human face: George Iron Walker, his black oilskin flapping in the Rainier's slipstream like a vampire.

Lily kept on swinging the SUV from side to side, but George Iron Walker was determined not to be shaken loose. He beat on the windshield with his fist, so that his heavy silver rings made a cracking noise on the glass, and he was roaring at her, although she couldn't make out what he was saying.

She swerved wildly for mile after mile. Still George Iron Walker held on, and still he kept beating at the windshield. She tried jamming her brakes on, and then speeding up again, but she couldn't shake him loose.

'— *kill you!*' she heard him shouting at her.

She kept on driving, but she knew that when she reached Mystery Lake, that was the end of the road, and there would be no place left for her to go.

But as the trees began to thin out on either side of the road, she saw two white lights up ahead of her. It was another vehicle, coming toward her. It had to be Nathan.

She switched off her own headlights. She didn't know if George Iron Walker realized what she was planning to do, but he reached inside his coat and took out a large knife with a heavy handle. He began to smash at the windshield again and again, in a frenzy. The safety-glass cracked all the way across, and then he smashed it yet again and it shattered and frosted over, and Lily was left blind. All she could see now was George Iron Walker's dark silhouette, and the rapidly brightening headlights of Nathan's Jeep.

'God help us, little William,' she said, and drove straight toward them.

It seemed like forever, but it was probably no more than ten seconds before they collided. Her windshield was filled with dazzling white light and then her airbag burst out in front of her face. She didn't hear anything, and even afterward she didn't remember hearing anything. All she could remember was being thrown violently backward and forward, the way that Jeff used to shake her when he was drunk and angry.

Then there was silence, except for the *tick-tick-ticking* of gradually cooling metal. She turned to little William and said, 'William? Are you OK?'

He looked up at her, wide-eyed, and nodded. For the first time that evening, he had been shocked into silence.

Lily was still sitting behind the wheel when her door was wrenched open with a loud creak. She lifted her arm, ready to defend herself, but it was Special Agent Kellogg.

'Lily? You're not hurt, are you?'

'My nose, that's all.'

'How about junior?'

'He's OK.'

'Here –' he held out his hand to her – 'let me help you guys out. It worked then – with the Wendigo?'

'It was touch and go for a while, but yes. It worked. Damn thing was all burned up.'

'The net held?'

'The net held. I think I did some damage to some poor guy's RV. But the net held.'

'That's terrific. You don't know how glad I am to see you.'

Stiffly, Lily climbed out of the Rainier and helped little William out, too.

'George Iron Walker?' she said.

'Sorry?'

'George Iron Walker – he was clinging on to the hood – I couldn't shake him off.'

Special Agent Kellogg said nothing but pointed to the front of their collided vehicles. She had hit his Jeep head-on, although he must have braked hard as soon as he saw her coming, because the damage wasn't as devastating as she had thought it would be: a badly dented hood, and a bumper that had dropped off.

But in between the Rainier's bull-bars and the Jeep's front

grille reared a huge black-and-brindled wolf, its head raised toward the sky, its eyes bulging, its bloody tongue lolling out of the side of its jaws. Its chest had been crushed almost completely flat.

'Don't know how that could have happened,' said Special Agent Kellogg. 'Damn thing must have been dancing in the middle of the road.'

Lily held William close to her, so that he wouldn't see it. 'George Iron Walker,' she said, huskily.

Special Agent Kellogg frowned at her. 'He took off as soon as you did. So did that Native American girl. I don't know how they did it. I turned around to watch you go, and when I turned back they weren't there any more. It was like they'd just *vanished.*'

Lily started to tremble. 'Do you think you could take us home now? God knows what little William here has been through.'

'Sure. We'll need to talk about this, though. Tomorrow, if you'd prefer it. But I'm going to have to find a way of explaining all of this.'

He walked back to his Jeep, reached inside the driver's door and turned the key. The engine started, and he walked back to help Lily into the passenger seat.

'We could always tell the truth,' said Lily.

Special Agent Kellogg climbed into the driver's seat and backed the Jeep away from Lily's Rainier. The brindled wolf remained where it was for a moment, standing upright, its nose pointed toward the treetops. Then it dropped heavily on to the ground, its fur matted with blood, like any other road-kill.

'The truth?' said Special Agent Kellogg, as they drove back along the logging road, between the trees. There was a strong smell of smoke in the air, and smoldering pine. 'In my experience, nobody wants to hear the truth. They just want to hear what they're comfortable with.'

* * *

The next morning was the first day of the Moon of the Red Grass Appearing. It was a dull, overcast day, but much warmer, and melted snow began to drip from the roof. Lily allowed Tasha and Sammy to sleep late, but little William had woken early and wanted his breakfast.

'Where's Mommy?' he asked her. 'Is Mommy coming?'

'Soon, sweetheart.' How do you tell a two-year-old boy that he's never going to see his mommy or his daddy ever again? He doesn't even understand the idea of 'heaven'.

But when Tasha and Sammy came down, they both played with him, and made him laugh. Lily stood and watched them, drinking her decaf, and wondered where William had actually been in the time when the Wendigo had taken him. *Asleep*, George Iron Walker had told her. *Dreaming*. But where? Even though she had seen the Wendigo for herself, she still found it difficult to think of other existences, beneath our feet, or beside us – especially if it were possible to move from one to the other, as simply as walking from one room into the next.

Shortly after eleven a.m. Special Agent Kellogg came by. He was wearing a brown tweed sport coat and a black rollneck sweater and, apart from a large crimson bruise on his left cheek, he looked relaxed and well, and smelled of Boss aftershave.

'How are you feeling?' he asked her.

'Good. Better. Relieved. And you?'

'Well . . . not too bad. I had to come up with some cock-and-bull story about suspecting that George Iron Walker was involved in kidnapping little William, and that they wanted to negotiate a ransom with you. The police will want to talk to you later, and children's services, but I've told them that you gave me some really heroic help, so I don't think that you'll have any serious problems.' He smiled. 'And that's true. You *were* a heroine. You were amazing.'

'I was scared half to death.'

'That's what makes you all the more of a heroine.'
Lily sat down on the couch next to him. 'I still can't really believe that it happened.'
'Oh, it happened all right. I went back to Mystery Lake late last night and had your SUV removed by a tow-truck. George Iron Walker's, too. I also talked to those people whose RV you totaled. Fortunately they didn't really understand what they were looking at. They simply thought your truck was on fire and you were panicking.'
'What about the Wendigo? Any sign?'
'Ash – that's all I saw. And what was left of my net.'
'How about the wolf?'
'Gone. Some predator probably dragged it off for a late supper.'
'I promise you, Nathan. That wolf was George Iron Walker. He could change his shape. Maybe it was some kind of hypnosis, but he could do it.'
'Well – I'll be going out to his place in Black Crow Valley this afternoon. If George Iron Walker is still there, alive and kicking, we'll know different. But if he isn't – who knows? Maybe he *was* a wolf.'
'If he *is* there, will you be charging him?'
'What with? Reckless endangerment with a Native American tree-spirit?'
'Nathan – he was going to have us all slaughtered.'
Special Agent Kellogg took hold of her hand and squeezed it. 'I know, Lily. But even if he *is* still alive, I doubt that he'll be coming after you again. I think all the scores have been pretty much settled, don't you?'
'I hope so.'
'What about you? Have you thought what you're going to do?'
Lily shrugged. 'I don't know. For starters, I have to take care of little William. I may have to look after his brother and sister too.'
'Hell of a houseful.'

'I know. I started off trying to get two children back and now it looks like I'm going to have five.'

'Guess I can give you a hand. I come from a family of seven. I know all about looking after little kids.'

'Nathan – that's an offer I might very well take you up on.'

That night, after she had put little William down and Tasha and Sammy had gone to bed, Lily poured herself a large glass of red wine, put her feet up by the fire and tuned her TV to *Sleepless in Seattle*. For one reason or another, she had never seen it before, and she felt like watching something silly and romantic.

She felt as if her whole life had been turned inside-out. Not only had she lost Agnes and Ned, and Jeff, and seen John Shooks killed, but she could never look at the world in the same way again. She would always feel that there was another country, an older country that was populated by spirits and wonder-workers and animals that could change their shape. She knew that it was very close beside her, but she would never be able to see it, because it was always edgewise-on.

She stifled a yawn. She really needed a good night's sleep. But she was just about to get out of her chair when she thought she heard a clicking noise, like the front door being unlocked.

She stood up, switched off the television and listened. Nothing. She must have imagined it. Now that the snow was melting so fast, the house was full of creaks and cracklings and sudden shifting sounds. All the same, she decided to fasten the chains and the bolts on the front door, and set the alarm for the night.

She went out into the hallway and listened again. She had the strongest feeling that there was somebody close by – somebody watching her, somebody trying to suppress their breathing.

'Tasha?' she called. 'Sammy?'

No reply. She shrugged to herself and crossed the hallway to the front door. She was annoyed to see that it wasn't quite closed properly. Those kids. They rushed in and out of the house every five minutes and they were always leaving the doors open. But she was just about to go over and close it when all of the lights went out.

She turned around, her skin prickling. 'Who's there?' she demanded.

Still there was no reply.

'I'm warning you, this house is connected directly to the police station, and all I have to do is push one button.'

Gradually, her eyes were becoming accustomed to the gloom. As they did so, she realized that somebody was standing in the kitchen doorway: a tall, dark figure, with an arrangement of horns on its head that looked like antlers. It stood perfectly still and made no sound at all.

'Who are you?' said Lily. 'Get out of my house, right now!'

The figure moved toward her. Then it spoke, in a harsh Minnesota accent. 'You don't remember me, Mrs Blake? You and me – we have some unfinished business.'

'You get the hell out of my house,' said Lily. 'You get out and you never come back.'

The figure came closer. 'I don't know how you escaped the divine retribution that you so justly deserved, Mrs Blake, but when I found out that you were still alive, I was sorely vexed, believe you me. Especially since it turned out that you really are a witch, after all. What you did to my friend, what you did to my office, what you did to your ex-husband – witchery, that's all, plain and simple. Fortunately – I still have the key that your ex-husband gave me before.'

'Victor Quinn,' said Lily. 'You sad, miserable excuse for a human being.'

'Oh, you think so? Well, let me tell you something: you are the spawn of Satan himself, and I am going to make sure that you never again have the opportunity to wreak the kind of destruction that you wreaked on those two innocent men whose only crime was that they wanted to be reunited with their own flesh and blood.

'But we're going to see some flesh and blood now, Mrs Blake, and that flesh and blood is going to be yours.'

Lily hesitated, feinted, and then she made a dash for the alarm panel beside the front door. But Victor Quinn was quicker. He seized her wrist just as she was about to push the panic button, and twisted her arm around behind her back, so fiercely that her hand was forced right up between her shoulder-blades. Then he clamped his other hand over her mouth, gripping her jaw. She could smell the same reek of tobacco that she had smelled on him before – tobacco, and stale sweat.

'Got your kids back, didn't you, Mrs Blake? But only through witchery. And now they're going to be orphans, which is your fault entirely.'

Lily struggled and kicked and tried to bite his hand, but Victor Quinn frogmarched her into the kitchen and forced her to sit down on a chair. He dragged a black rag out of his pocket and gagged her with it, tying it in a painfully tight double knot at the back of her head. Then he produced two military-style belts, khaki webbing with brass buckles, strapping one around her arms and her upper body and the other around her ankles.

I can't believe this is happening. Not again. Not the same nightmare repeating itself. I destroyed the Wendigo. Don't tell me I'm going to die like this.

Victor Quinn switched on the kitchen lights. This time he hadn't bothered with the transparent plastic mask that he had worn before. He had a plain, pasty face, with pale-blue eyes and a bulbous nose. The devil's horns on his head were nothing but sticks, fastened with adhesive tape. Lily thought, *You could be anybody. I could have passed you in the street a hundred times and I never would have noticed you.*

Victor Quinn reached under the kitchen table and hefted

up a red plastic gasoline container. 'This time, we're going to do it right. This time, we're going to make sure that you start burning and keep on burning until there's nothing left of you but ashes.'

He unscrewed the cap, and without any ceremony he sloshed the gasoline all over Lily's head, soaking her. Her eyes smarted and the stench was so strong that she almost vomited behind her gag.

Victor Quinn took out a plastic cigarette lighter and flicked it into flame. 'So where'd you like me to apply this, Mrs Blake? Feet? Hair? How about the tip of your witch's nose?'

Lily could only struggle against the straps and grunt at him. *There are children in the house. For God's sake, even if you kill me, think of the children.*

'I think the hair is good. That way, you'll burn like a candle.'

He reached forward, holding out the cigarette lighter at arm's length and pulling back his coat-cuff with the other hand so it wouldn't be scorched when Lily burst into flame.

Oh God, please don't let this hurt too much.

There was a deafening bang. Victor Quinn flew sideways as if somebody had seized him by his coat collar and flung him on to the floor. He lay behind the kitchen table, and all that Lily could see of him was his feet shuddering.

Special Agent Kellogg came into the kitchen, holding his Desert Eagle with both hands. He stepped over to Victor Quinn and peered down at him. Then he holstered his gun and came back to Lily. He tugged off her gag, unfastened the webbing belts, and helped her to stand up.

'Is he dead?' asked Lily. She didn't want to look at him.

'Unless he can live for the rest of his life with half of his head missing, I would say so.'

'It's Victor Quinn. It's the man from FLAME – the one who tried to burn me before.'

'Looks like he got what he deserved, then.'

'How did you . . .? Thank God you did.'

'I came around to tell you about your SUV, and some other stuff about children's services. The door was open and I know how freaky you are about security. Come on, Lily, let's get you out of here. You need to wash that gas off.'

She was shaking so much that Special Agent Kellogg almost had to carry her upstairs. They were only halfway up when Tasha came out of her room in her pink-striped pajamas.

'Mommy? What's happening? I heard this really loud bang.'

Sammy's door opened and Sammy came out. 'I heard a really loud bang too!'

'Mommy, you *smell*! You smell like gasoline! What's going on?'

Lily climbed the last few stairs to the landing. 'I'll tell you what: I'm going to take a shower and change my clothes. Something nasty has happened and I don't want you to go downstairs. But I promise you this: nothing nasty is ever going to happen to us again. We're safe now.'

She turned to Special Agent Kellogg.

'Your mom's right,' he said. 'I have a couple of calls to make, then I'll come upstairs again and make sure you're OK.'

Lily went into her bathroom, stripped off her gasoline-soaked sweater and pants, and reached in to turn on the shower. As she did so, she looked into the mirror over the washbasin, the same mirror in which she had seen the Wendigo.

She didn't smile. She had no expression at all. She looked like a different person.

In the early hours of the morning, while it was still dark, she suddenly sat up in bed. Something had woken her, and she didn't know what. She sat there, listening, for almost a minute. Then – somewhere in the neighborhood – she heard the high, eerie howling of a wolf.

NEATH PORT TALBOT LIBRARY
AND INFORMATION SERVICES

1	6/07	25		49		73	
2		26		50		74	
3		27		51		75	
4		28		52		76	
5		29		53		77	
6		30		54		78	
7	9/8	31		55		79	
8		32		56		80	
9		33		57		81	
10		34		58		82	
11		35		59		83	
12		36		60		84	
13		37		61		85	
14		38		62		86	
15		39		63		87	
16		40		64		88	
17		41		65		89	
18		42		66		90	
19		43		67		91	
20		44		68		92	
21		45		69		COMMUNITY SERVICES	
22		46		70			
23		47		71		NPT/111	
24		48		72			